ballad of

YaYa

Book 7: The Trap

Written by
Jean-Marie Omont

Illustrated by
Golo Zhao

Created and Edited by
Patrick Marty and Charlotte Girard

Translation and Layout by Mike Kennedy

MAGNETIC™

www.magnetic-press.com

AFTER RUNNING AWAY FROM WICKED STRANGERS, YAYA ESCAPED BY JUMPING OFF A CLIFF INTO THE RIVER BELOW. SHE MIRACULOUSLY SURVIVED THE FALL, BUT LOST HER MEMORY IN THE PROCESS! WANDERING THE COLD, SNOWY WILDERNESS, SHE WAS RESCUED BY A BIG STRANGER... SOMEONE SHE SHOULD HAVE RECOGNIZED AS THE GANGSTER ZHU! BUT BECAUSE OF HER AMNESIA, SHE DIDN'T REALIZE HE WAS THE VILLAIN SHE HAD BEEN RUNNING AWAY FROM ALL THE WAY FROM SHANGHAI!

MEANWHILE, HER FRIEND TUDUO AND HIS NEW FRIEND OYSTER GRAVY SET OUT TO FIND YAYA AND TO KEEP THEIR PROMISE TO HELP FIND HER PARENTS IN HONG KONG...

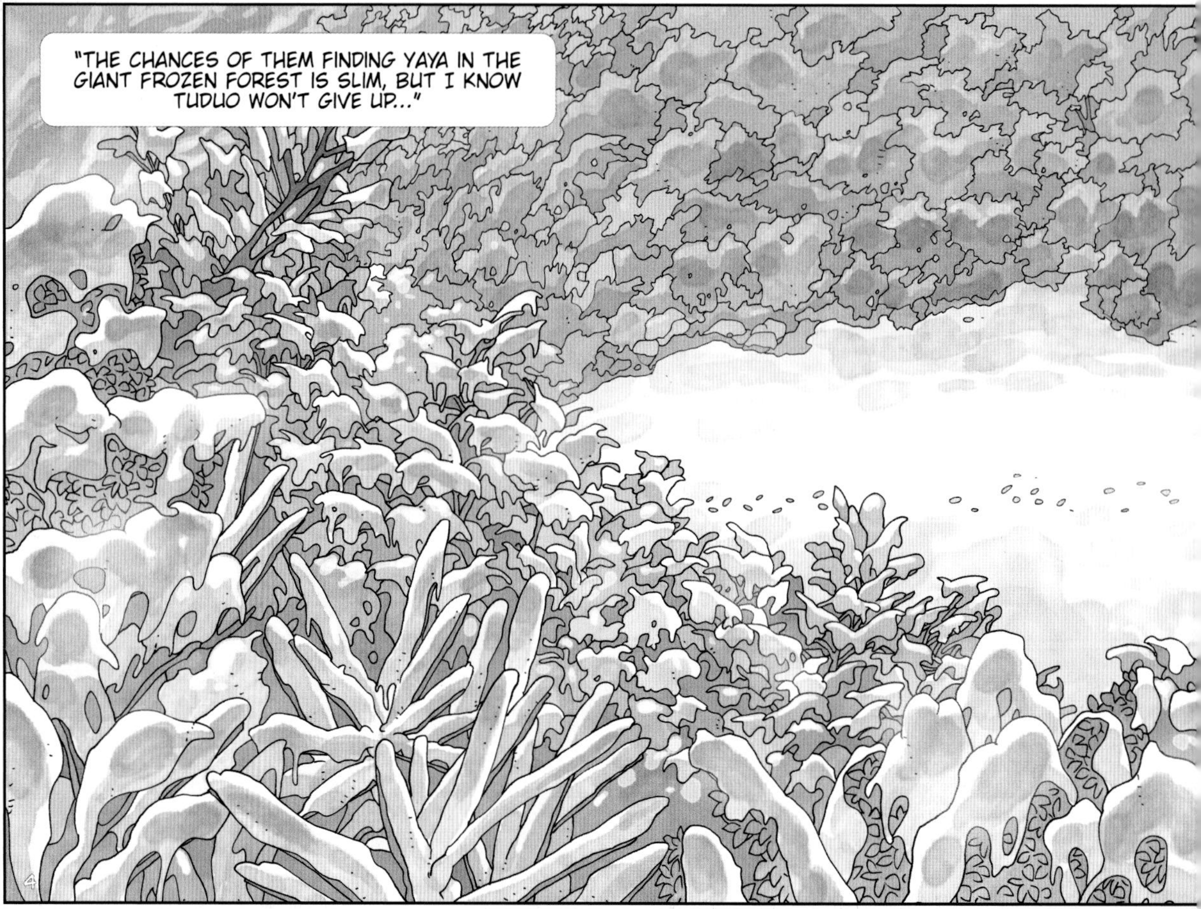
"THE CHANCES OF THEM FINDING YAYA IN THE GIANT FROZEN FOREST IS SLIM, BUT I KNOW TUDUO WON'T GIVE UP..."

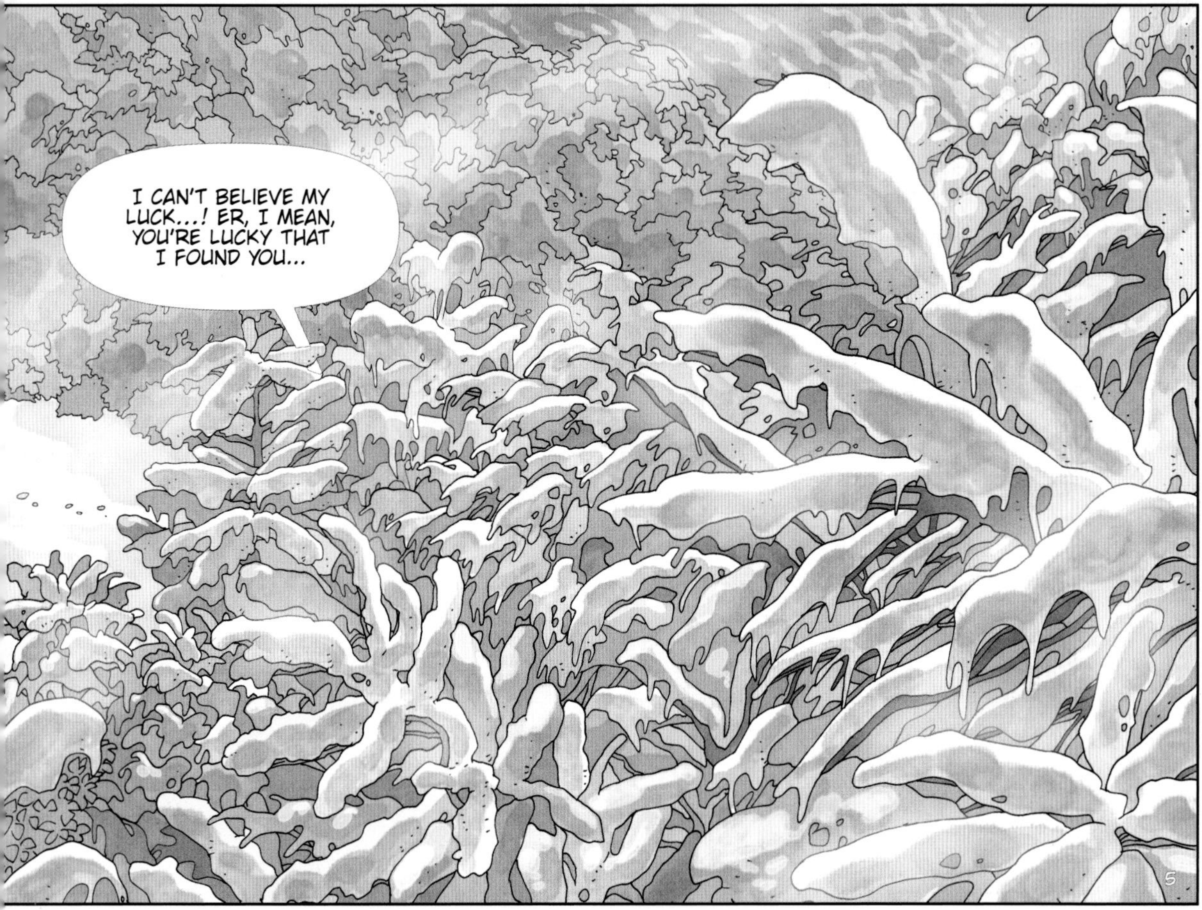
I CAN'T BELIEVE MY LUCK...! ER, I MEAN, YOU'RE LUCKY THAT I FOUND YOU...

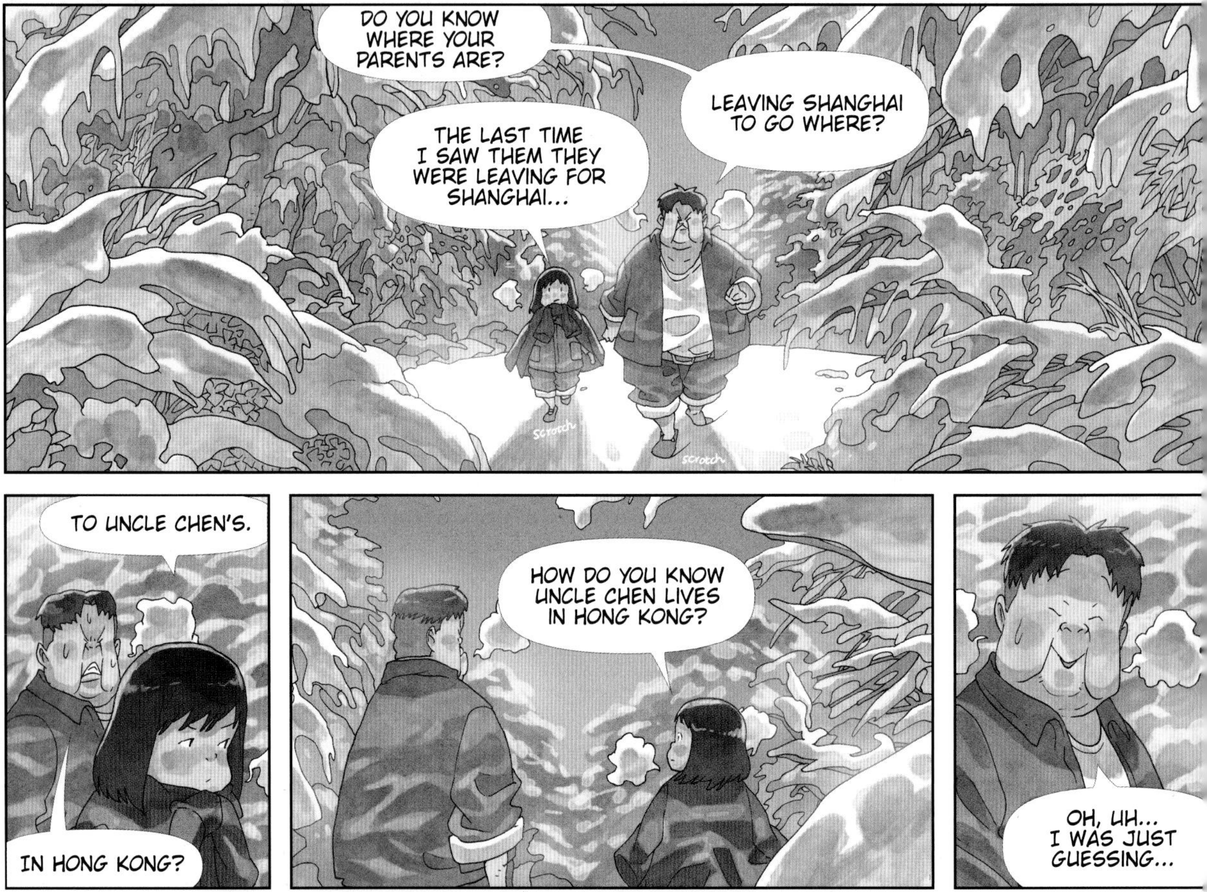
DO YOU KNOW WHERE YOUR PARENTS ARE?
THE LAST TIME I SAW THEM THEY WERE LEAVING FOR SHANGHAI...
LEAVING SHANGHAI TO GO WHERE?
scrotch
scrotch
TO UNCLE CHEN'S.
IN HONG KONG?
HOW DO YOU KNOW UNCLE CHEN LIVES IN HONG KONG?
OH, UH... I WAS JUST GUESSING...

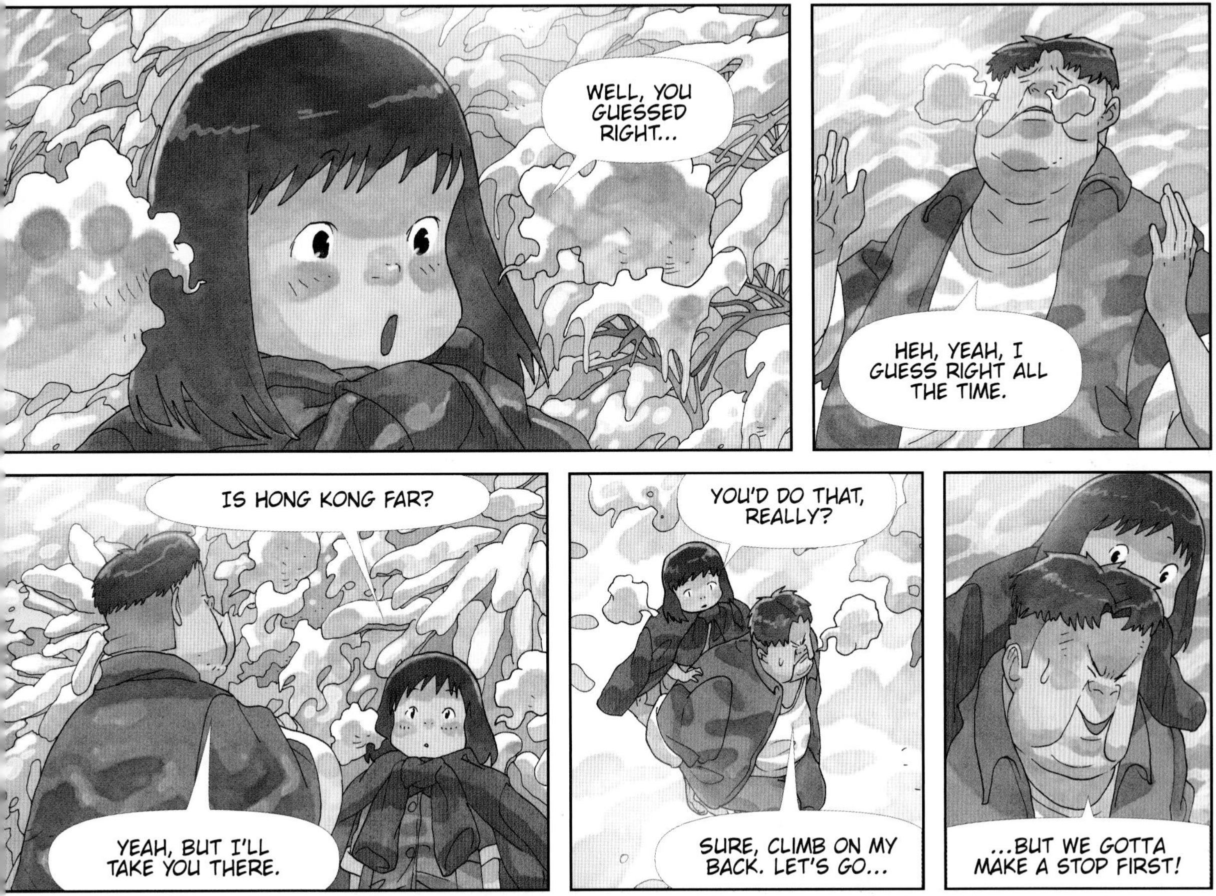
WELL, YOU GUESSED RIGHT...
HEH, YEAH, I GUESS RIGHT ALL THE TIME.
IS HONG KONG FAR?
YEAH, BUT I'LL TAKE YOU THERE.
YOU'D DO THAT, REALLY?
SURE, CLIMB ON MY BACK. LET'S GO...
...BUT WE GOTTA MAKE A STOP FIRST!

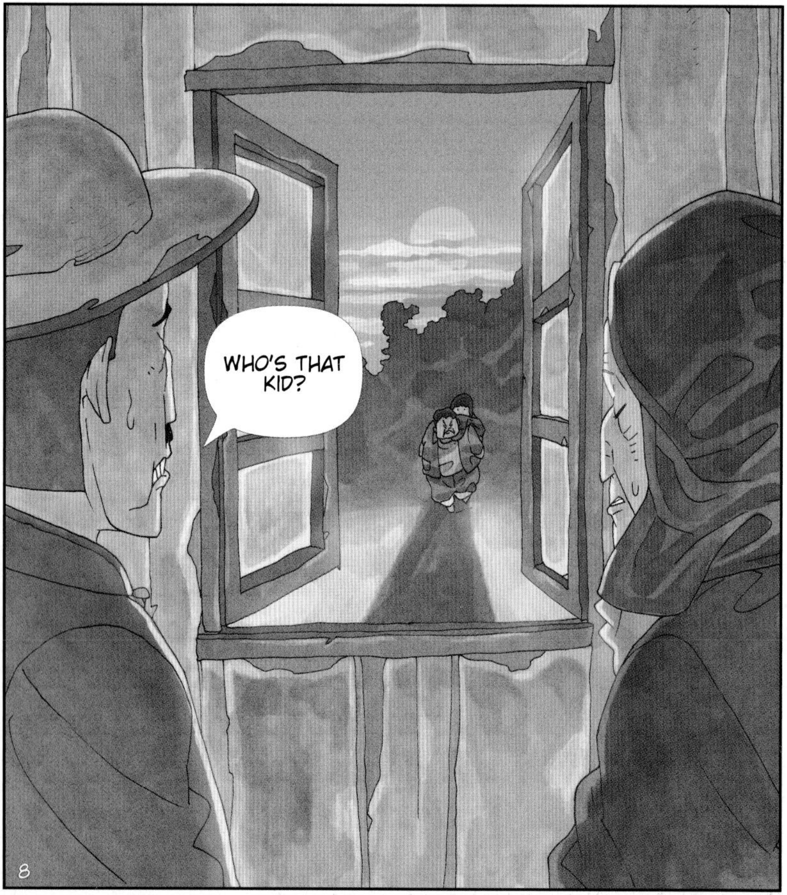
WHO'S THAT KID?

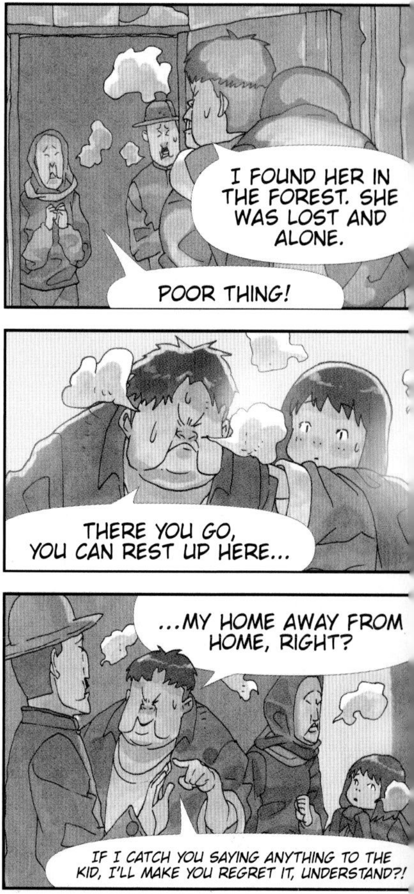
I FOUND HER IN THE FOREST. SHE WAS LOST AND ALONE.
POOR THING!
THERE YOU GO, YOU CAN REST UP HERE...
...MY HOME AWAY FROM HOME, RIGHT?
IF I CATCH YOU SAYING ANYTHING TO THE KID, I'LL MAKE YOU REGRET IT, UNDERSTAND?!

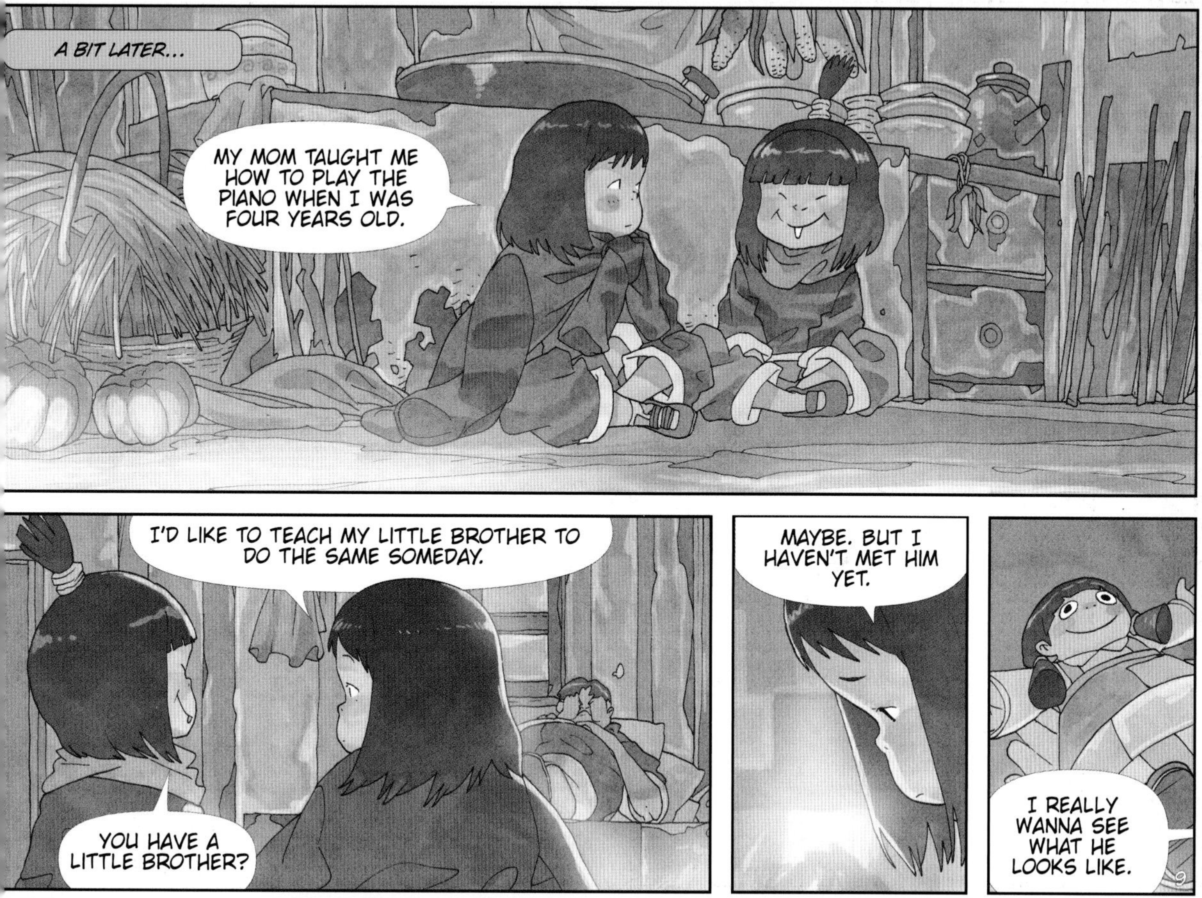
A BIT LATER...
MY MOM TAUGHT ME HOW TO PLAY THE PIANO WHEN I WAS FOUR YEARS OLD.
I'D LIKE TO TEACH MY LITTLE BROTHER TO DO THE SAME SOMEDAY.
YOU HAVE A LITTLE BROTHER?
MAYBE. BUT I HAVEN'T MET HIM YET.
I REALLY WANNA SEE WHAT HE LOOKS LIKE.

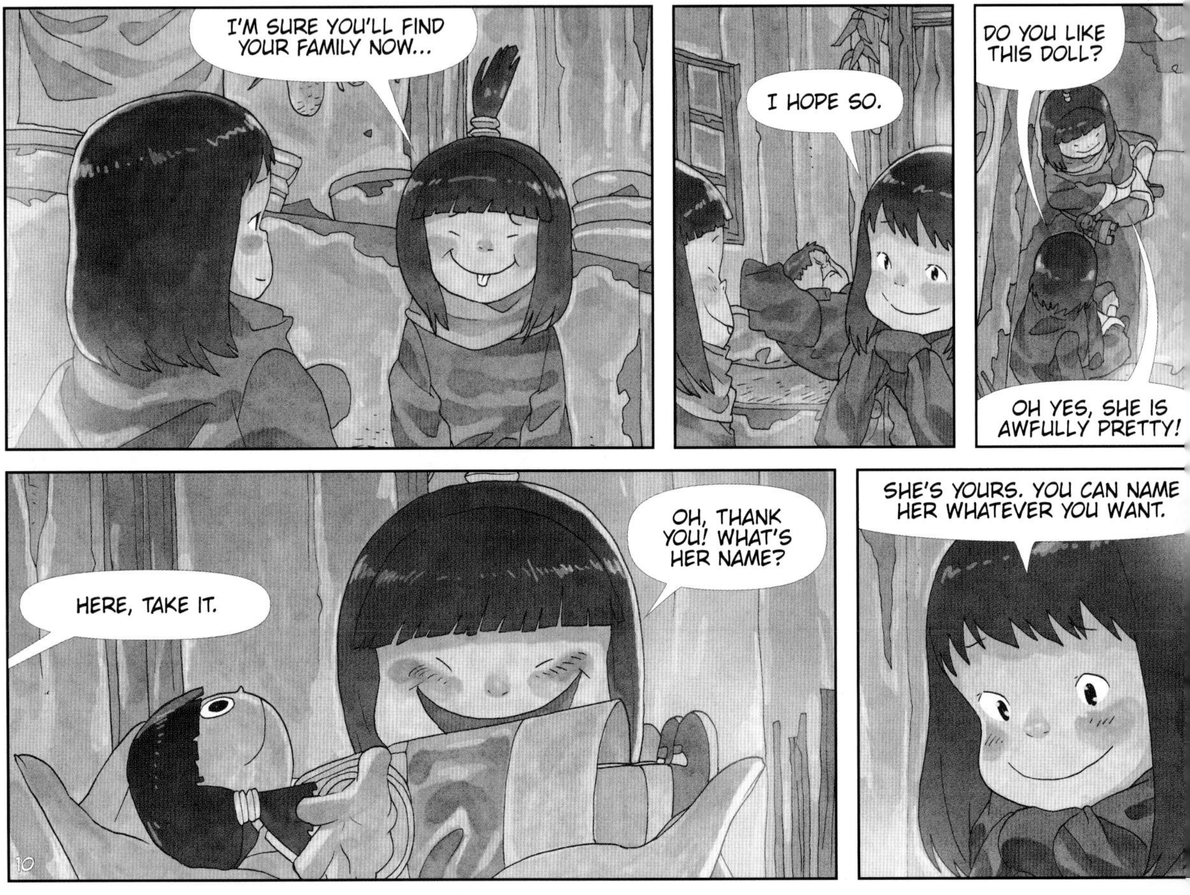
I'M SURE YOU'LL FIND YOUR FAMILY NOW...
I HOPE SO.
DO YOU LIKE THIS DOLL?
OH YES, SHE IS AWFULLY PRETTY!
HERE, TAKE IT.
OH, THANK YOU! WHAT'S HER NAME?
SHE'S YOURS. YOU CAN NAME HER WHATEVER YOU WANT.

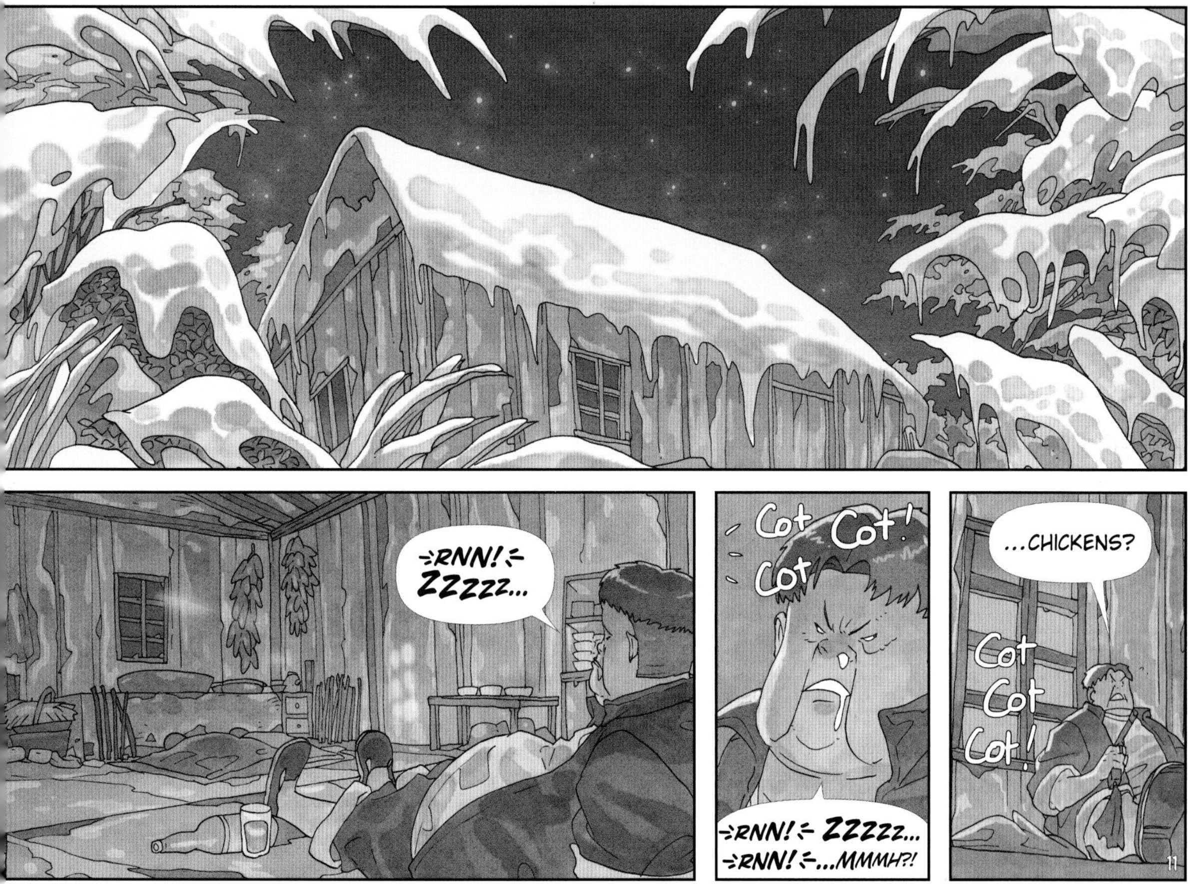
RNN! ZZZZZ...
Cot Cot! Cot
RNN! ZZZZZ... RNN! ...MMMH?!
...CHICKENS?
Cot Cot Cot!

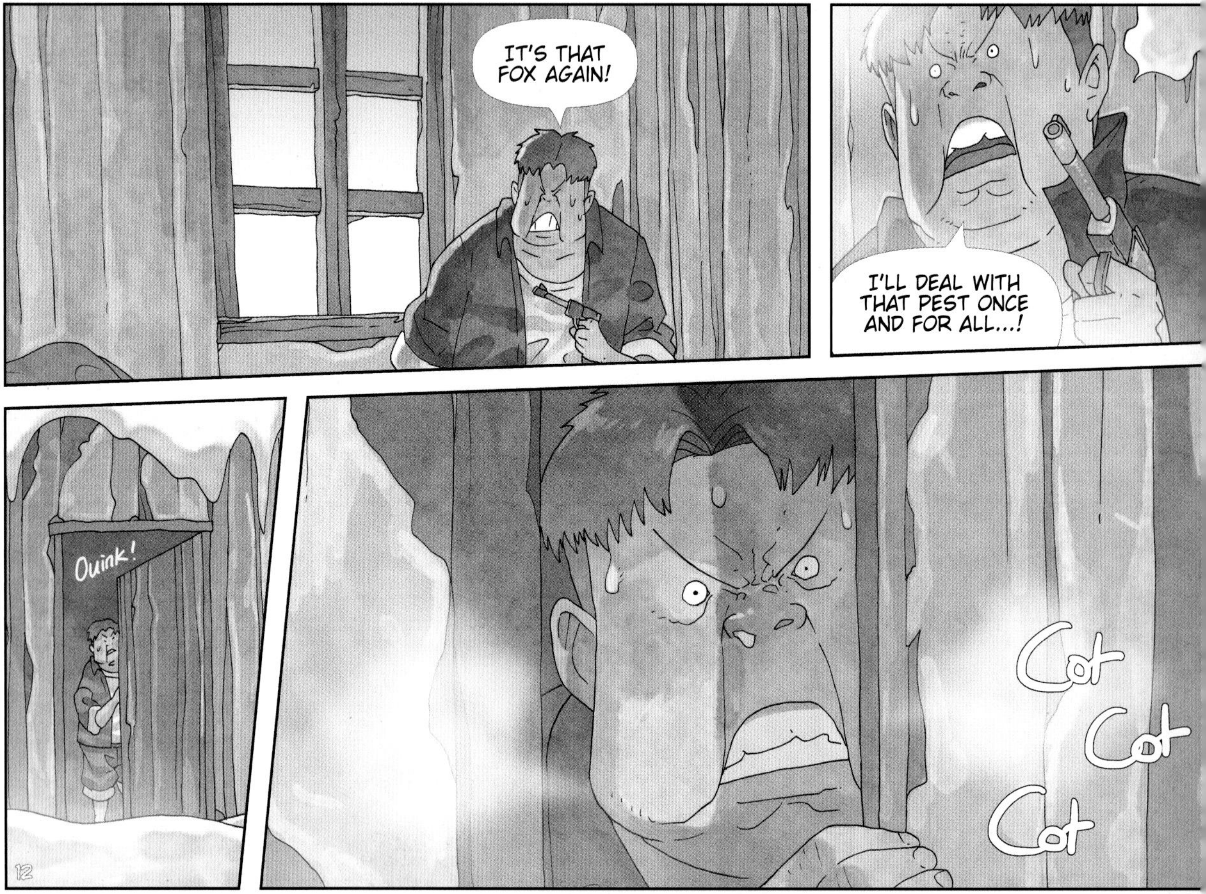

IT'S THAT FOX AGAIN!
I'LL DEAL WITH THAT PEST ONCE AND FOR ALL...!
Ouink!
Cot
Cot
Cot

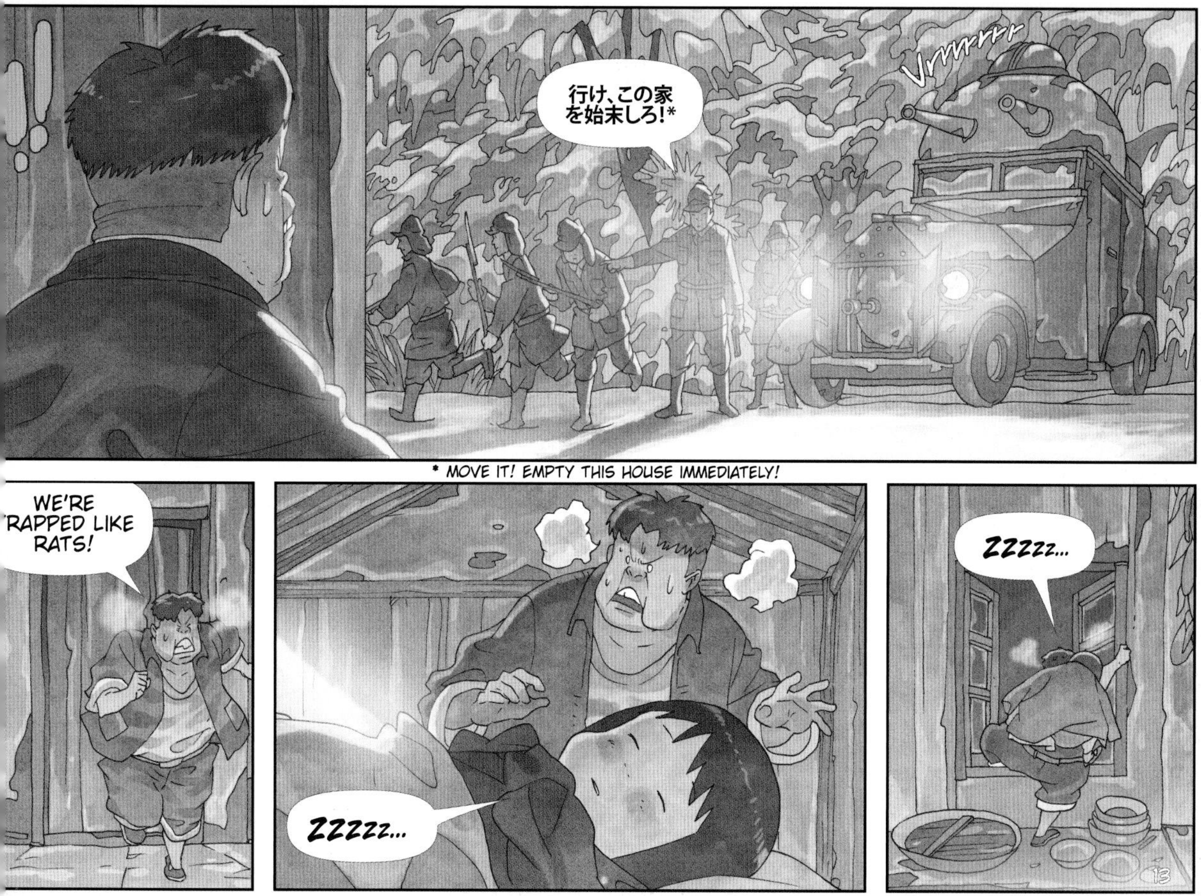
!!
Vrrrrrrr
行け、この家を始末しろ!*
* MOVE IT! EMPTY THIS HOUSE IMMEDIATELY!
WE'RE TRAPPED LIKE RATS!
ZZZzz...
ZZZzz...

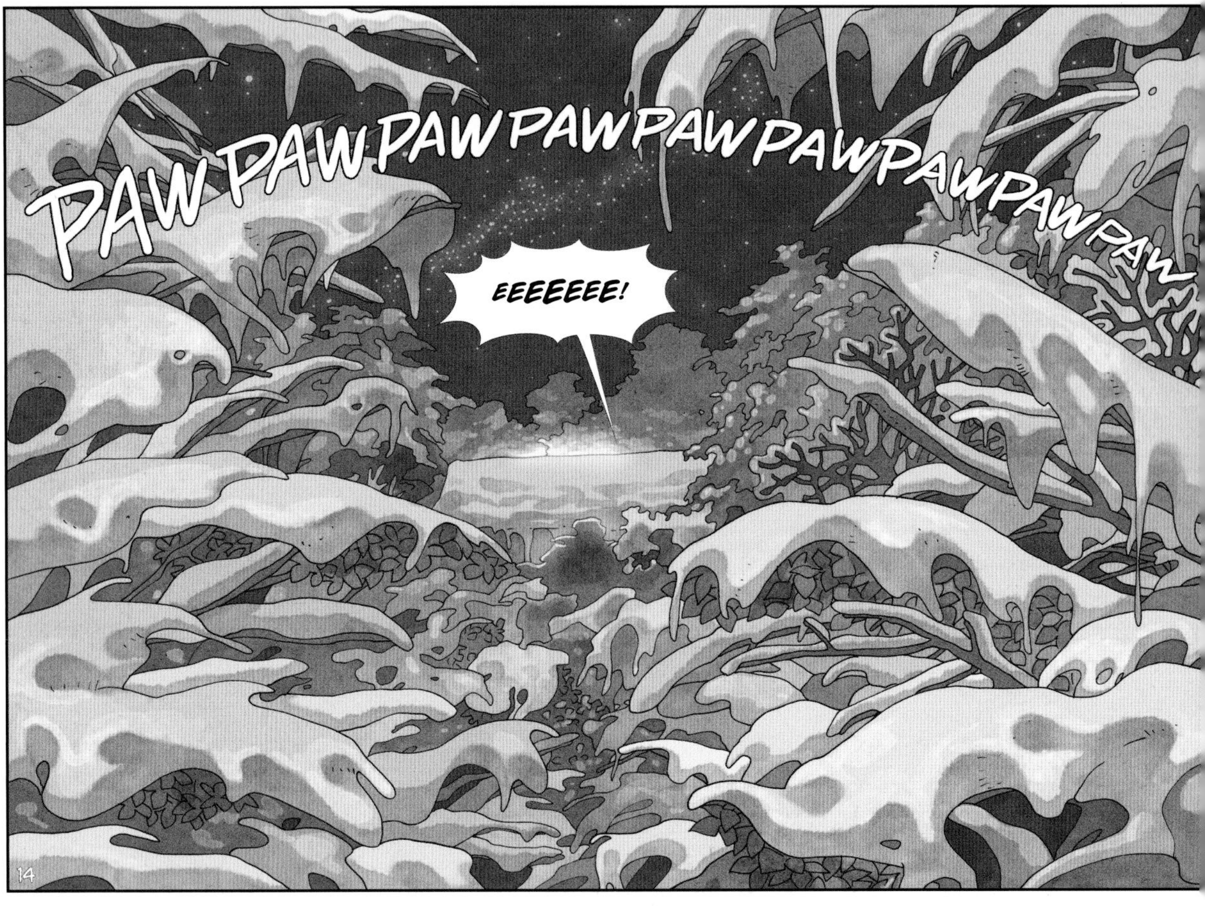
PAW PAW PAW PAW PAW PAW PAW PAW PAW
EEEEEEE!

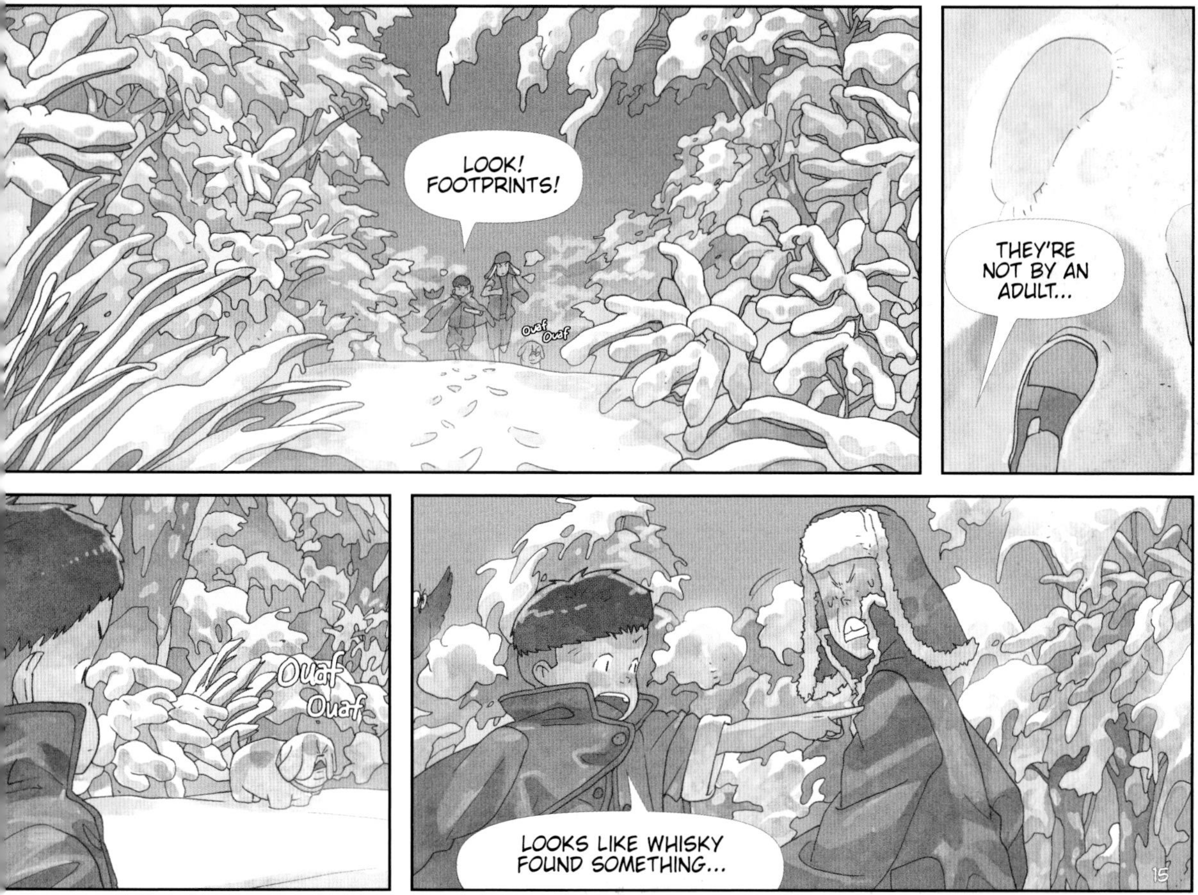
LOOK! FOOTPRINTS!
Ouaf Ouaf
THEY'RE NOT BY AN ADULT...
Ouaf
Ouaf
LOOKS LIKE WHISKY FOUND SOMETHING...

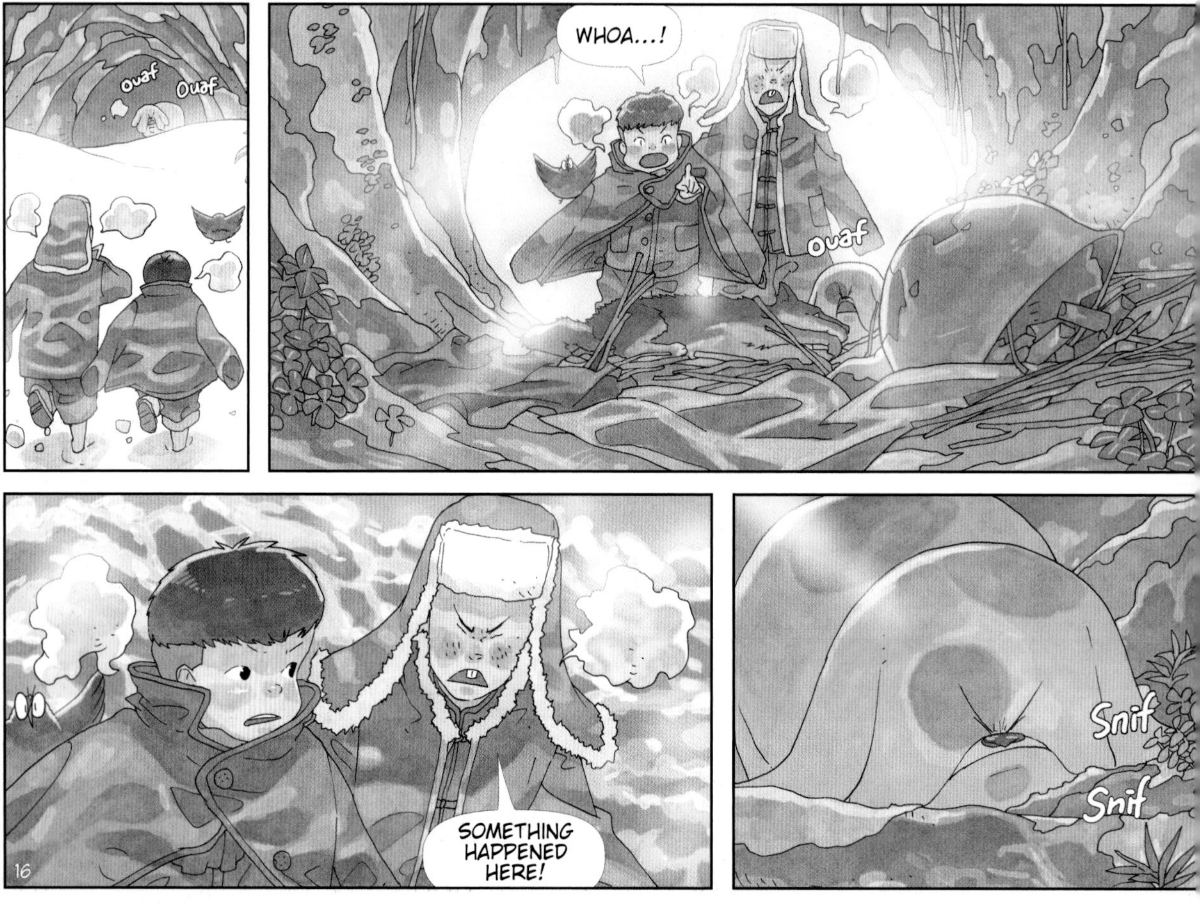
Ouaf
Ouaf
WHOA...!
Ouaf
SOMETHING HAPPENED HERE!
Snif
Snif

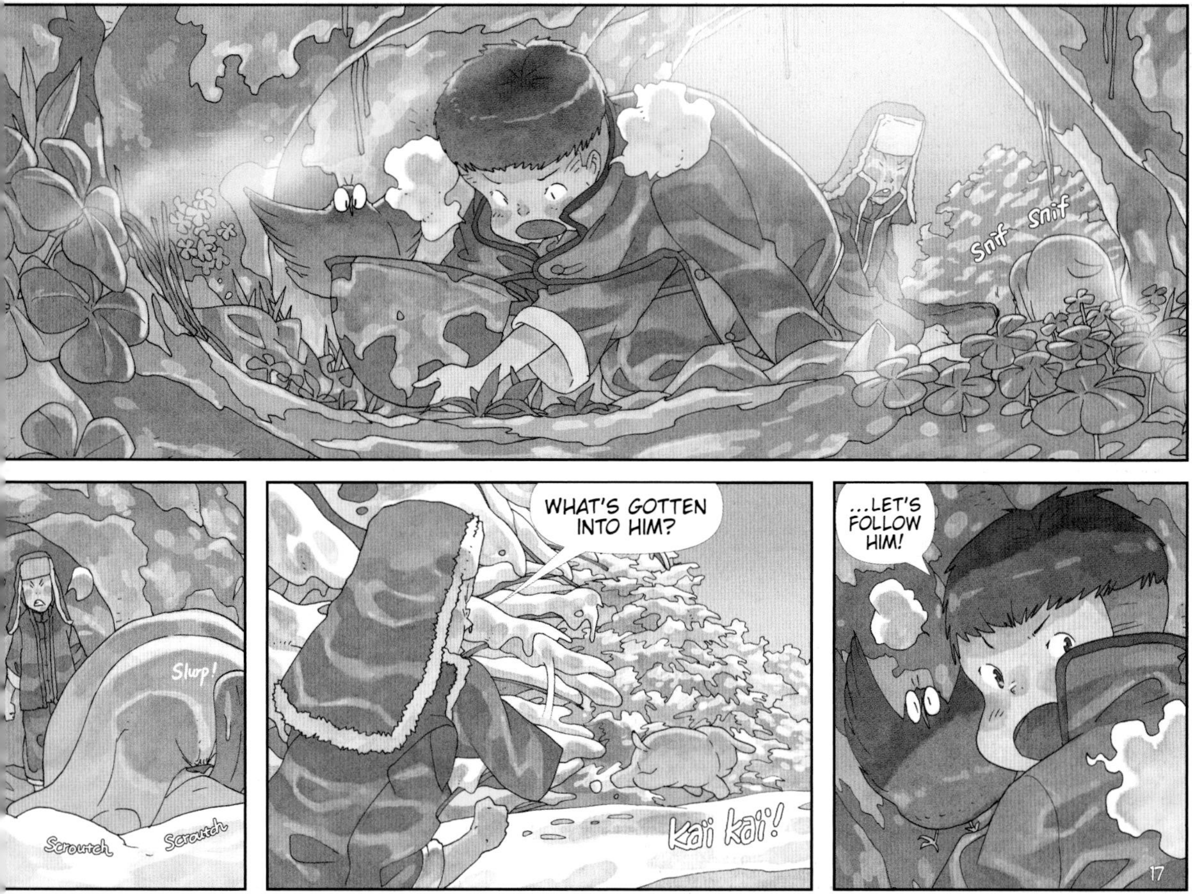
Snif Snif
Slurp!
Scroutch Scroutch
WHAT'S GOTTEN INTO HIM?
Kaï kaï!
...LET'S FOLLOW HIM!

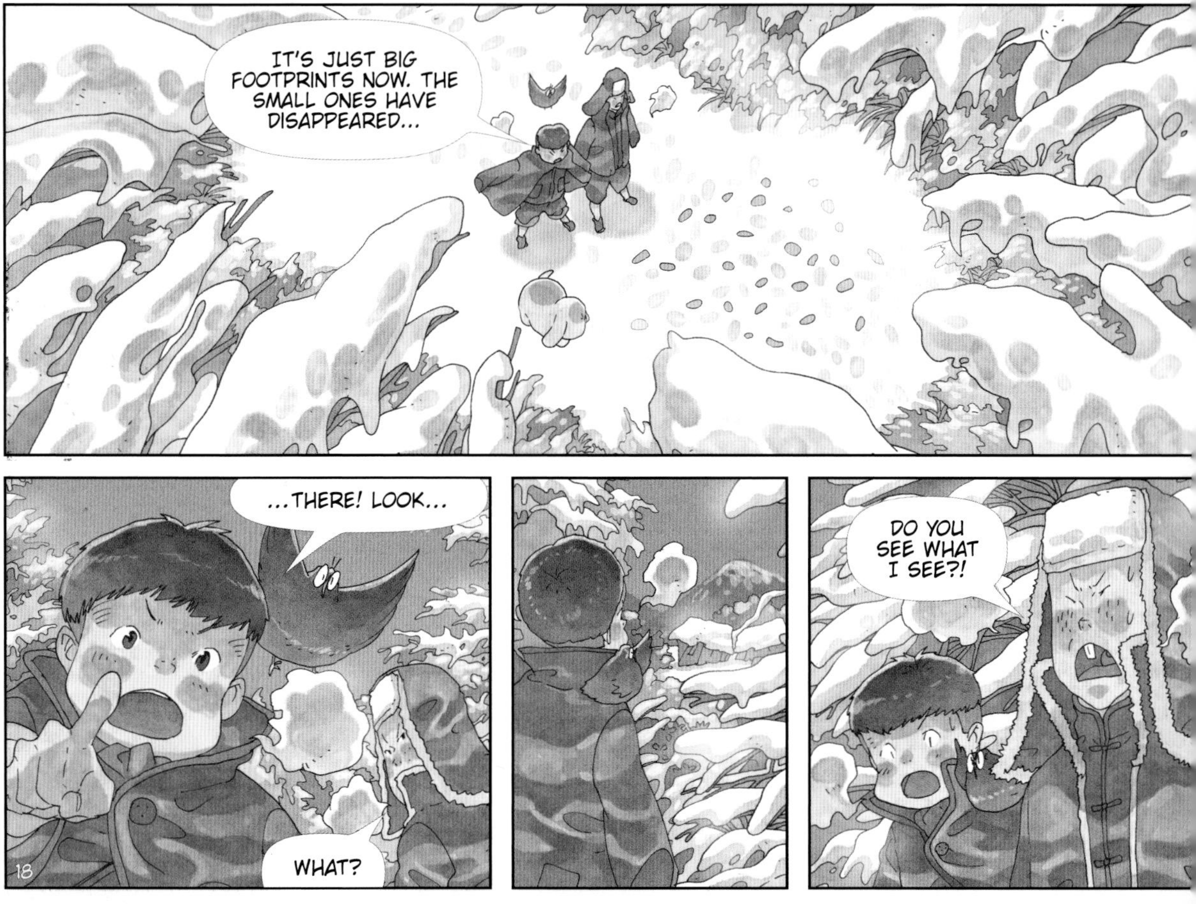
IT'S JUST BIG FOOTPRINTS NOW. THE SMALL ONES HAVE DISAPPEARED...
...THERE! LOOK...
WHAT?
DO YOU SEE WHAT I SEE?!

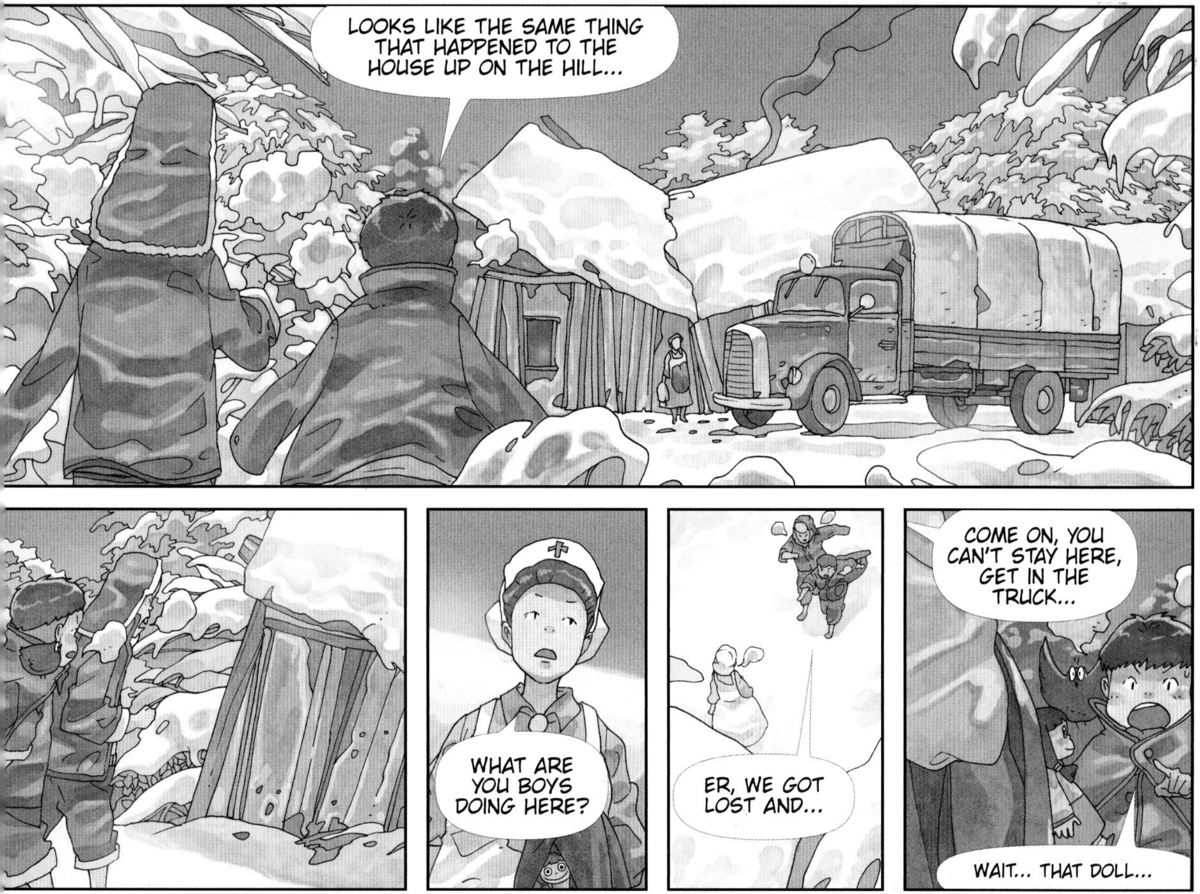
LOOKS LIKE THE SAME THING THAT HAPPENED TO THE HOUSE UP ON THE HILL...
WHAT ARE YOU BOYS DOING HERE?
ER, WE GOT LOST AND...
COME ON, YOU CAN'T STAY HERE, GET IN THE TRUCK...
WAIT... THAT DOLL...

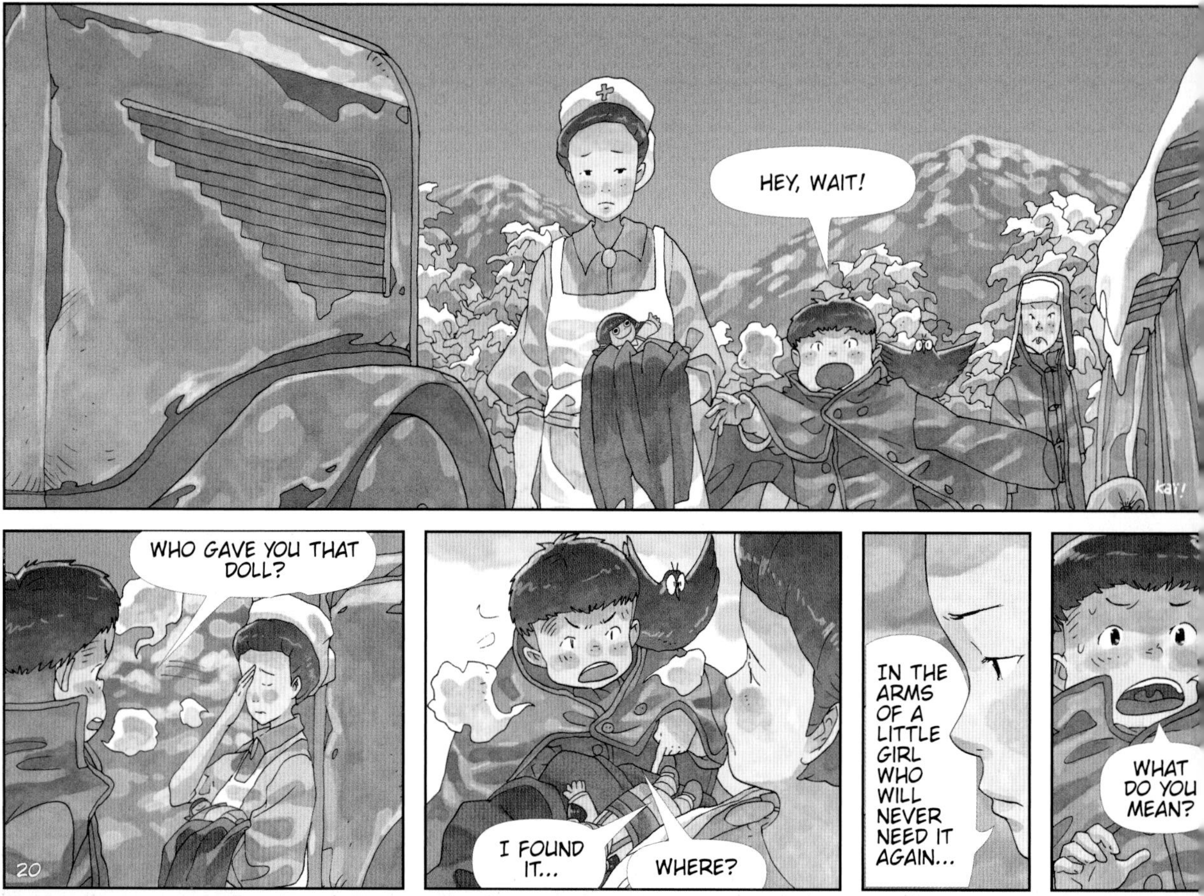
HEY, WAIT!
kaï!
WHO GAVE YOU THAT DOLL?
I FOUND IT...
WHERE?
IN THE ARMS OF A LITTLE GIRL WHO WILL NEVER NEED IT AGAIN...
WHAT DO YOU MEAN?

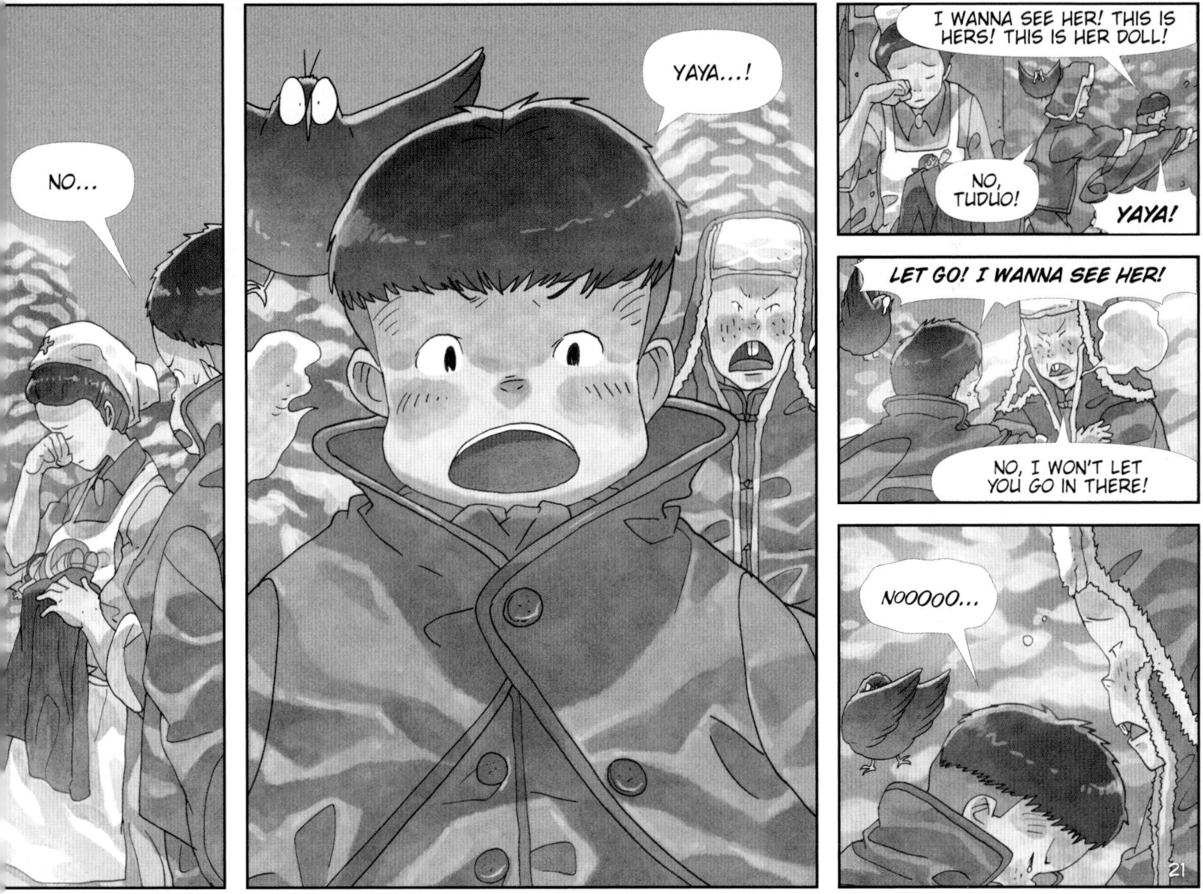

NO...
YAYA...!
I WANNA SEE HER! THIS IS HERS! THIS IS HER DOLL!
NO, TUDUO!
YAYA!
LET GO! I WANNA SEE HER!
NO, I WON'T LET YOU GO IN THERE!
NOOOOO...

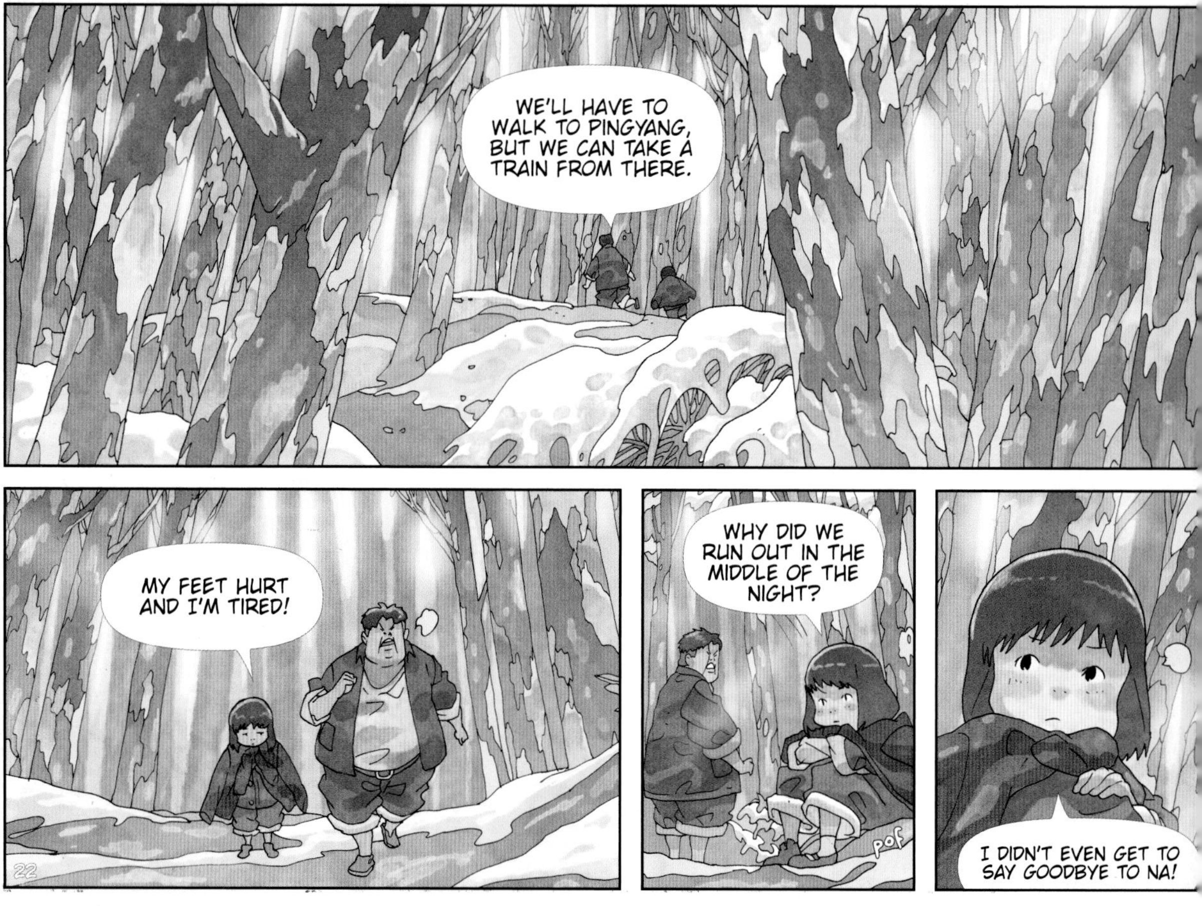

WE'LL HAVE TO WALK TO PINGYANG, BUT WE CAN TAKE A TRAIN FROM THERE.
MY FEET HURT AND I'M TIRED!
WHY DID WE RUN OUT IN THE MIDDLE OF THE NIGHT?
pof
I DIDN'T EVEN GET TO SAY GOODBYE TO NA!

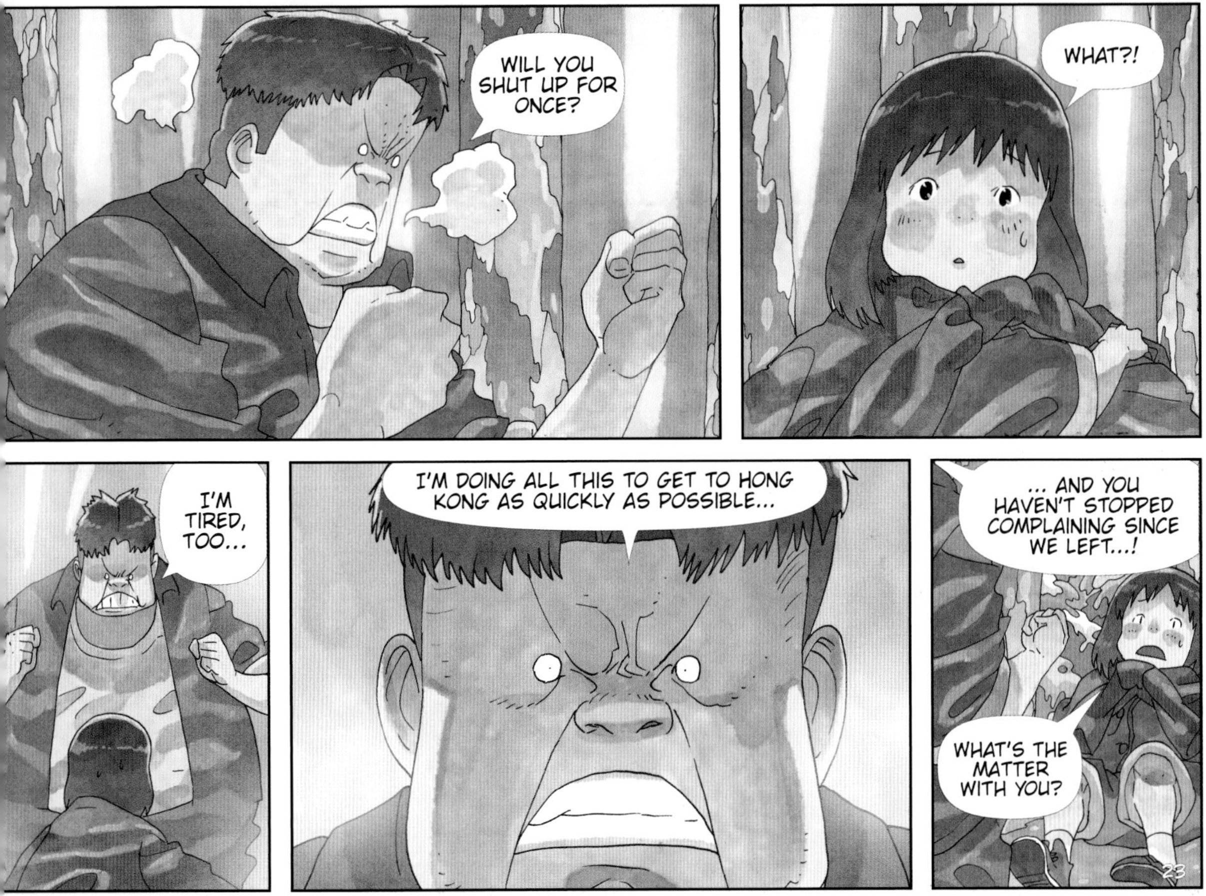
WILL YOU SHUT UP FOR ONCE?
WHAT?!
I'M TIRED, TOO...
I'M DOING ALL THIS TO GET TO HONG KONG AS QUICKLY AS POSSIBLE...
... AND YOU HAVEN'T STOPPED COMPLAINING SINCE WE LEFT...!
WHAT'S THE MATTER WITH YOU?
23

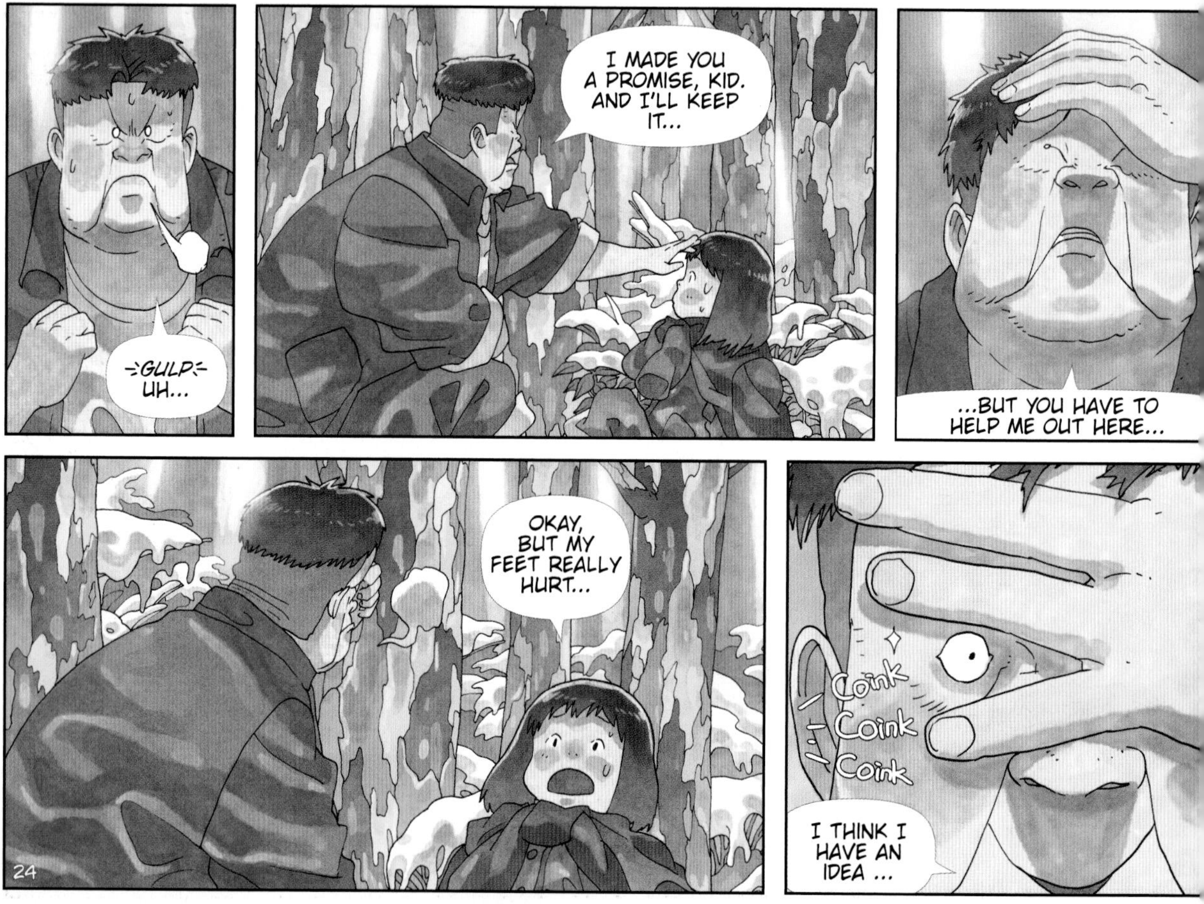

=GULP=
UH...
I MADE YOU A PROMISE, KID. AND I'LL KEEP IT...
...BUT YOU HAVE TO HELP ME OUT HERE...
OKAY, BUT MY FEET REALLY HURT...
Coink
Coink
Coink
I THINK I HAVE AN IDEA ...

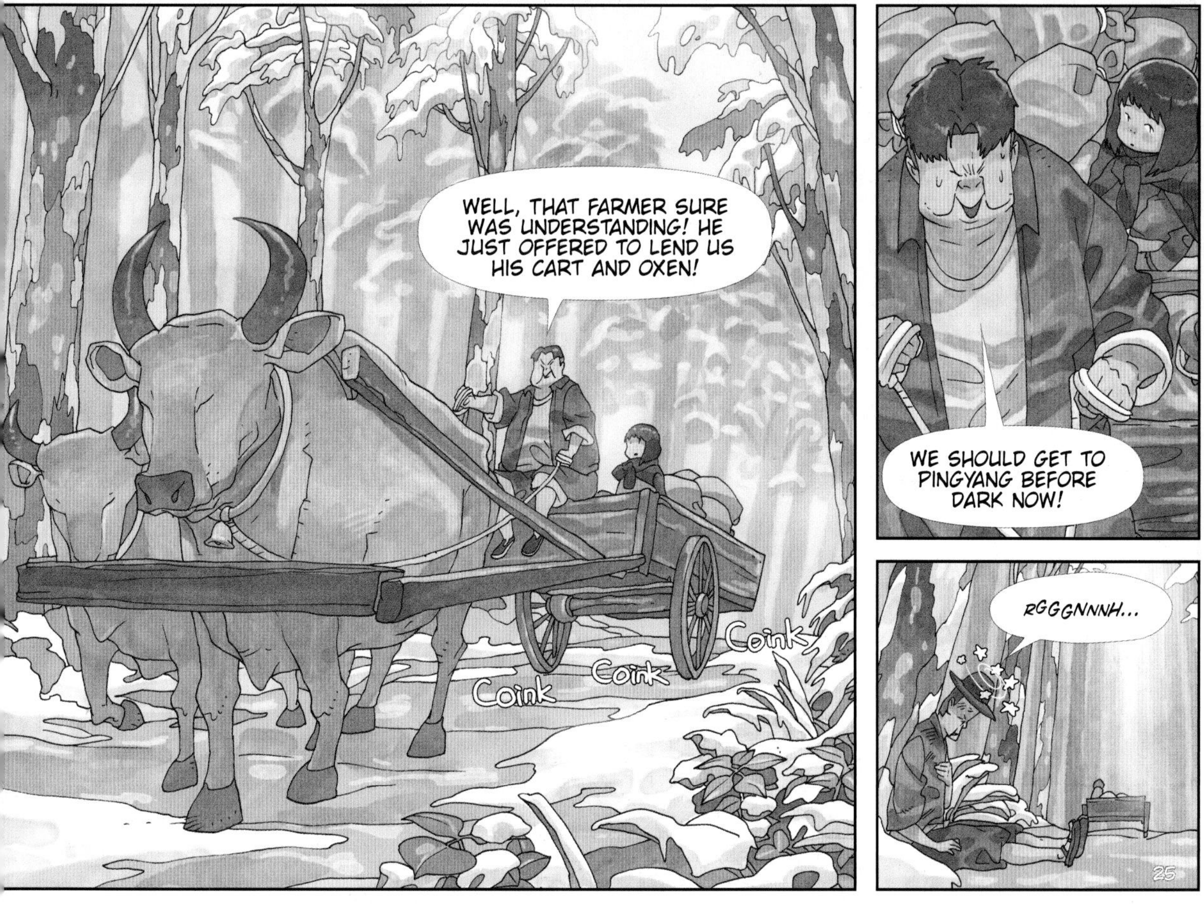
WELL, THAT FARMER SURE WAS UNDERSTANDING! HE JUST OFFERED TO LEND US HIS CART AND OXEN!
Coink
Coink
Coink
WE SHOULD GET TO PINGYANG BEFORE DARK NOW!
RGGGNNNH...

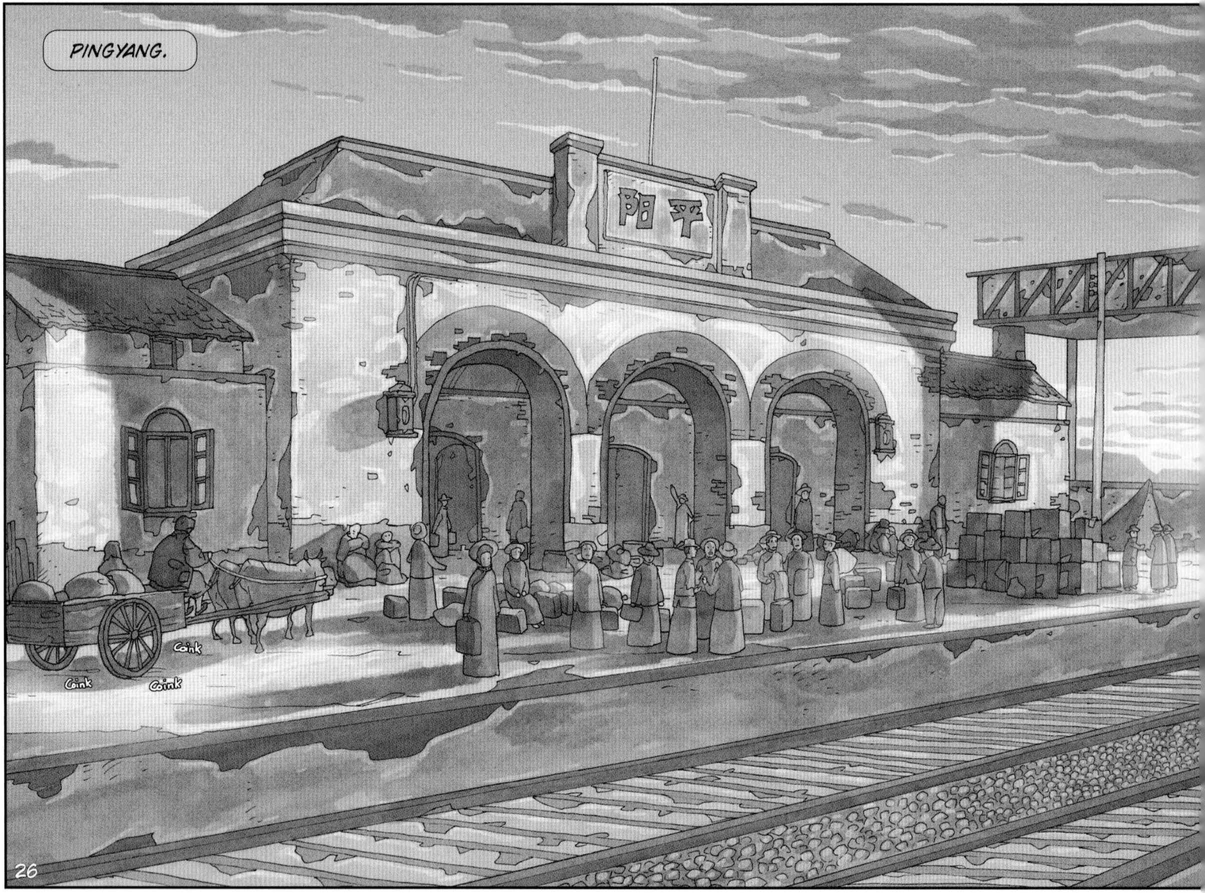
PINGYANG.
阳平
Coink
Coink
Coink

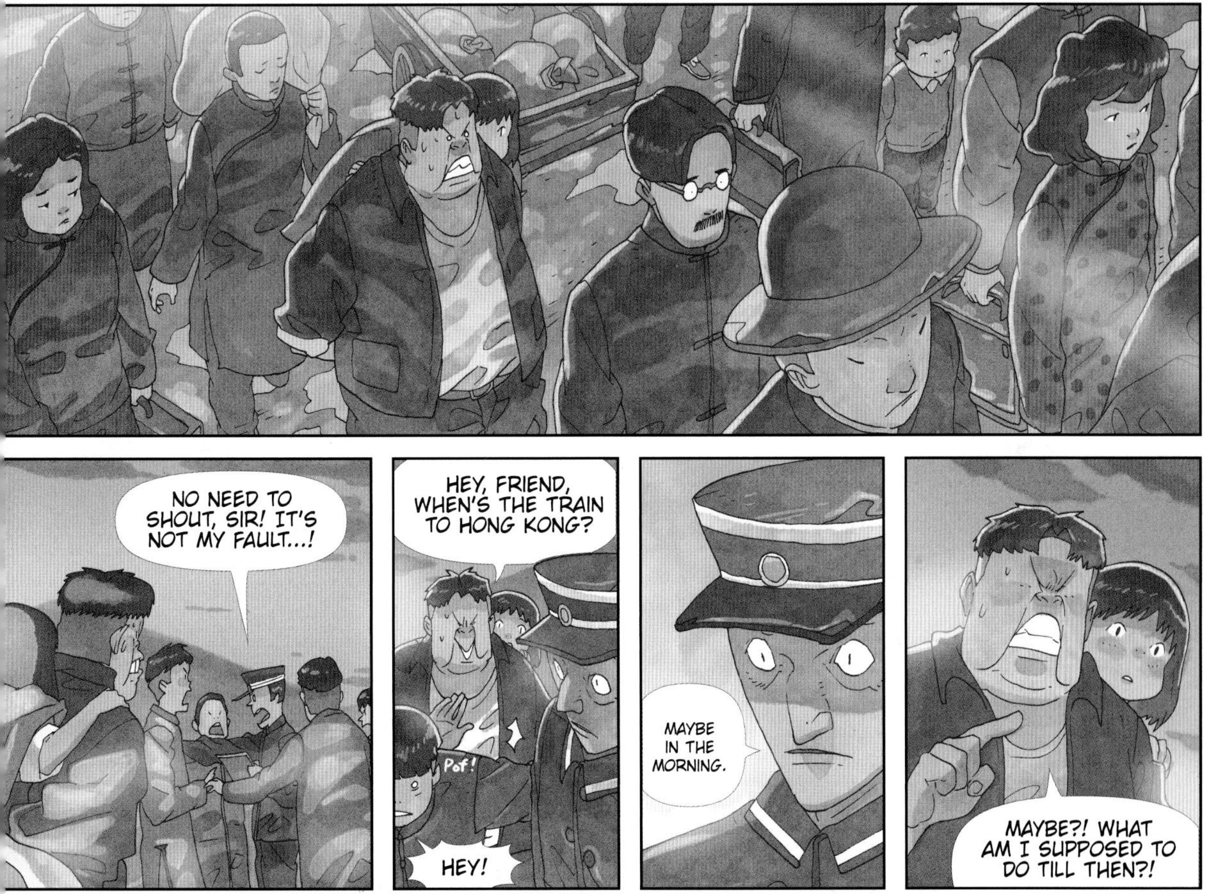
NO NEED TO SHOUT, SIR! IT'S NOT MY FAULT...!
HEY, FRIEND, WHEN'S THE TRAIN TO HONG KONG?
Pof!
HEY!
MAYBE IN THE MORNING.
MAYBE?! WHAT AM I SUPPOSED TO DO TILL THEN?!

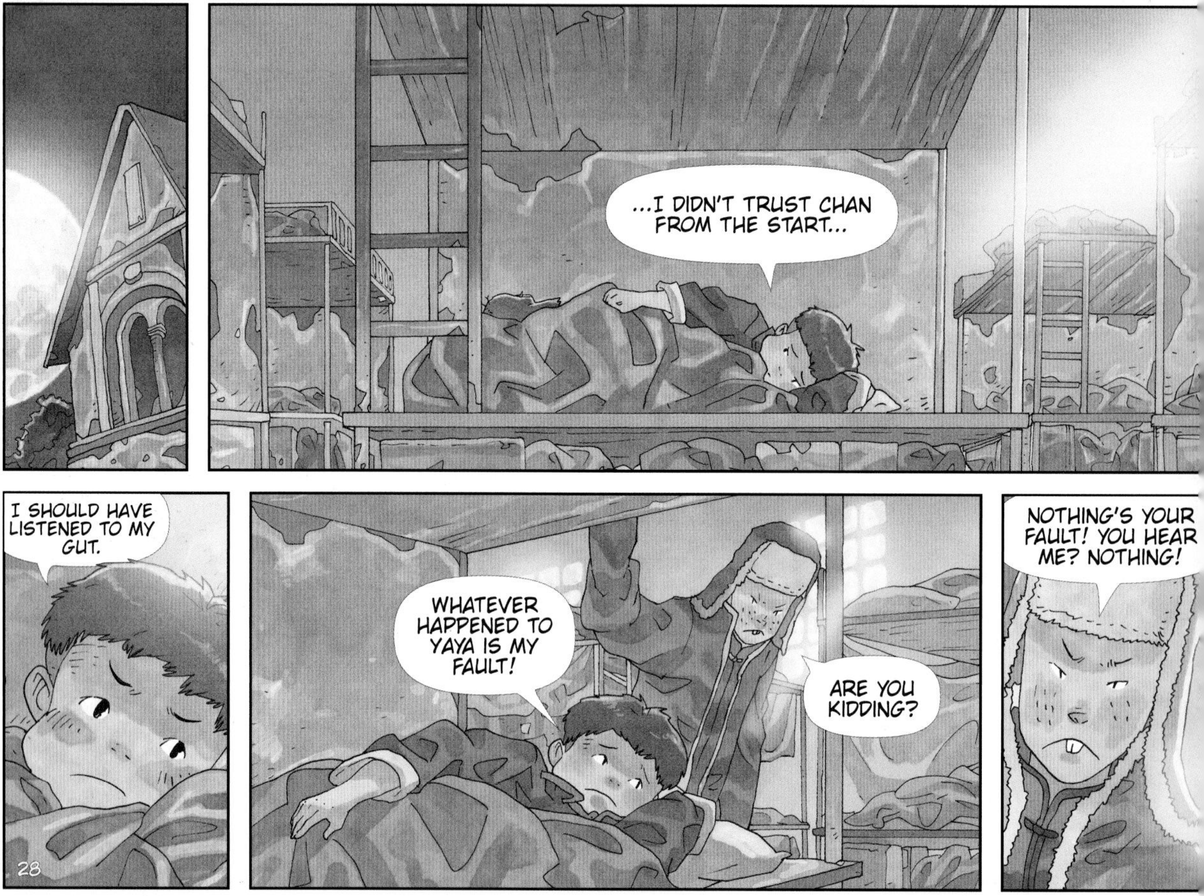
...I DIDN'T TRUST CHAN FROM THE START...
I SHOULD HAVE LISTENED TO MY GUT.
WHATEVER HAPPENED TO YAYA IS MY FAULT!
ARE YOU KIDDING?
NOTHING'S YOUR FAULT! YOU HEAR ME? NOTHING!

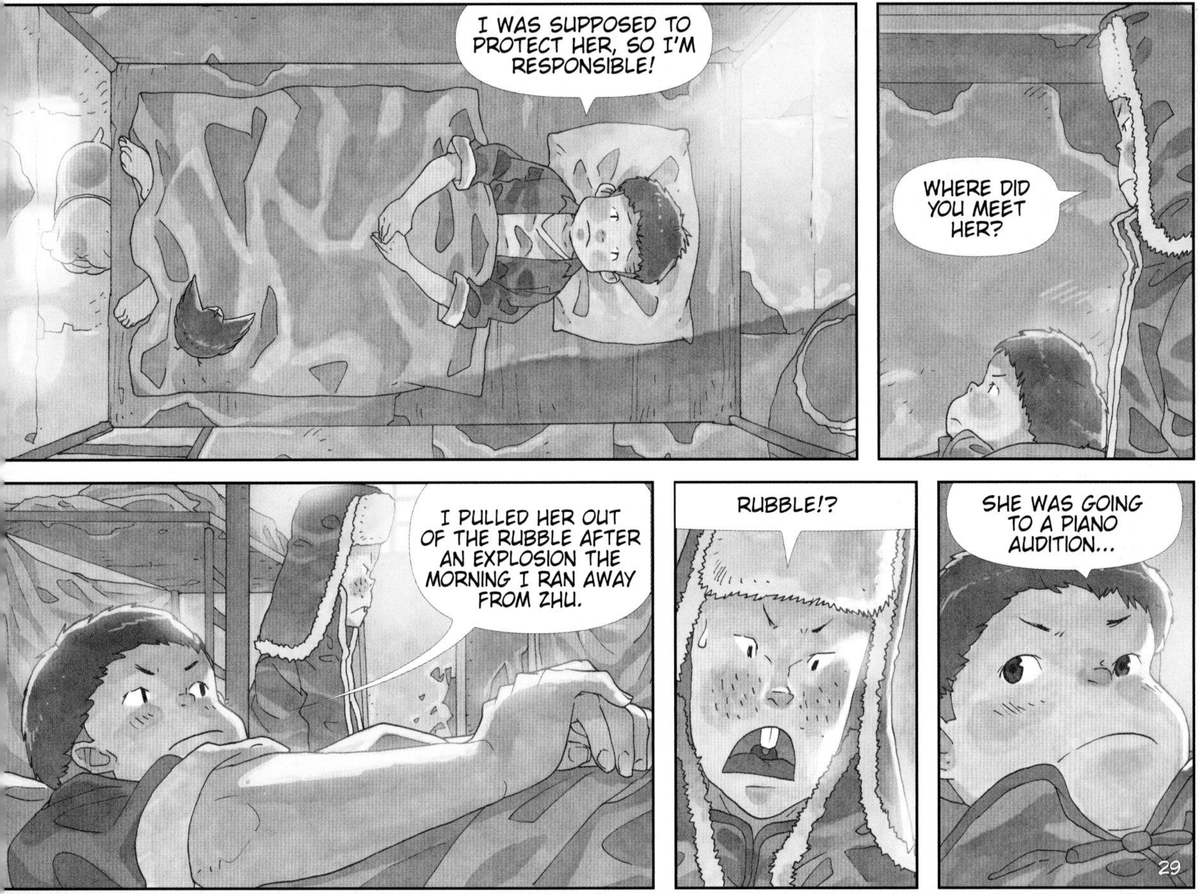

I WAS SUPPOSED TO PROTECT HER, SO I'M RESPONSIBLE!
WHERE DID YOU MEET HER?
I PULLED HER OUT OF THE RUBBLE AFTER AN EXPLOSION THE MORNING I RAN AWAY FROM ZHU.
RUBBLE!?
SHE WAS GOING TO A PIANO AUDITION...

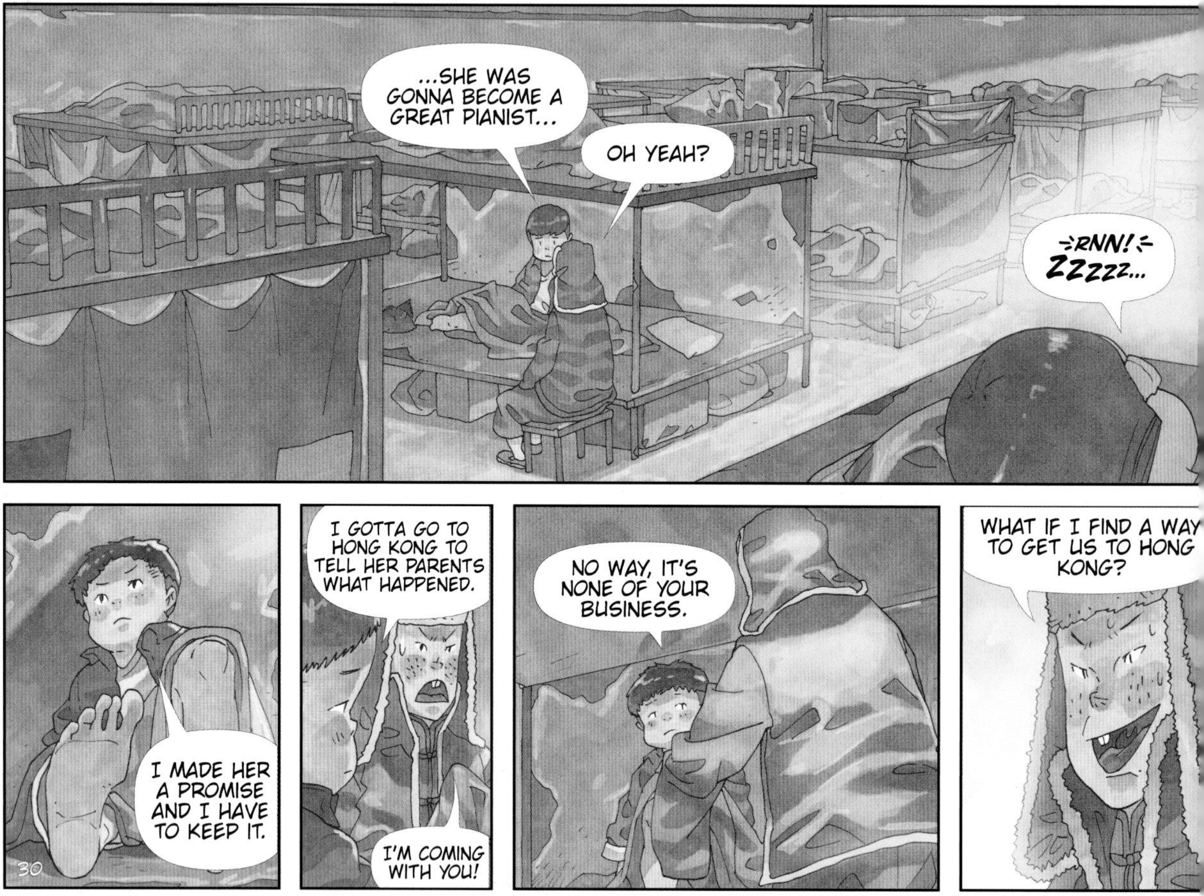
...SHE WAS GONNA BECOME A GREAT PIANIST...
OH YEAH?
RNN! ZZzzz...
I MADE HER A PROMISE AND I HAVE TO KEEP IT.
I GOTTA GO TO HONG KONG TO TELL HER PARENTS WHAT HAPPENED.
I'M COMING WITH YOU!
NO WAY, IT'S NONE OF YOUR BUSINESS.
WHAT IF I FIND A WAY TO GET US TO HONG KONG?

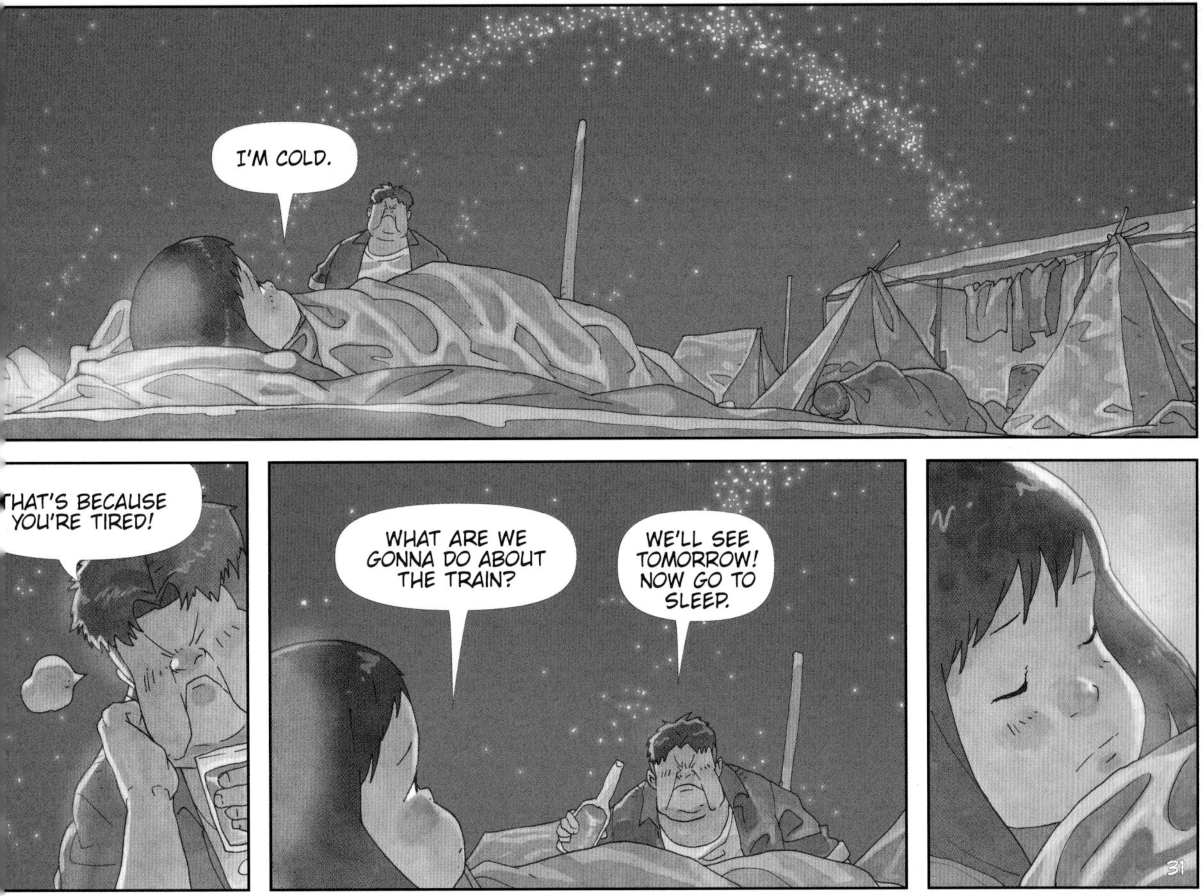
I'M COLD.
THAT'S BECAUSE YOU'RE TIRED!
WHAT ARE WE GONNA DO ABOUT THE TRAIN?
WE'LL SEE TOMORROW! NOW GO TO SLEEP.

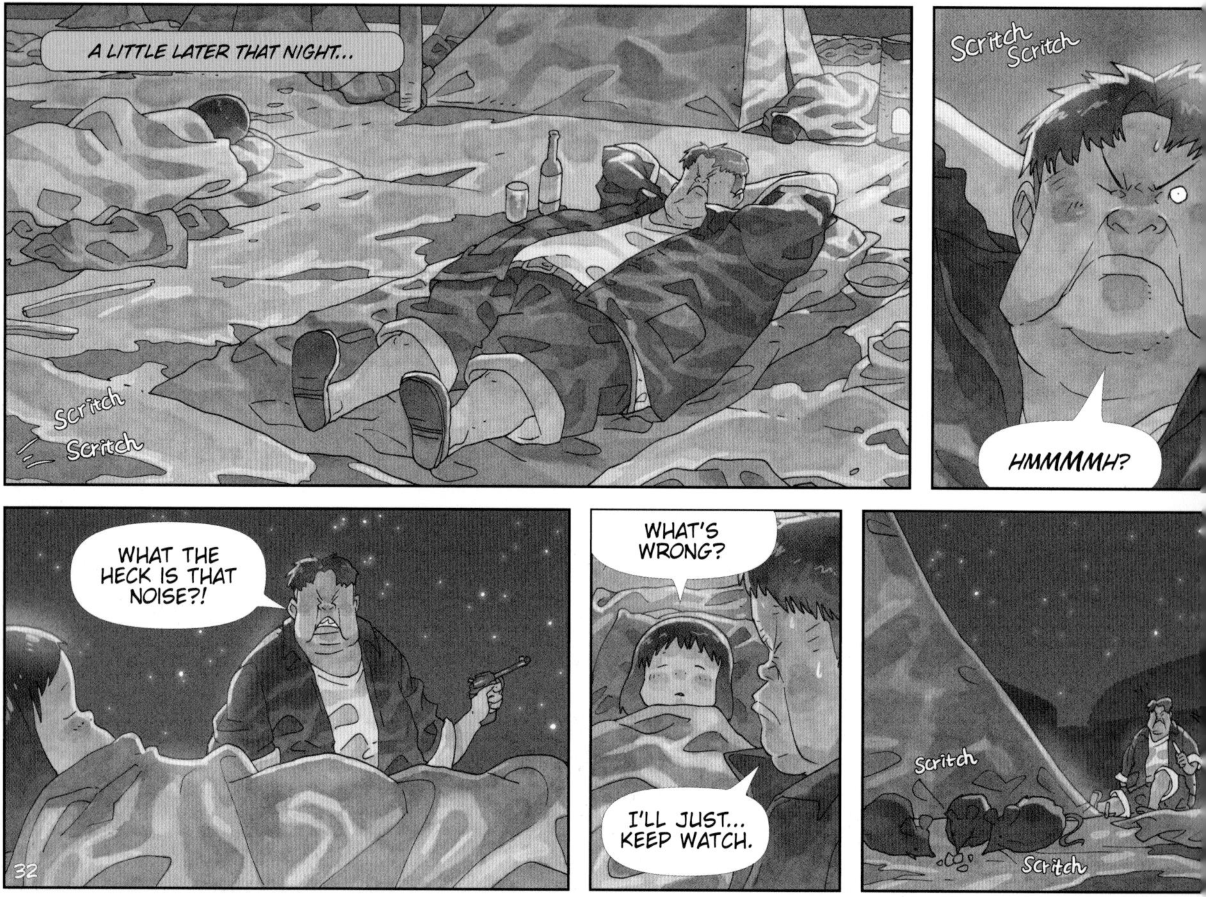
A LITTLE LATER THAT NIGHT...
Scritch
Scritch
Scritch
Scritch
HMMMMH?
WHAT THE HECK IS THAT NOISE?!
WHAT'S WRONG?
I'LL JUST... KEEP WATCH.
Scritch
Scritch

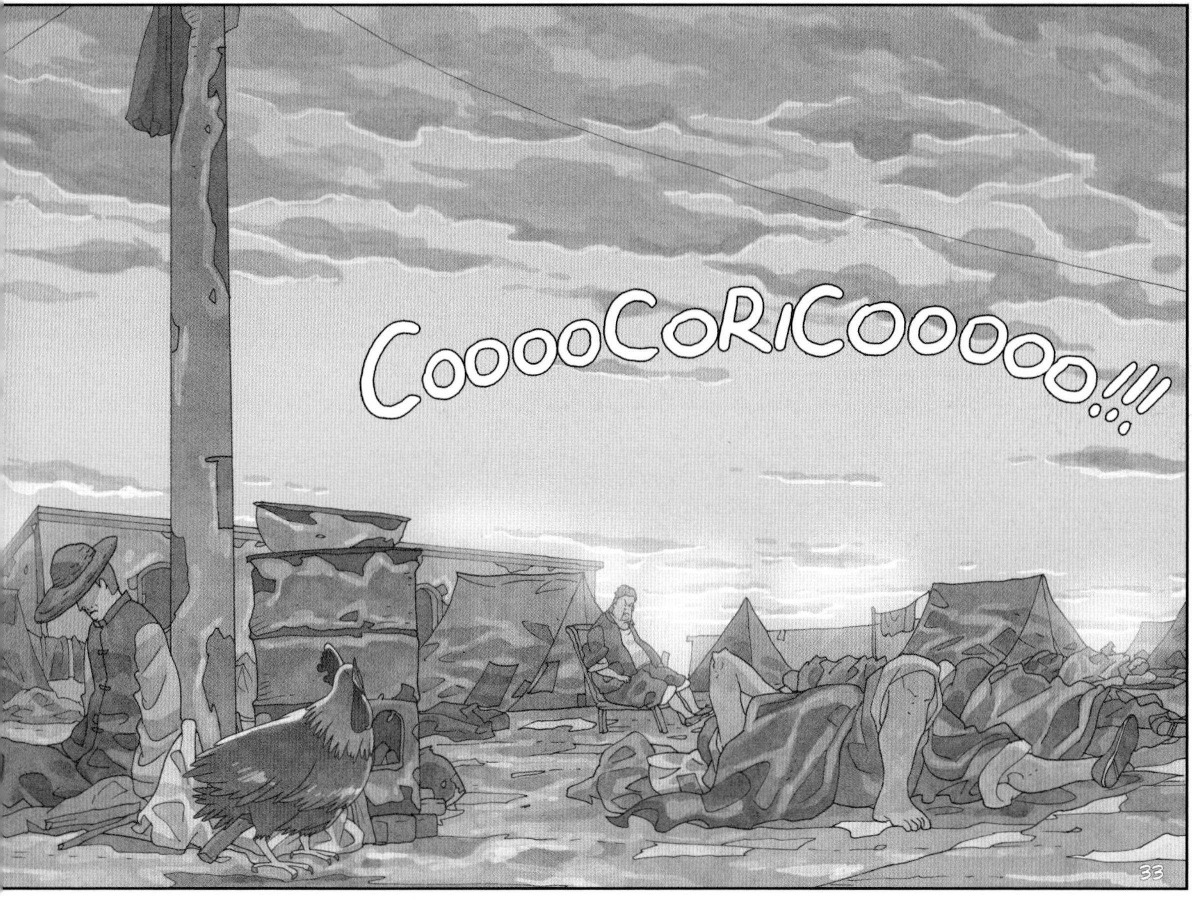
COOOOCORICOOOOOO...!!!

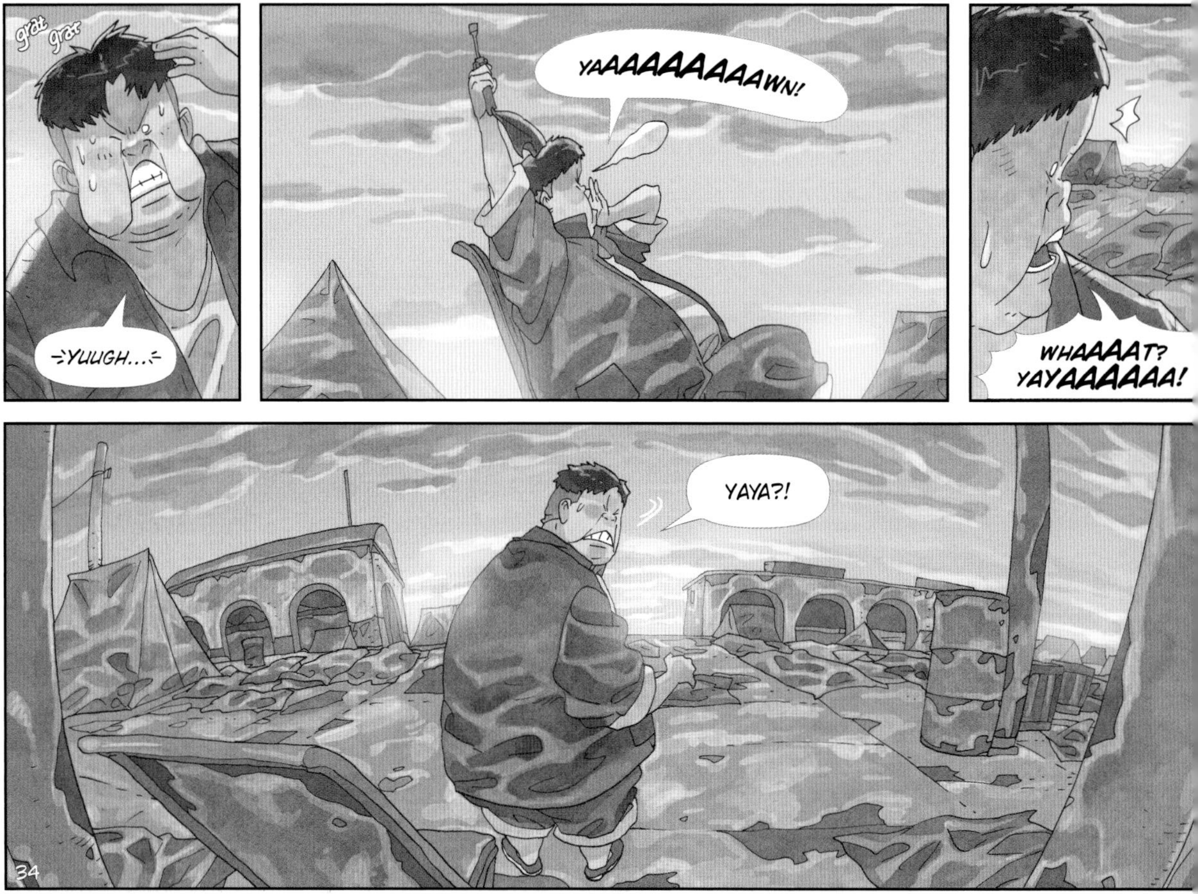
grat grat
YUUGH...
YAAAAAAAAAAWN!
WHAAAAT?
YAYAAAAAA!
YAYA?!

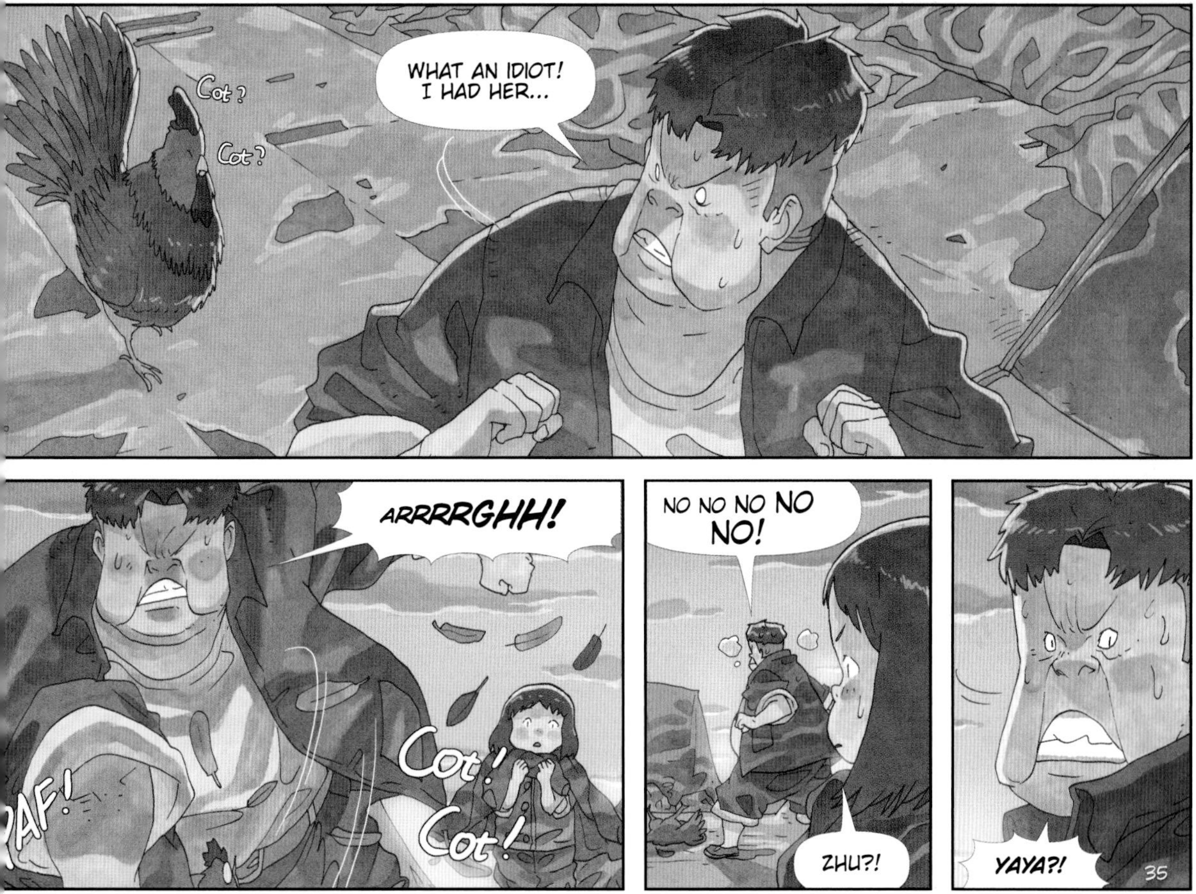
Cot?
Cot?
WHAT AN IDIOT! I HAD HER...
ARRRRGHH!
PAF!
Cot!
Cot!
NO NO NO NO NO!
ZHU?!
YAYA?!

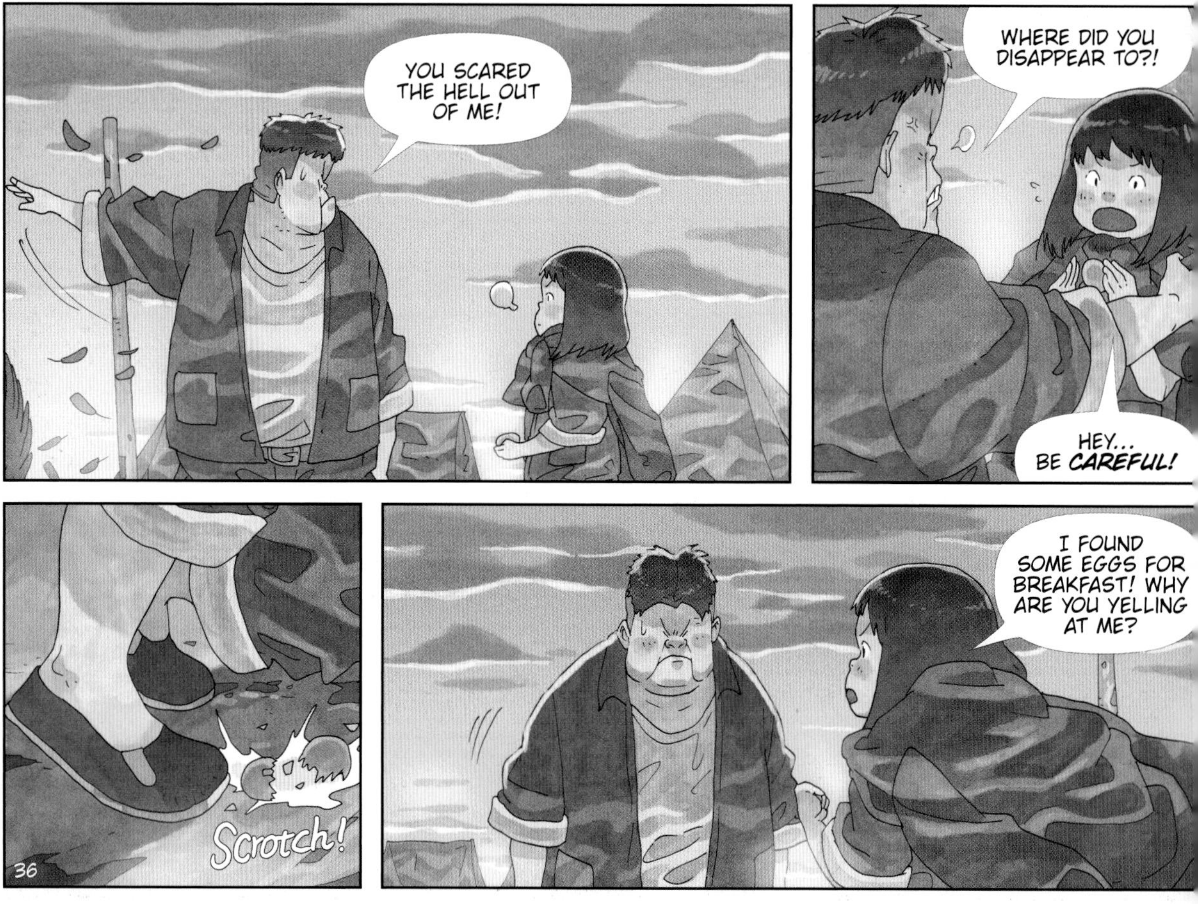
YOU SCARED THE HELL OUT OF ME!
WHERE DID YOU DISAPPEAR TO?!
HEY... BE **CAREFUL!**
Scrotch!
I FOUND SOME EGGS FOR BREAKFAST! WHY ARE YOU YELLING AT ME?

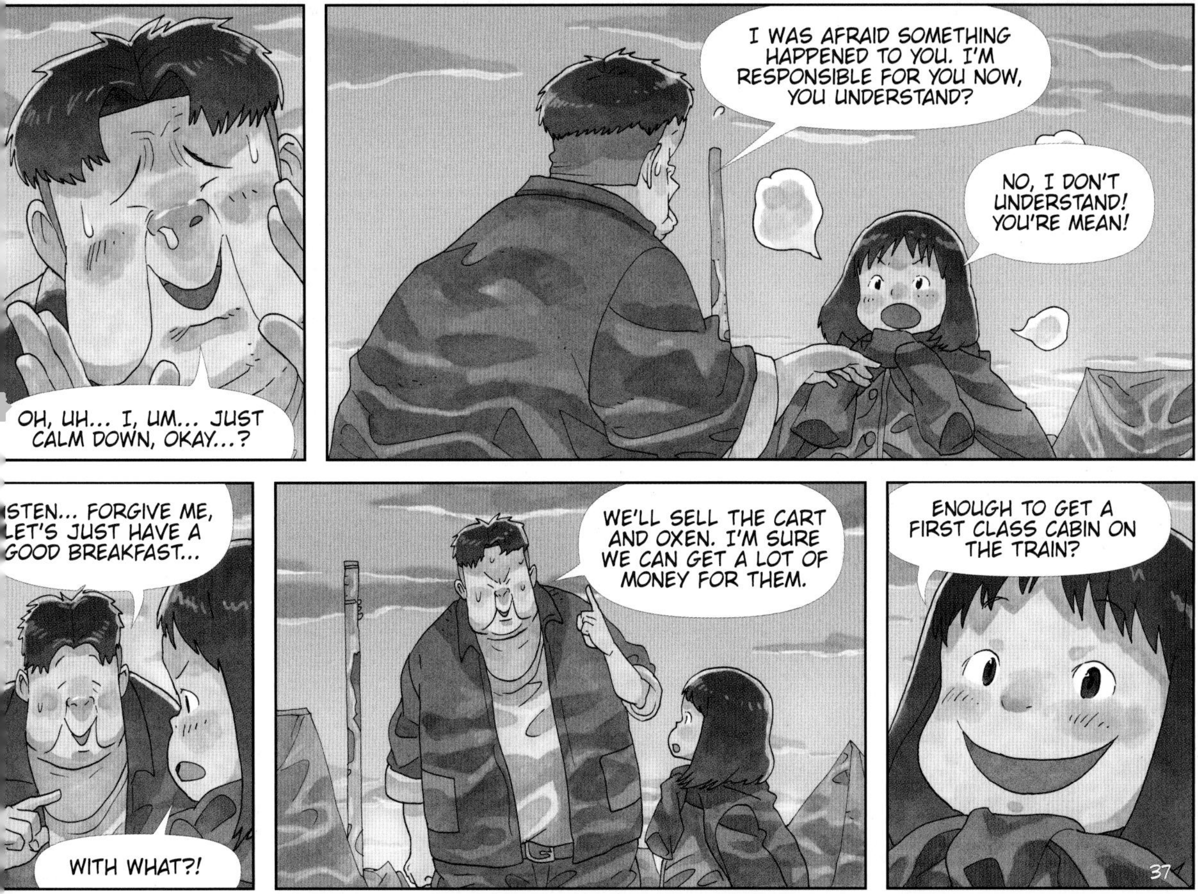
OH, UH... I, UM... JUST CALM DOWN, OKAY...?
I WAS AFRAID SOMETHING HAPPENED TO YOU. I'M RESPONSIBLE FOR YOU NOW, YOU UNDERSTAND?
NO, I DON'T UNDERSTAND! YOU'RE MEAN!
STEN... FORGIVE ME, LET'S JUST HAVE A GOOD BREAKFAST...
WITH WHAT?!
WE'LL SELL THE CART AND OXEN. I'M SURE WE CAN GET A LOT OF MONEY FOR THEM.
ENOUGH TO GET A FIRST CLASS CABIN ON THE TRAIN?

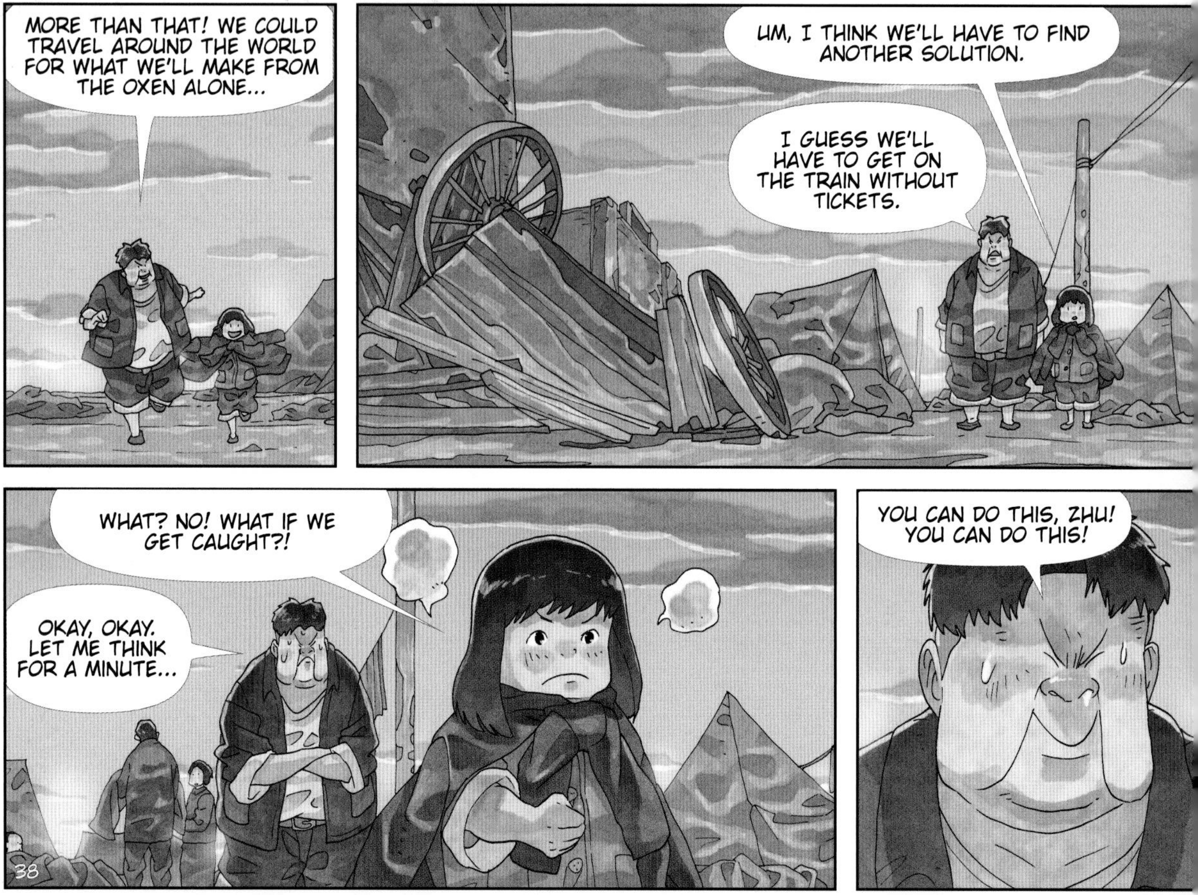
MORE THAN THAT! WE COULD TRAVEL AROUND THE WORLD FOR WHAT WE'LL MAKE FROM THE OXEN ALONE...
UM, I THINK WE'LL HAVE TO FIND ANOTHER SOLUTION.
I GUESS WE'LL HAVE TO GET ON THE TRAIN WITHOUT TICKETS.
WHAT? NO! WHAT IF WE GET CAUGHT?!
OKAY, OKAY. LET ME THINK FOR A MINUTE...
YOU CAN DO THIS, ZHU! YOU CAN DO THIS!

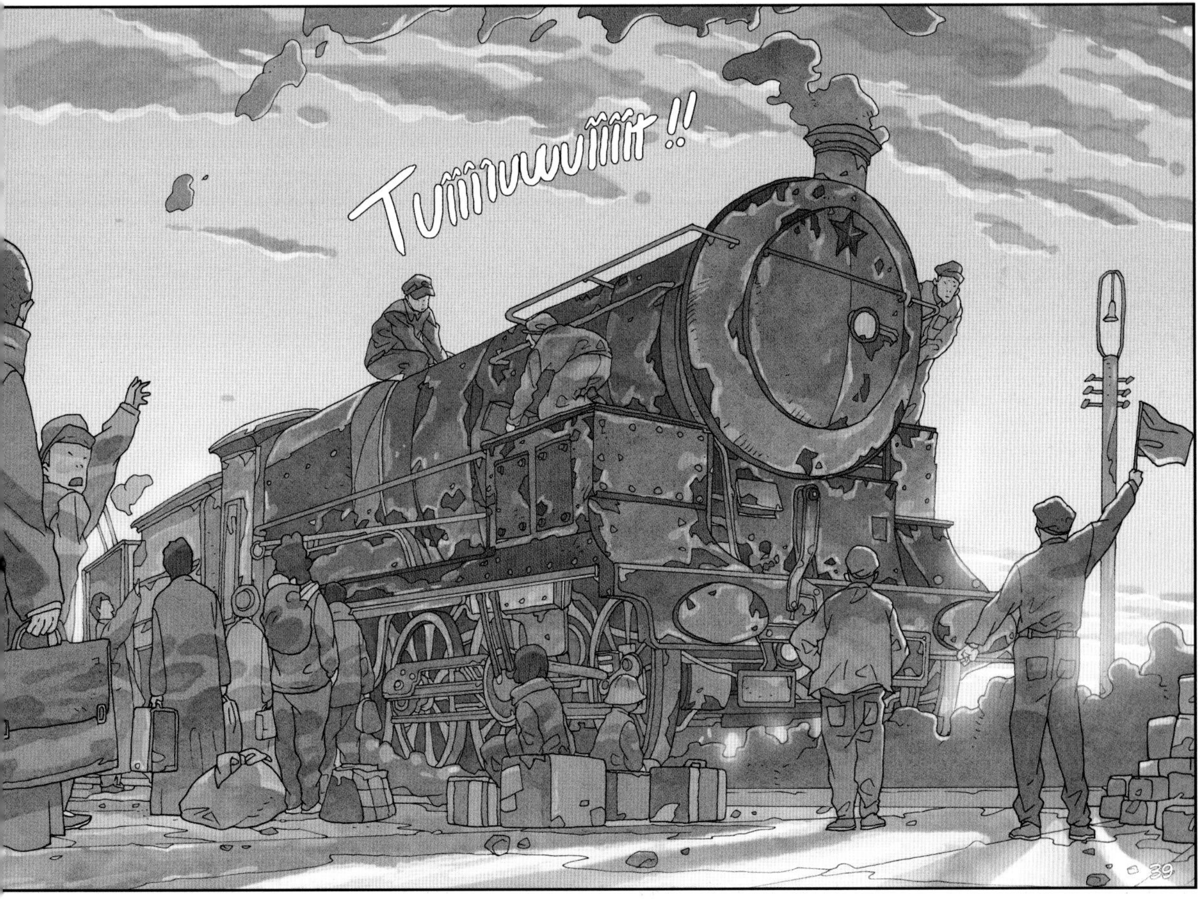
Tuĩîîruuuĩĩîît !!

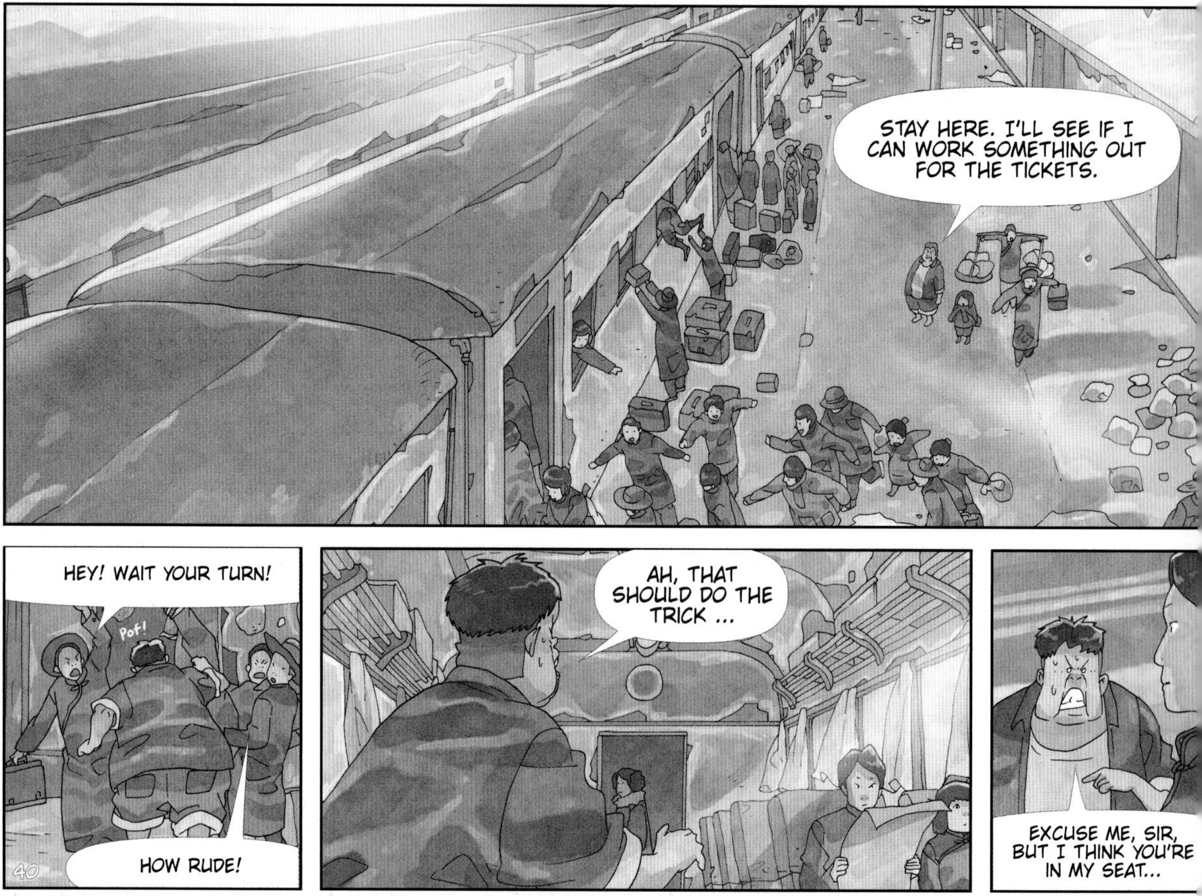
STAY HERE. I'LL SEE IF I CAN WORK SOMETHING OUT FOR THE TICKETS.
HEY! WAIT YOUR TURN!
Pof!
HOW RUDE!
AH, THAT SHOULD DO THE TRICK ...
EXCUSE ME, SIR, BUT I THINK YOU'RE IN MY SEAT...

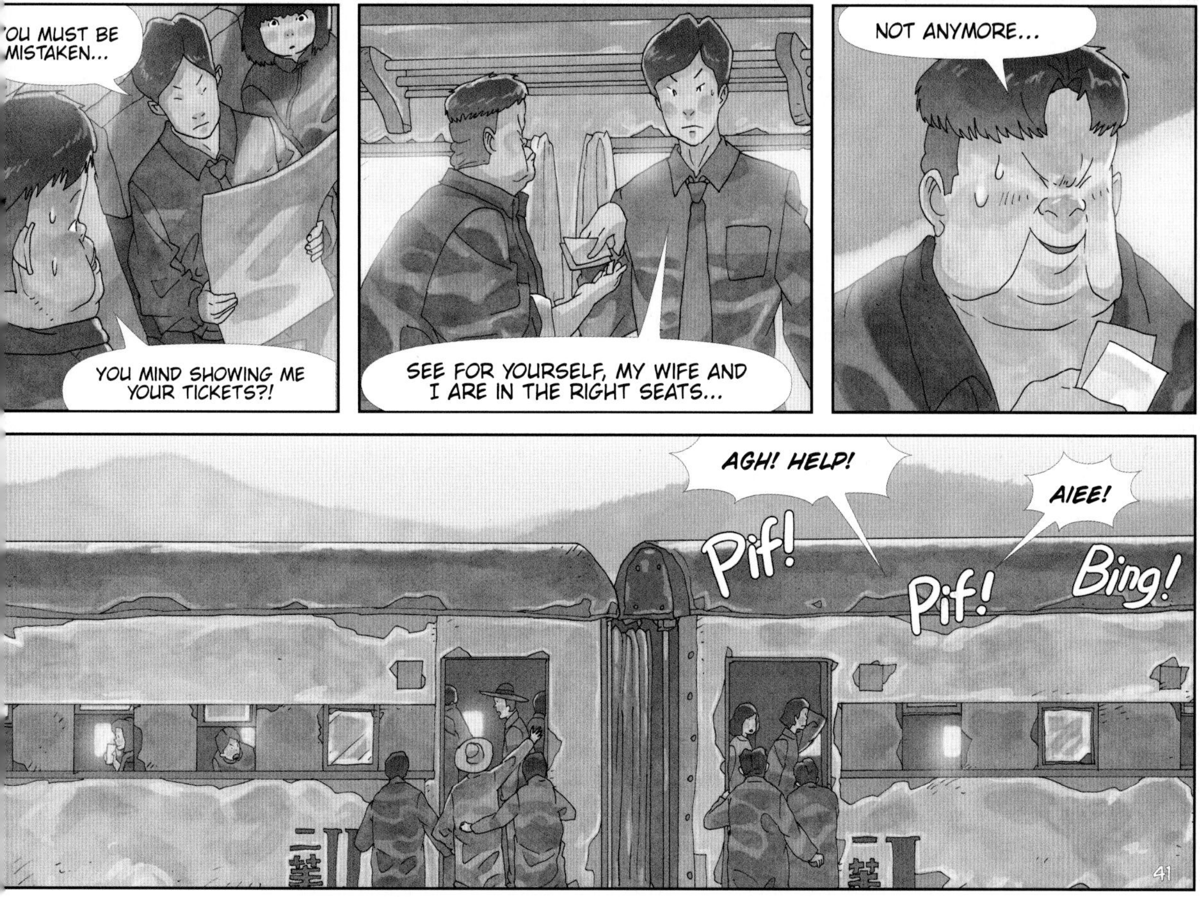
OU MUST BE MISTAKEN...
YOU MIND SHOWING ME YOUR TICKETS?!
SEE FOR YOURSELF, MY WIFE AND I ARE IN THE RIGHT SEATS...
NOT ANYMORE...
AGH! HELP!
AIEE!
Pif!
Pif!
Bing!

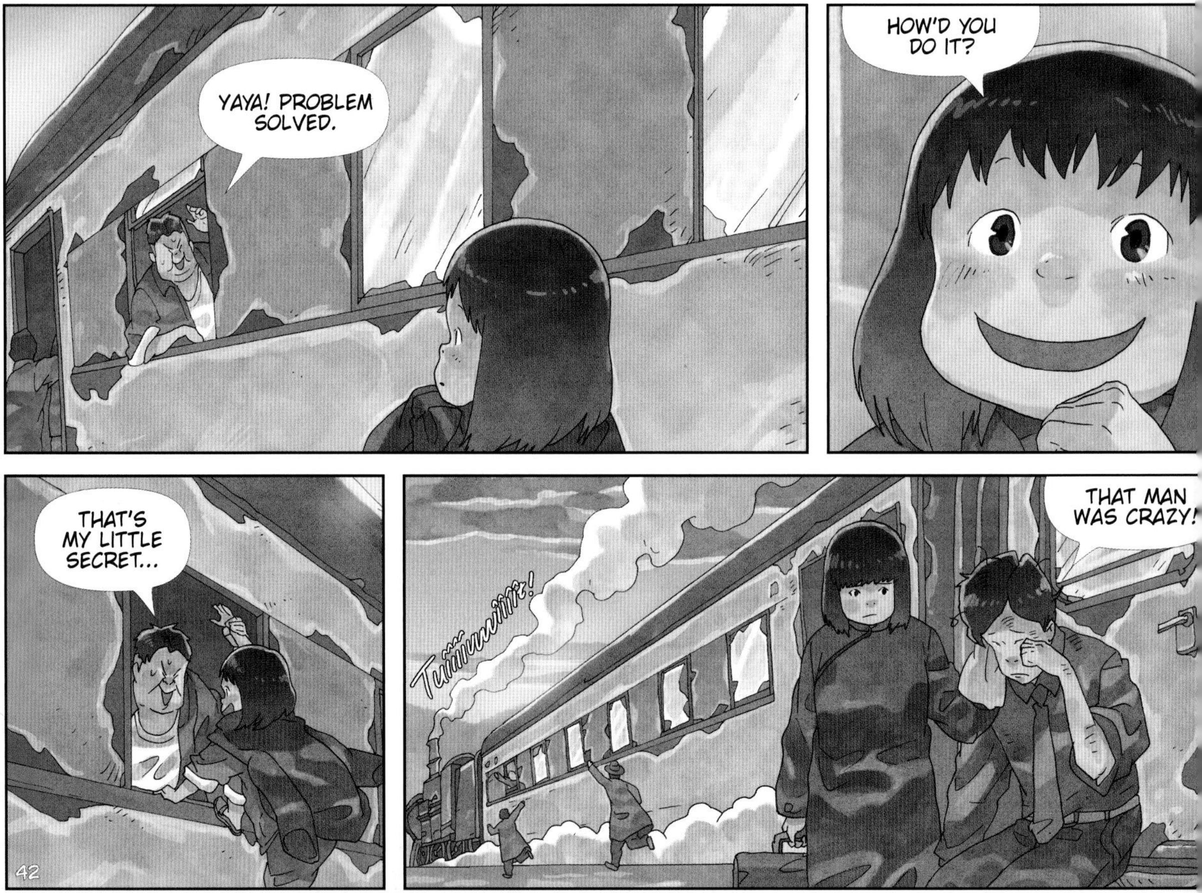
YAYA! PROBLEM SOLVED.
HOW'D YOU DO IT?
THAT'S MY LITTLE SECRET...
Tuiiiuuuiiiit!
THAT MAN WAS CRAZY!

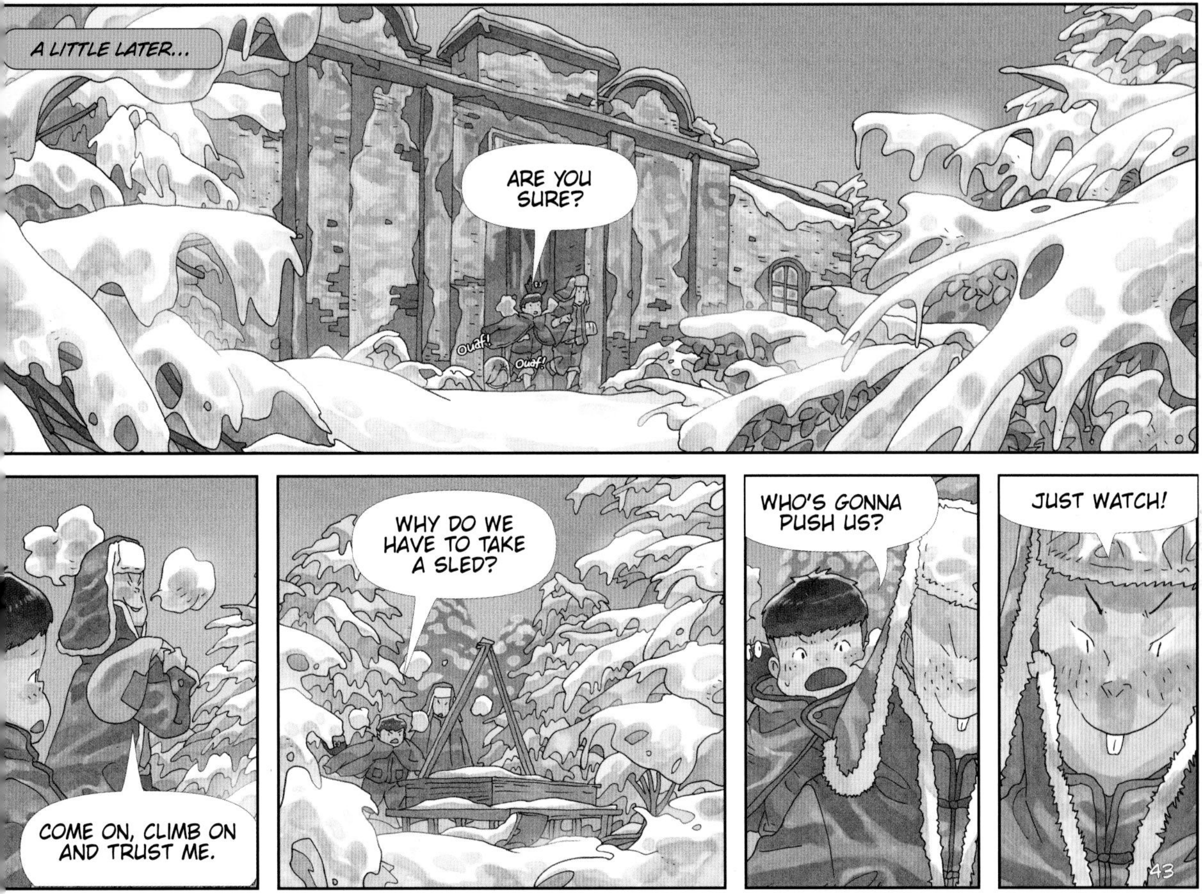
A LITTLE LATER...
ARE YOU SURE?
Ouaf!
Ouaf!
COME ON, CLIMB ON AND TRUST ME.
WHY DO WE HAVE TO TAKE A SLED?
WHO'S GONNA PUSH US?
JUST WATCH!

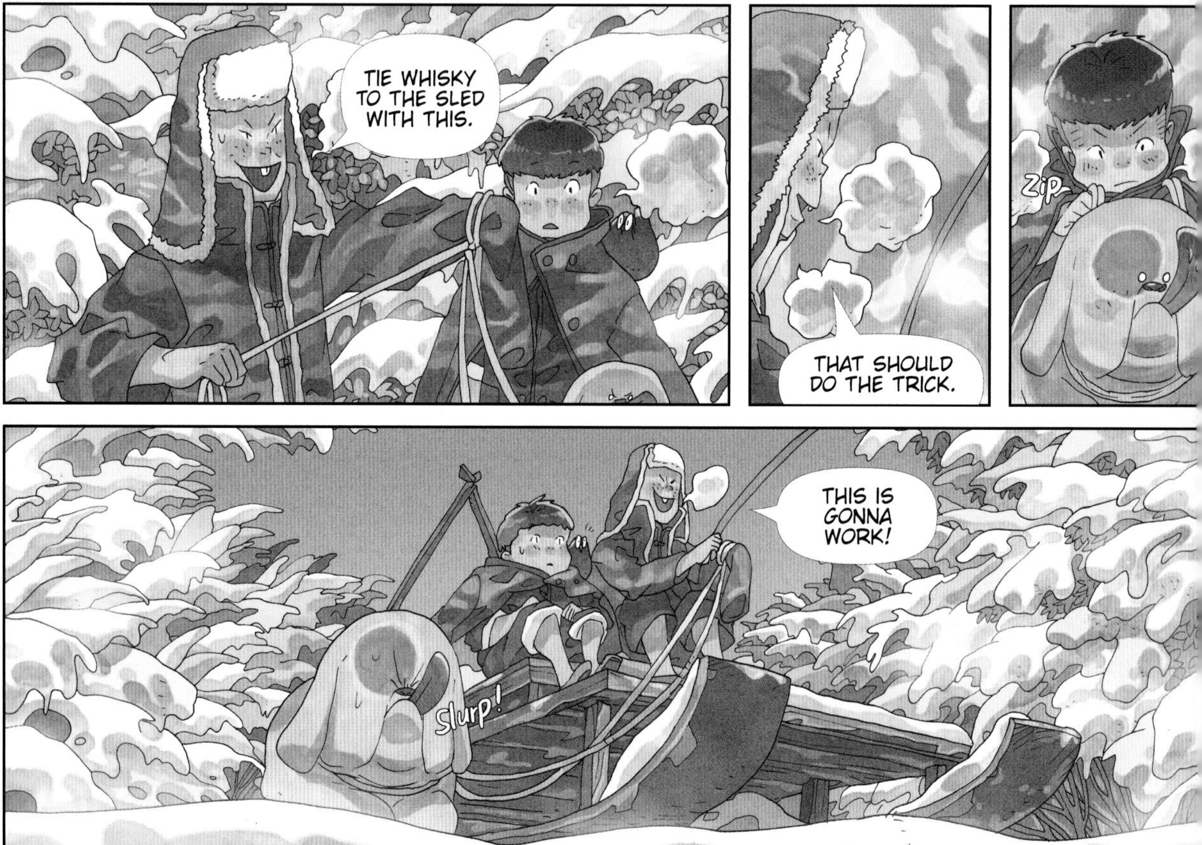
TIE WHISKY TO THE SLED WITH THIS.
THAT SHOULD DO THE TRICK.
ZIP
THIS IS GONNA WORK!
Slurp!

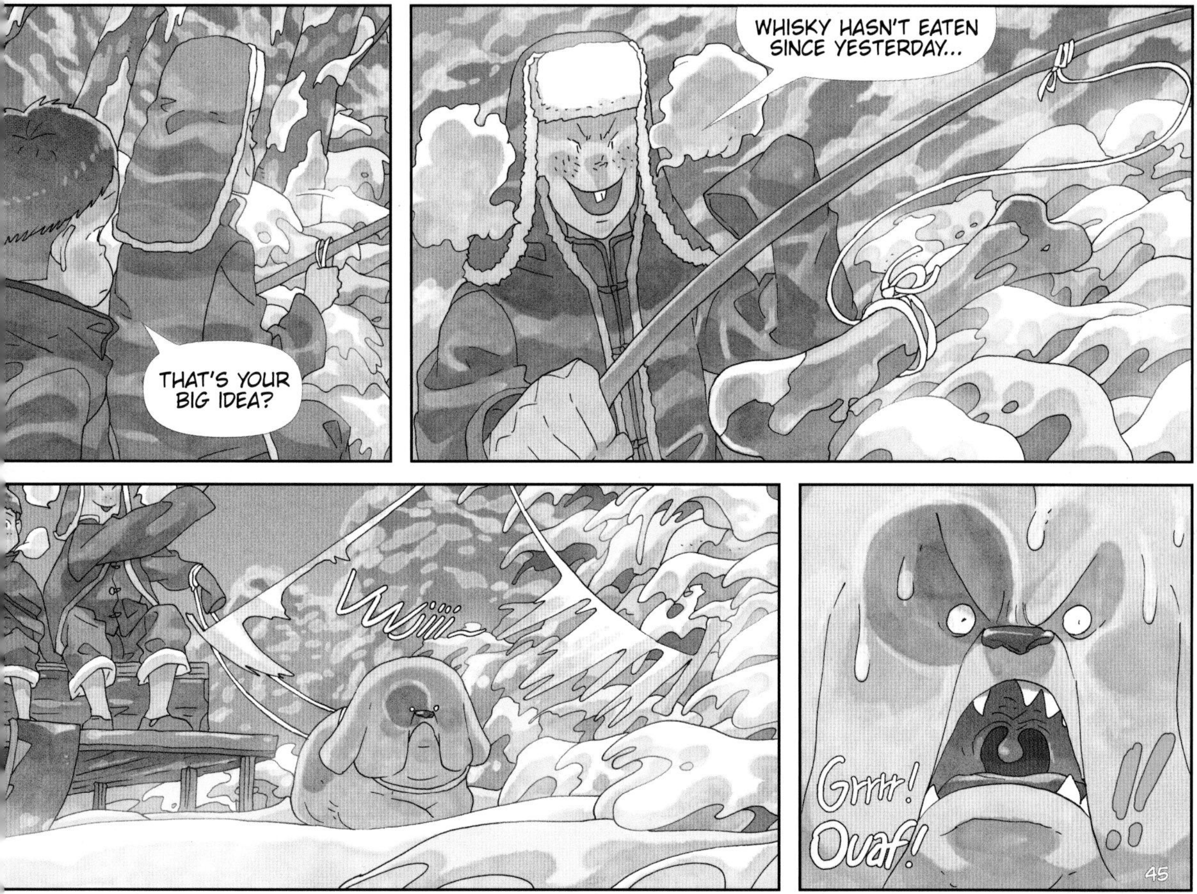
THAT'S YOUR BIG IDEA?
WHISKY HASN'T EATEN SINCE YESTERDAY...
Grrrr!
Ouaf!
!!

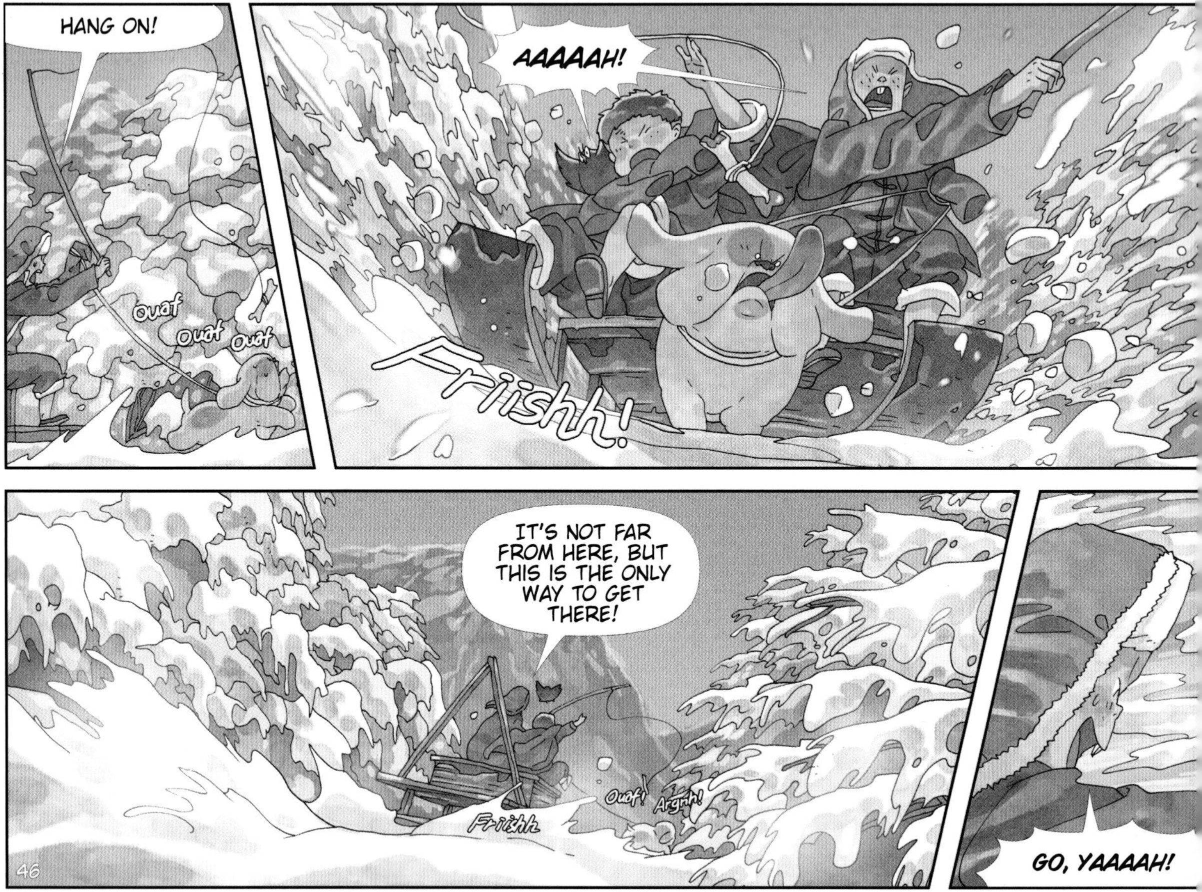
HANG ON!
Ouaf
Ouaf
Ouaf
AAAAAH!
Friishh!
IT'S NOT FAR FROM HERE, BUT THIS IS THE ONLY WAY TO GET THERE!
Friishh
Ouaf!
Argnh!
GO, YAAAAH!

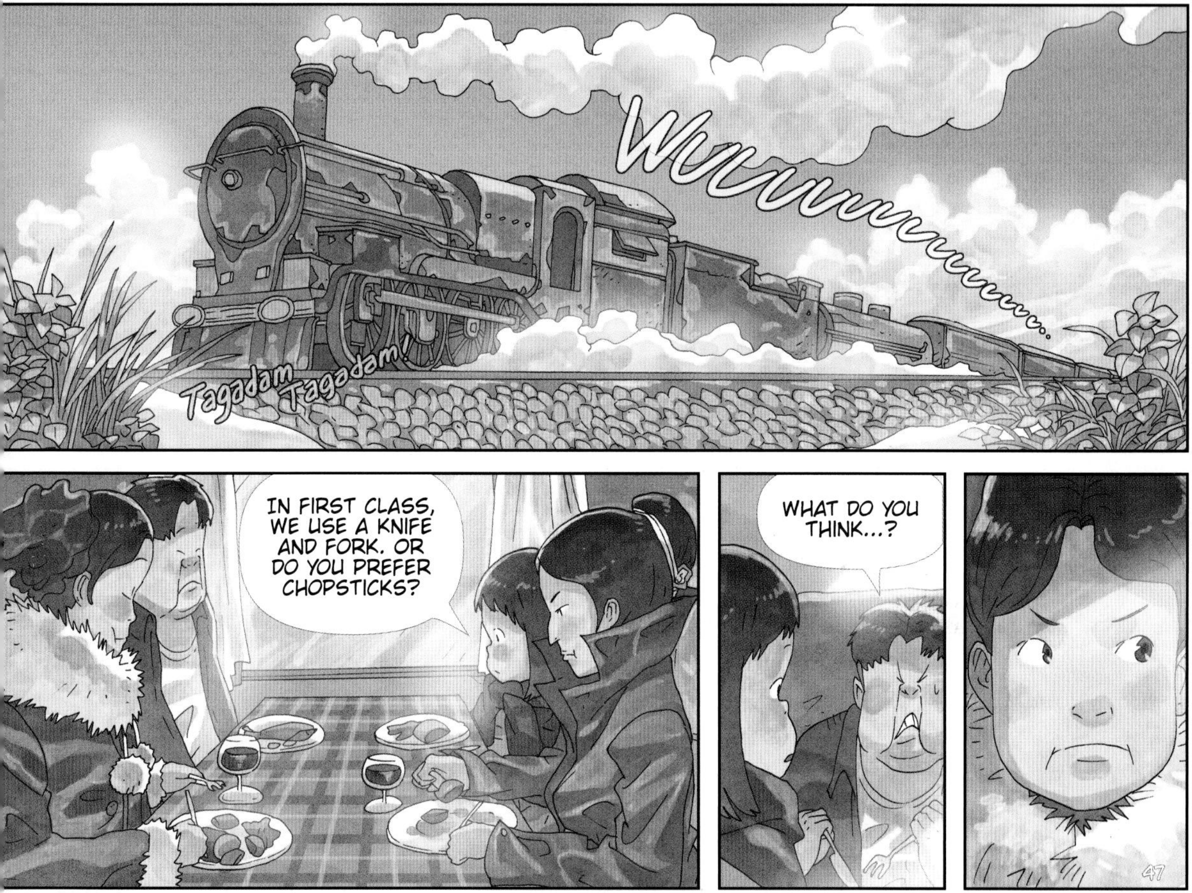
WUUUUUUUUUUUU...
Tagadam Tagadam!
IN FIRST CLASS, WE USE A KNIFE AND FORK. OR DO YOU PREFER CHOPSTICKS?
WHAT DO YOU THINK...?

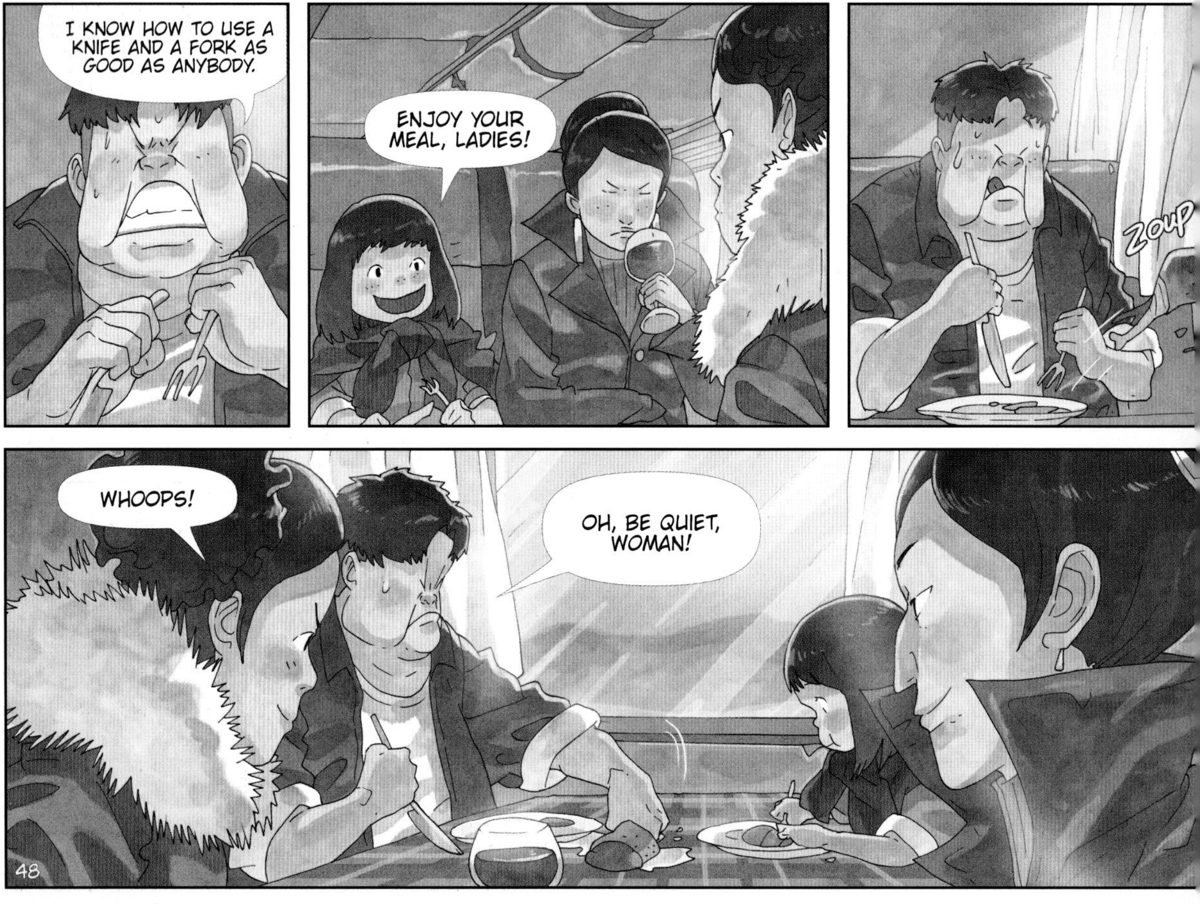
I KNOW HOW TO USE A KNIFE AND A FORK AS GOOD AS ANYBODY.
ENJOY YOUR MEAL, LADIES!
ZOUP
WHOOPS!
OH, BE QUIET, WOMAN!

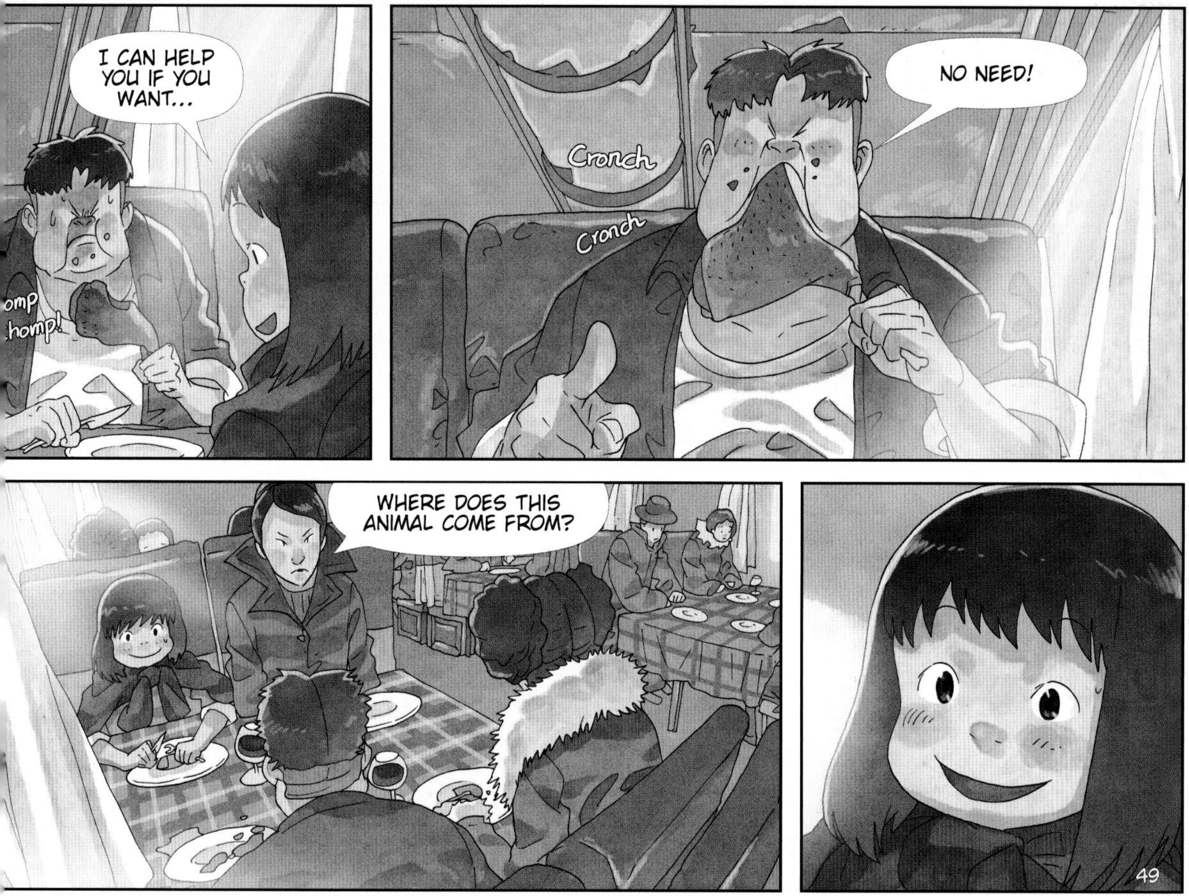
I CAN HELP YOU IF YOU WANT...
omp
chomp!
NO NEED!
Cronch
Cronch
WHERE DOES THIS ANIMAL COME FROM?

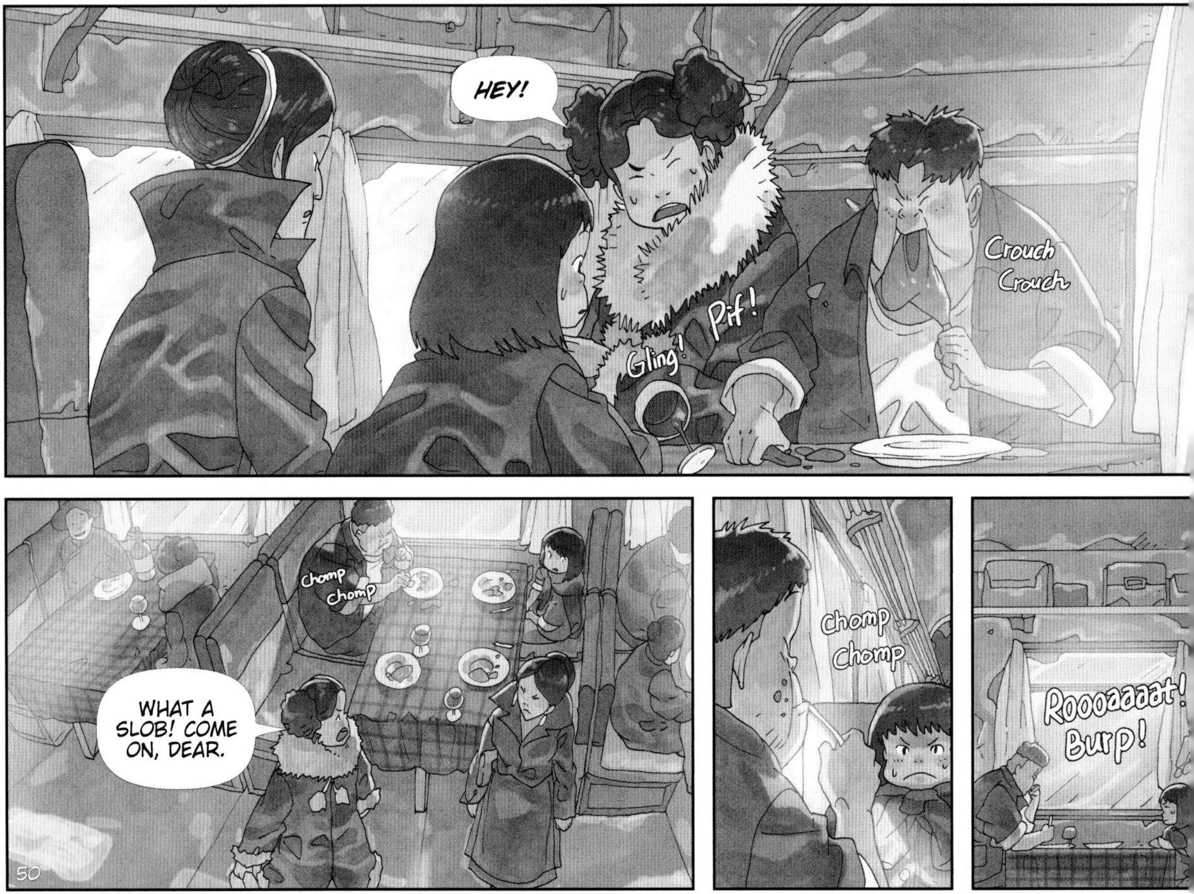
HEY!
Crouch
Crouch
Pif!
Gling!
Chomp
chomp
WHAT A SLOB! COME ON, DEAR.
Chomp
Chomp
Roooaaaat!
Burp!

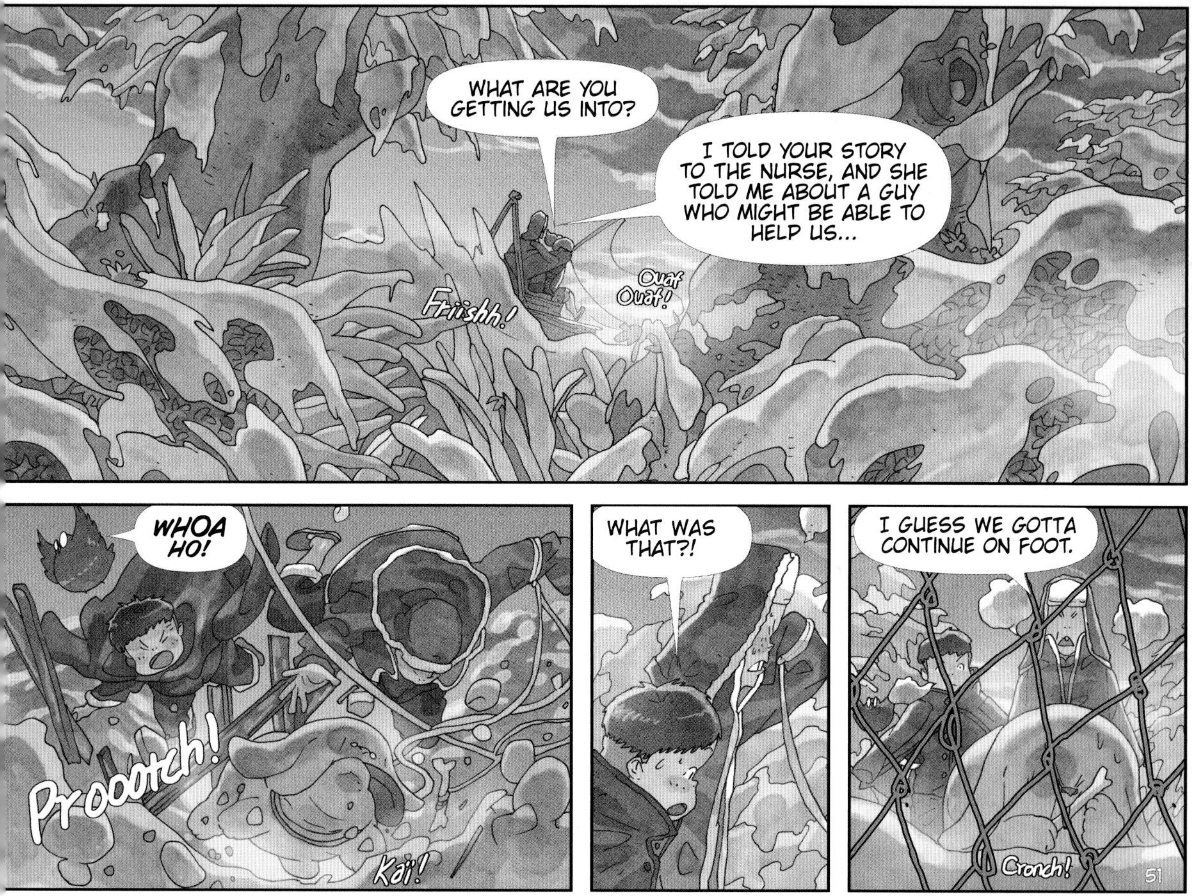
WHAT ARE YOU GETTING US INTO?
I TOLD YOUR STORY TO THE NURSE, AND SHE TOLD ME ABOUT A GUY WHO MIGHT BE ABLE TO HELP US...
Friishh!
Ouaf Ouaf!
WHOA HO!
Prooootch!
Kaï!
WHAT WAS THAT?!
I GUESS WE GOTTA CONTINUE ON FOOT.
Cronch!

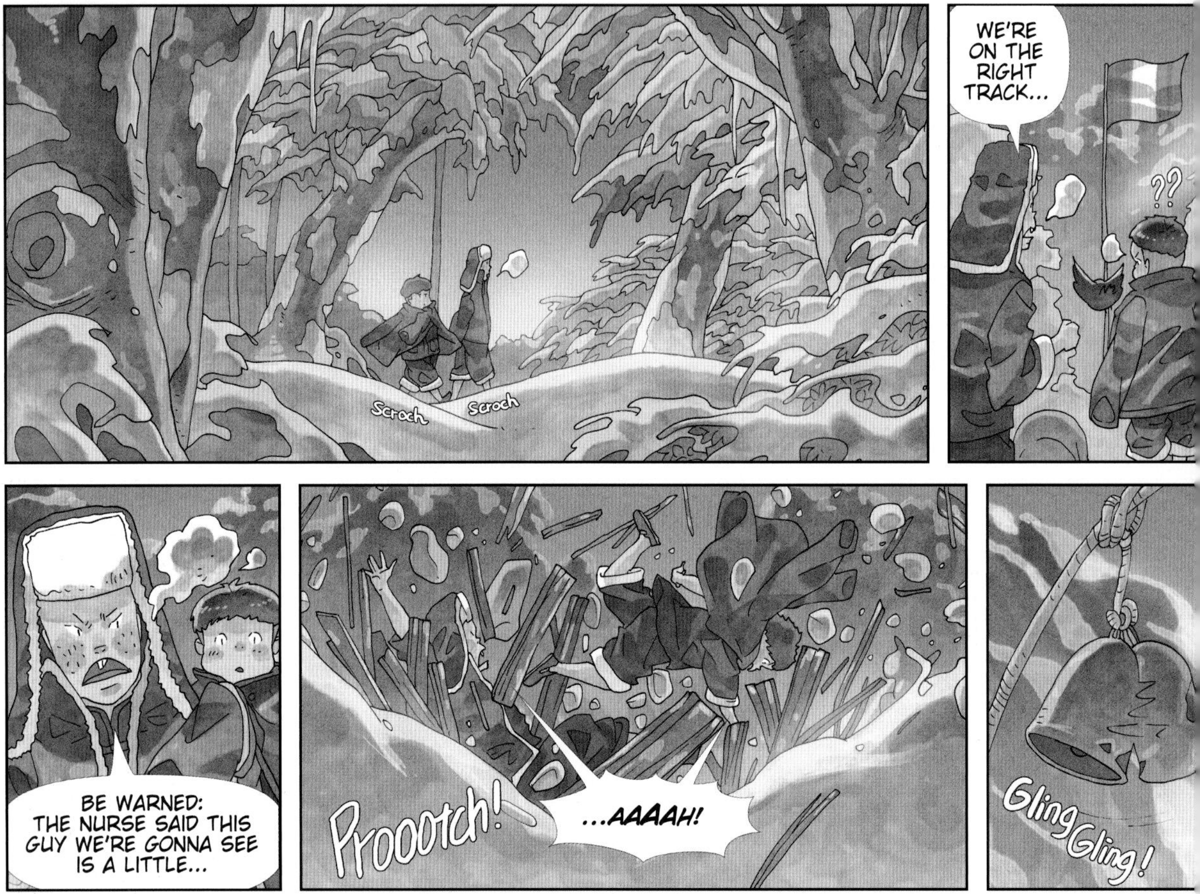
Scroch
Scroch
WE'RE ON THE RIGHT TRACK...
??
BE WARNED: THE NURSE SAID THIS GUY WE'RE GONNA SEE IS A LITTLE...
Prooootch!
...AAAAH!
Gling Gling!

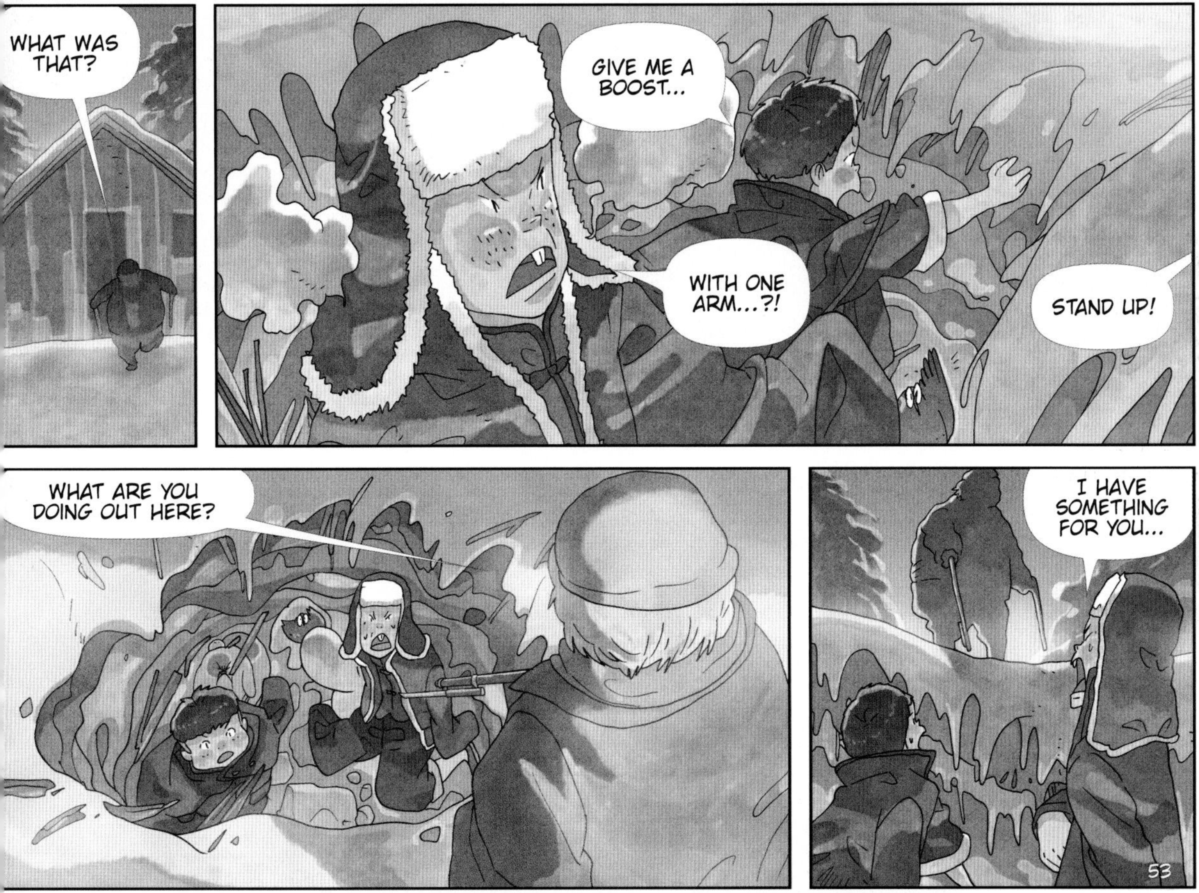
WHAT WAS THAT?
GIVE ME A BOOST...
WITH ONE ARM...?!
STAND UP!
WHAT ARE YOU DOING OUT HERE?
I HAVE SOMETHING FOR YOU...

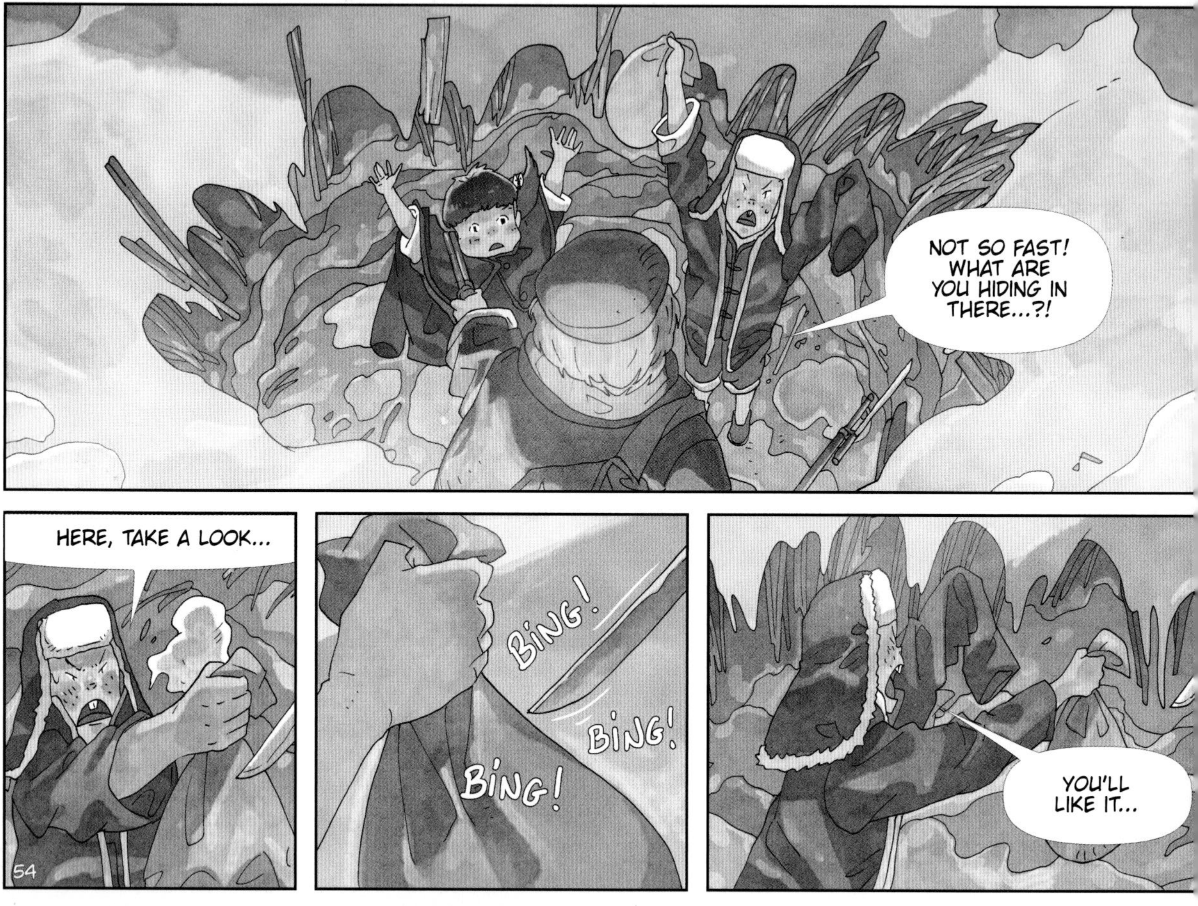
NOT SO FAST! WHAT ARE YOU HIDING IN THERE...?!
HERE, TAKE A LOOK...
BING!
BING!
BING!
YOU'LL LIKE IT...

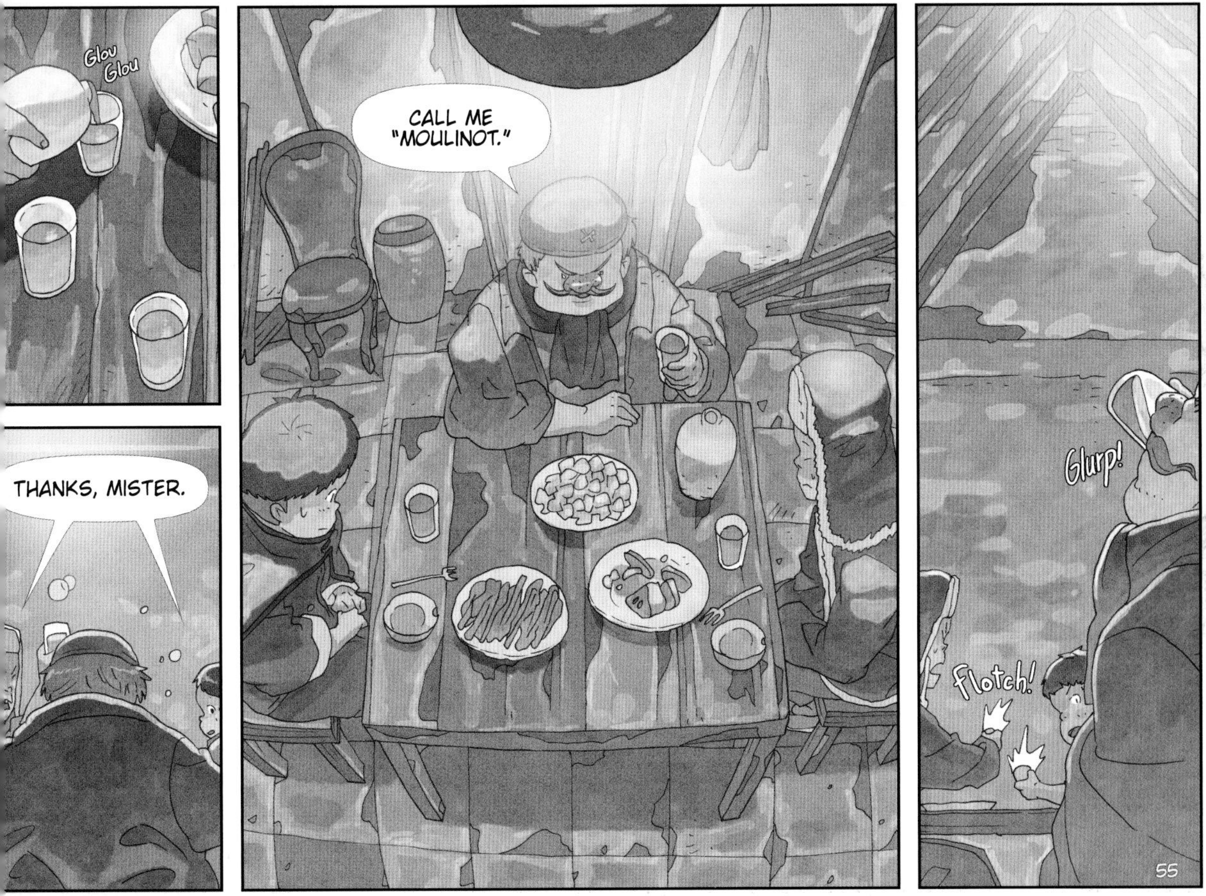
Glou
Glou
THANKS, MISTER.
CALL ME "MOULINOT."
Glurp!
Flotch!

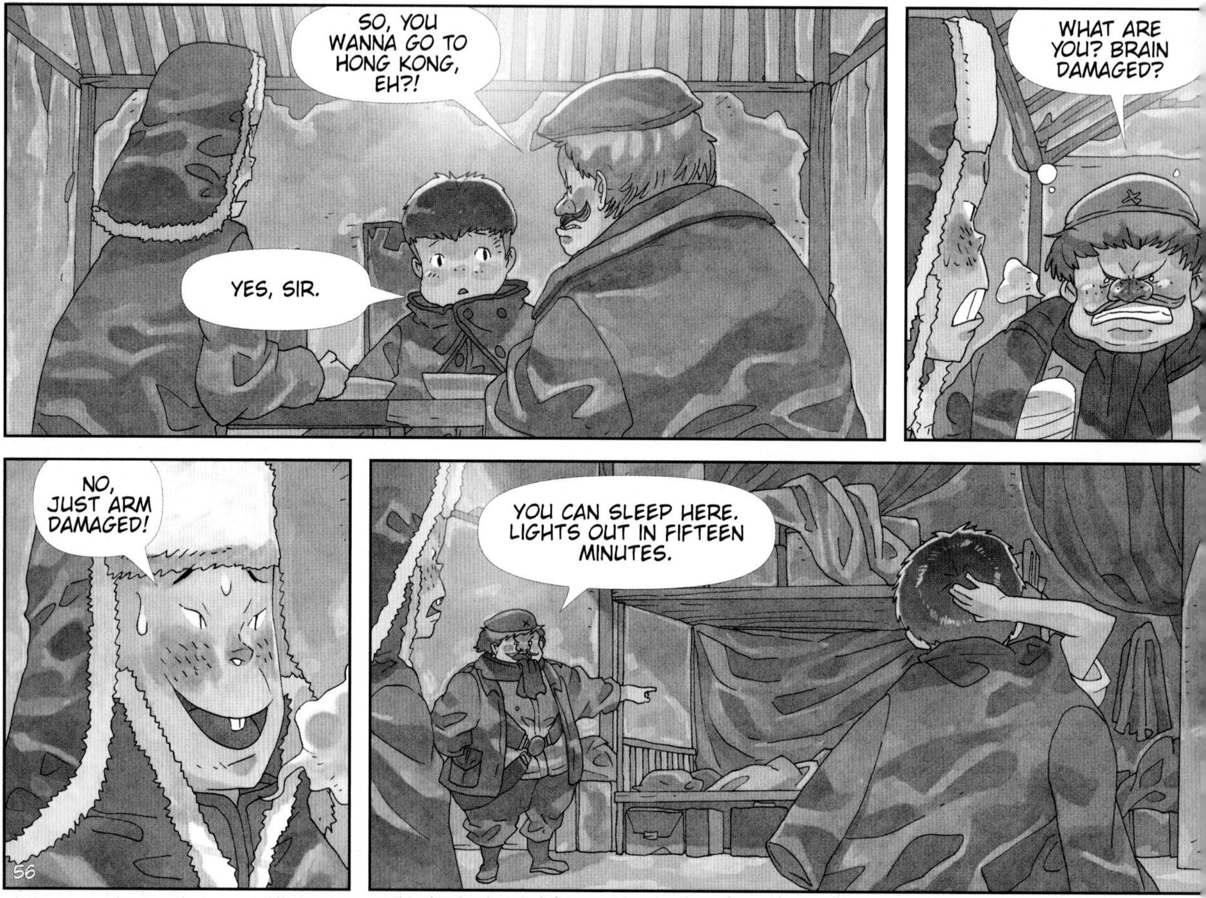
SO, YOU WANNA GO TO HONG KONG, EH?!
YES, SIR.
WHAT ARE YOU? BRAIN DAMAGED?
NO, JUST ARM DAMAGED!
YOU CAN SLEEP HERE. LIGHTS OUT IN FIFTEEN MINUTES.

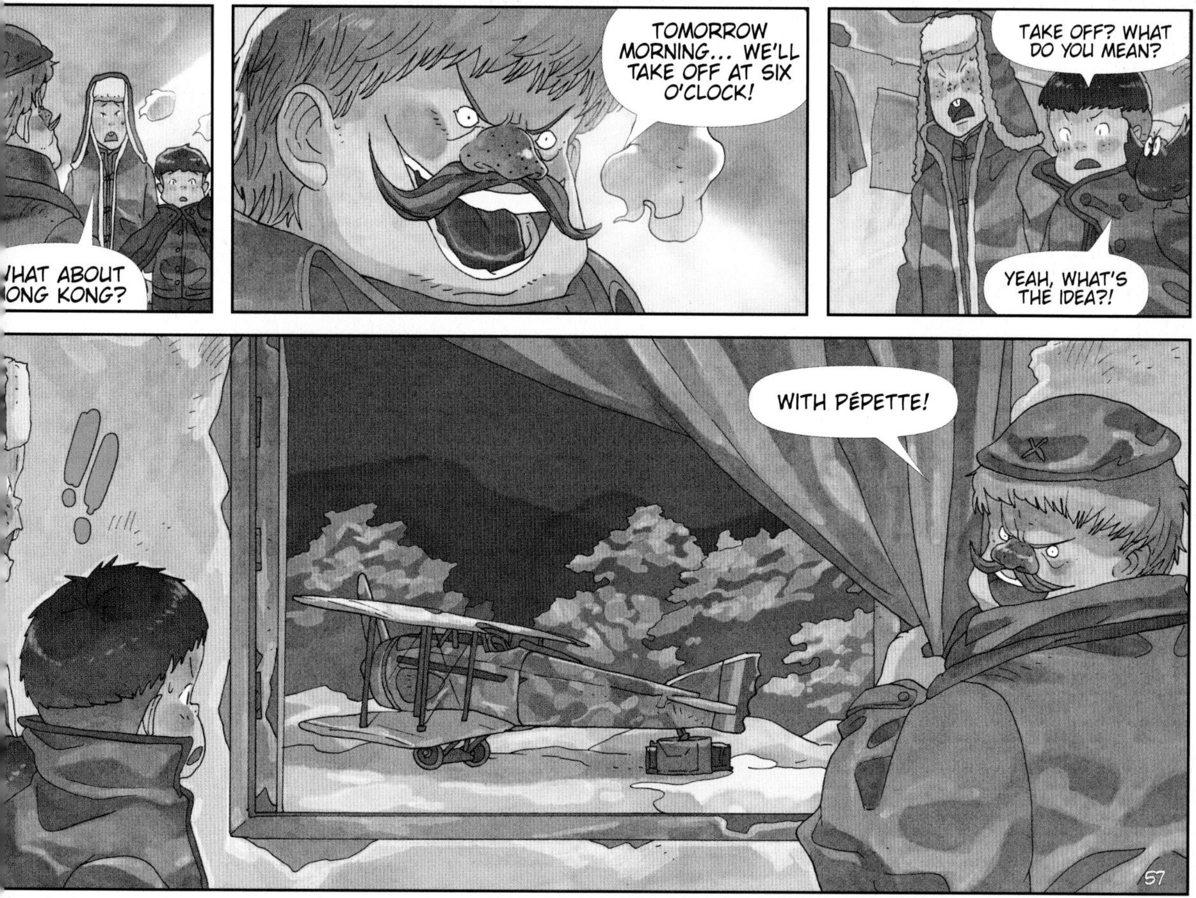
HAT ABOUT ONG KONG?
TOMORROW MORNING... WE'LL TAKE OFF AT SIX O'CLOCK!
TAKE OFF? WHAT DO YOU MEAN?
YEAH, WHAT'S THE IDEA?!
WITH PÉPETTE!

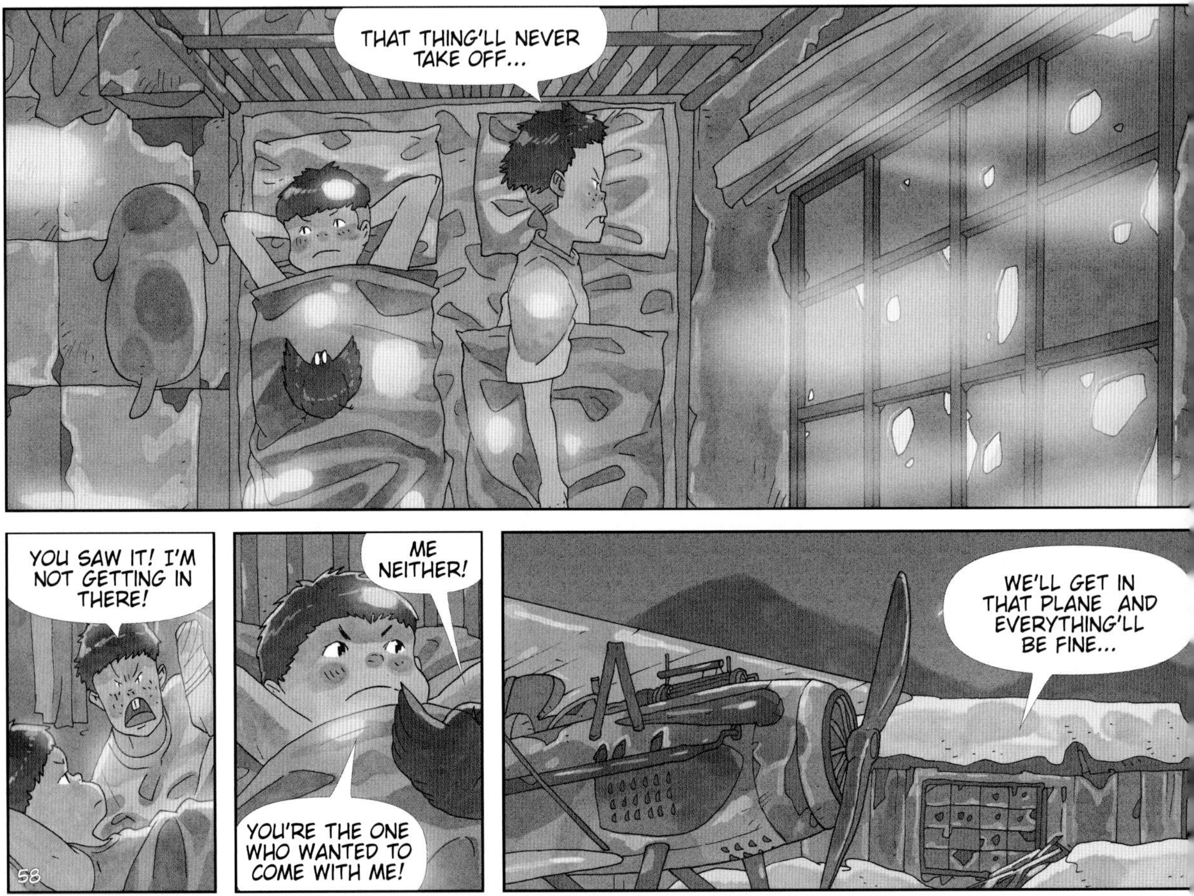

THAT THING'LL NEVER TAKE OFF...
YOU SAW IT! I'M NOT GETTING IN THERE!
ME NEITHER!
YOU'RE THE ONE WHO WANTED TO COME WITH ME!
WE'LL GET IN THAT PLANE AND EVERYTHING'LL BE FINE...

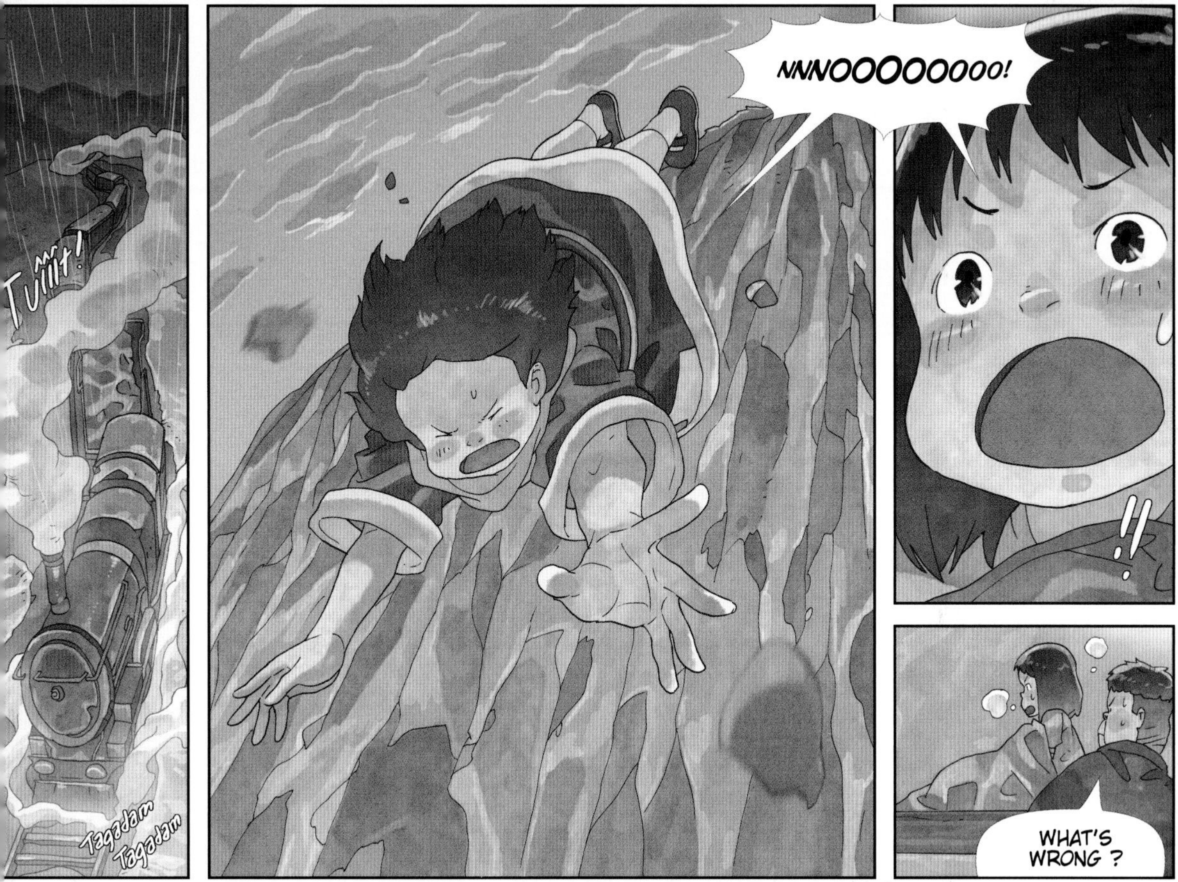
Tuiiiit!
Tagadam
Tagadam
NNNOOOOOOOO!
!!
WHAT'S WRONG ?

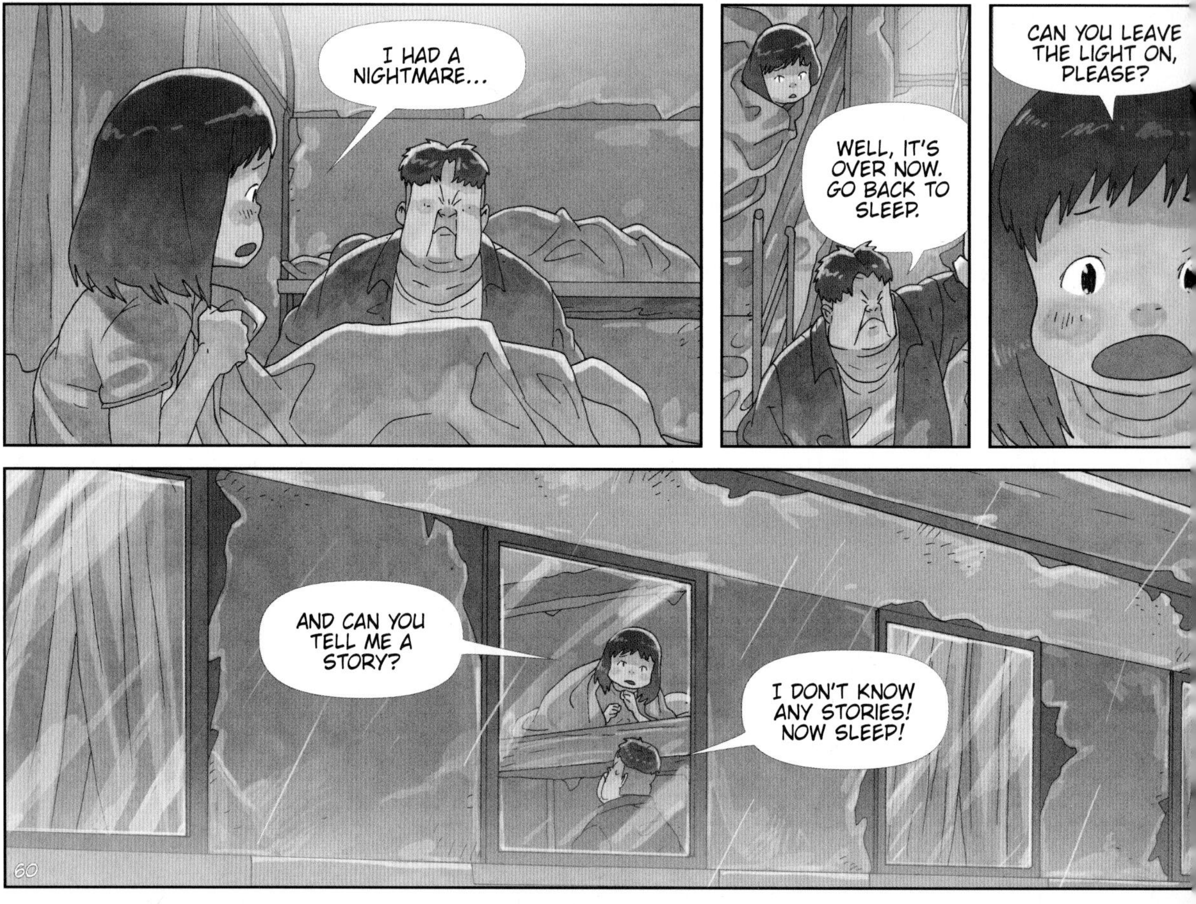
I HAD A NIGHTMARE...
WELL, IT'S OVER NOW. GO BACK TO SLEEP.
CAN YOU LEAVE THE LIGHT ON, PLEASE?
AND CAN YOU TELL ME A STORY?
I DON'T KNOW ANY STORIES! NOW SLEEP!

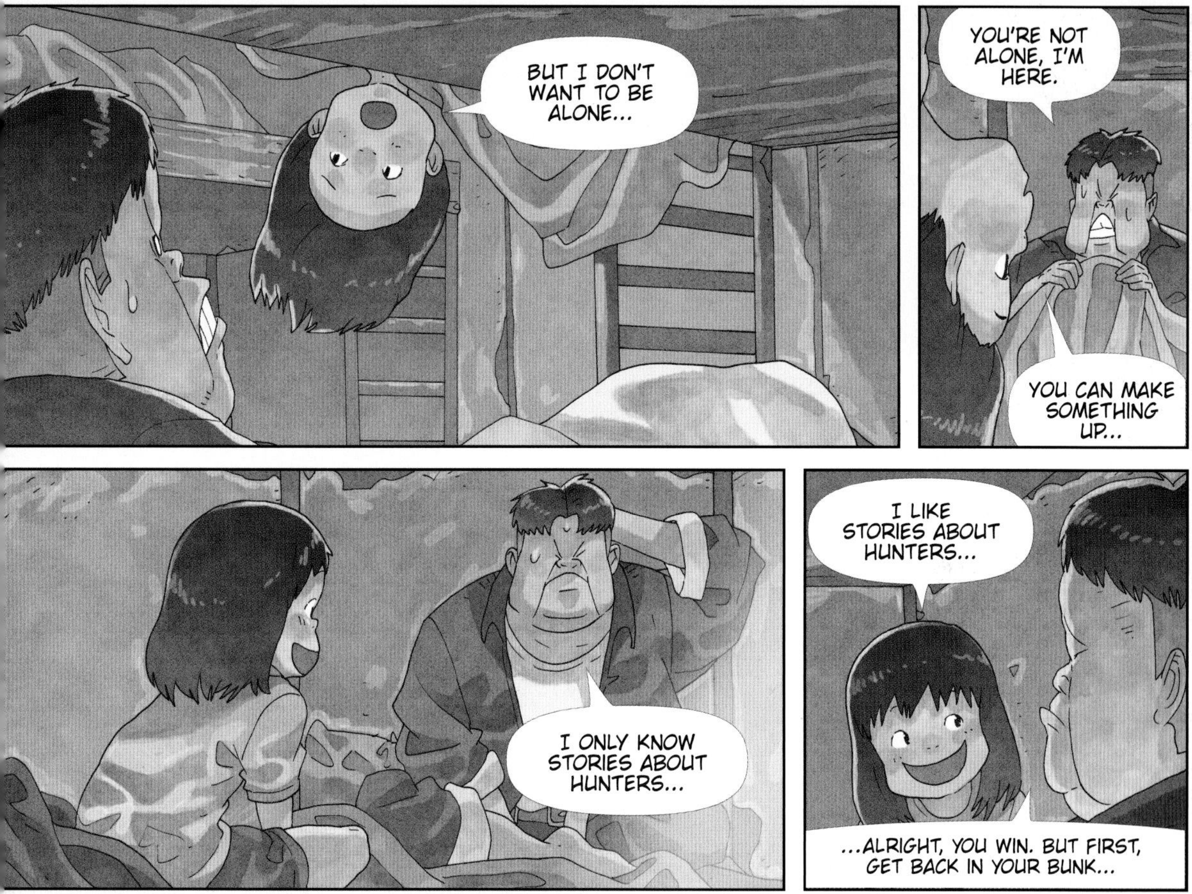
BUT I DON'T WANT TO BE ALONE...
YOU'RE NOT ALONE, I'M HERE.
YOU CAN MAKE SOMETHING UP...
I ONLY KNOW STORIES ABOUT HUNTERS...
I LIKE STORIES ABOUT HUNTERS...
...ALRIGHT, YOU WIN. BUT FIRST, GET BACK IN YOUR BUNK...

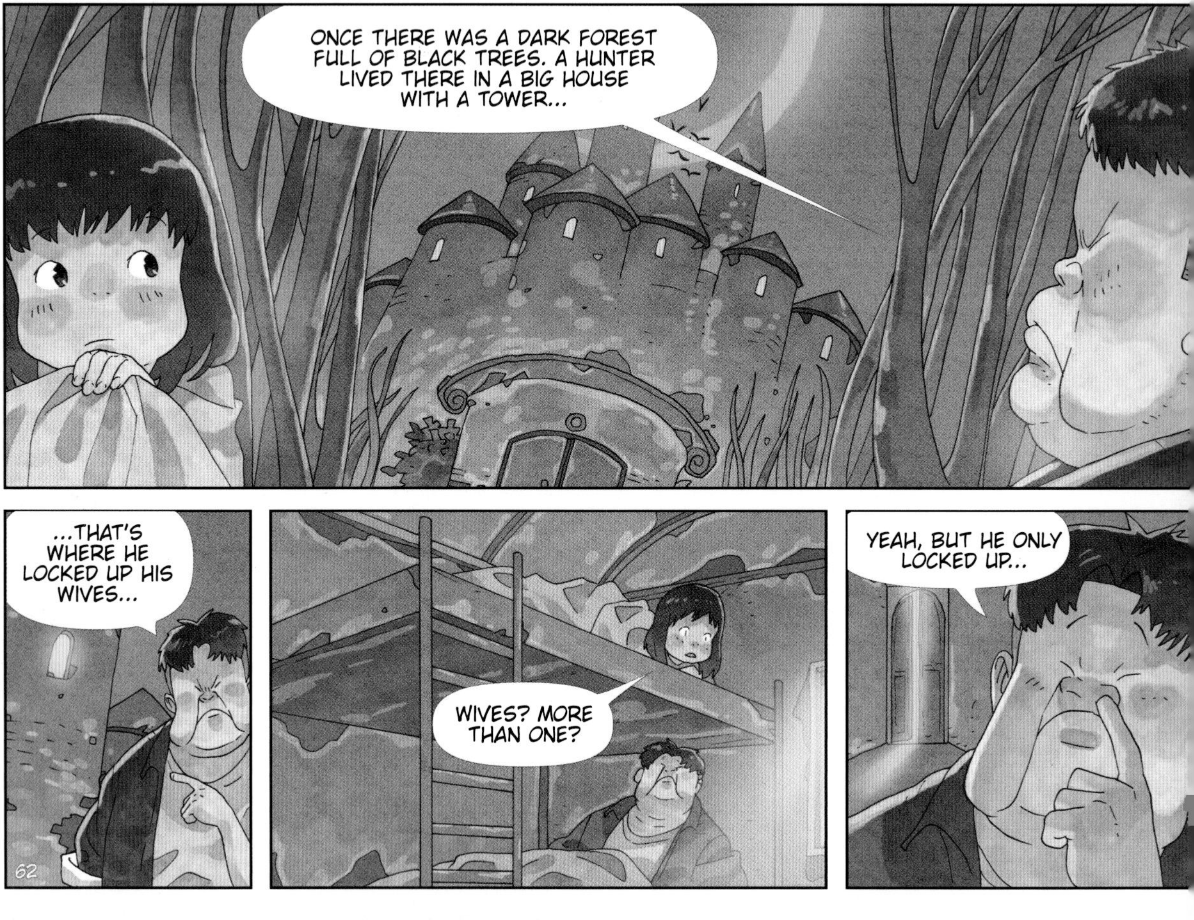
ONCE THERE WAS A DARK FOREST FULL OF BLACK TREES. A HUNTER LIVED THERE IN A BIG HOUSE WITH A TOWER...
...THAT'S WHERE HE LOCKED UP HIS WIVES...
WIVES? MORE THAN ONE?
YEAH, BUT HE ONLY LOCKED UP...

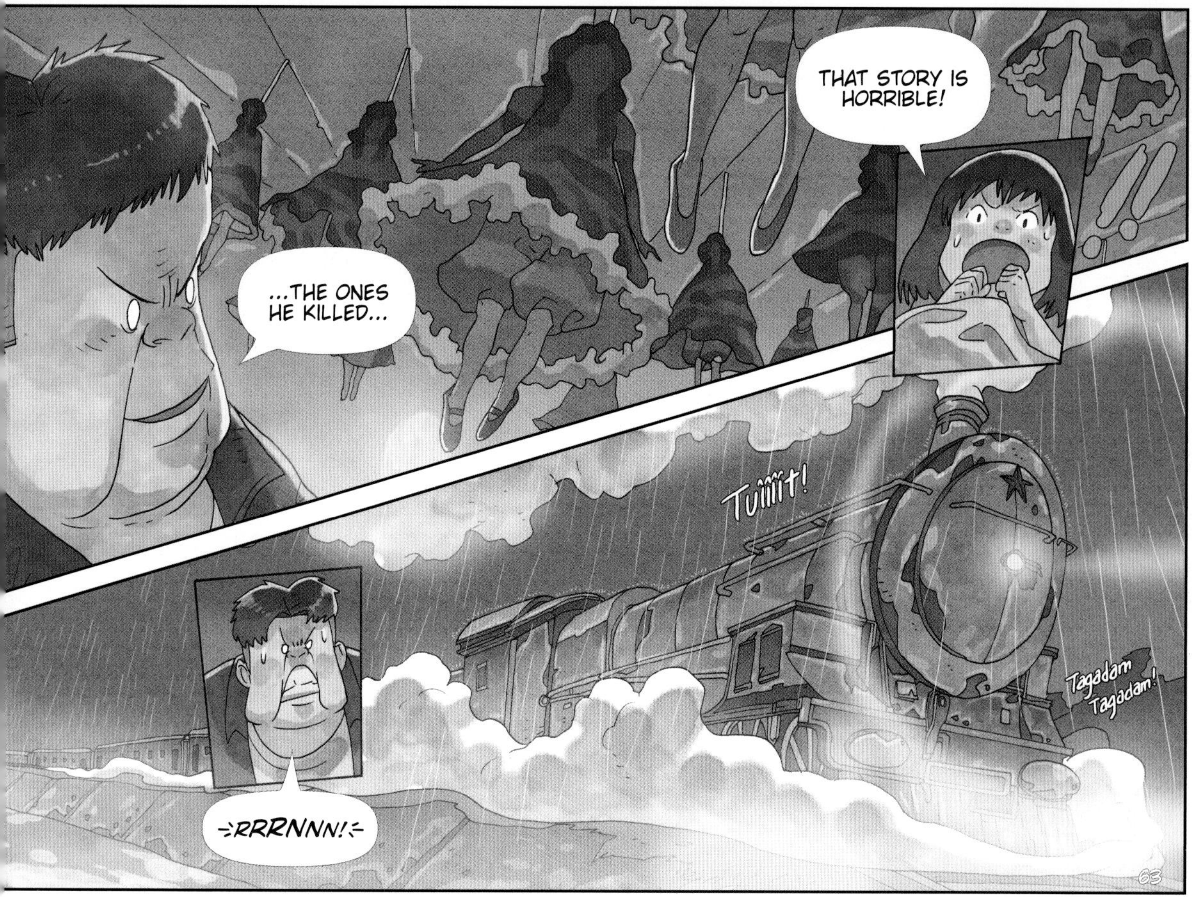
...THE ONES
HE KILLED...
THAT STORY IS
HORRIBLE!
Tuïïïït!
Tagadam
Tagadam!
RRRNNN!

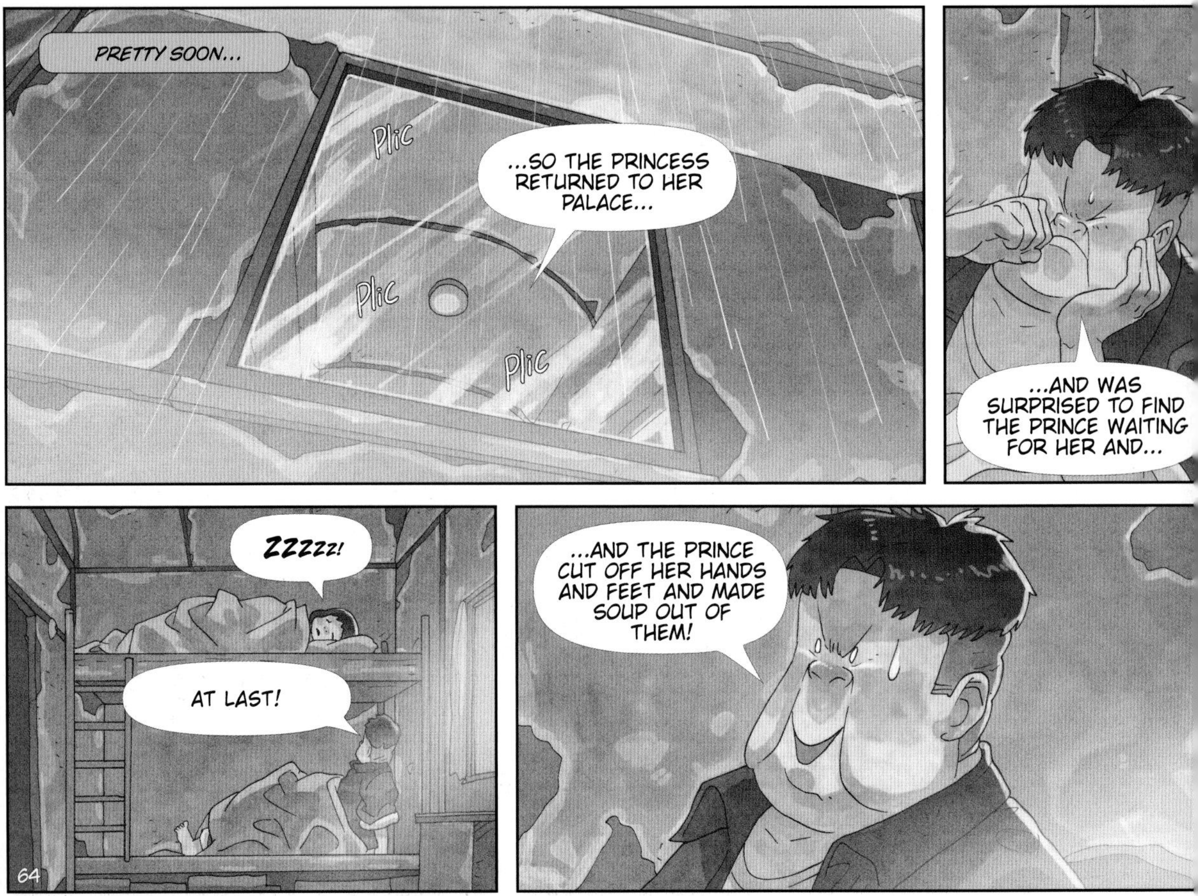
PRETTY SOON...
Plic
Plic
Plic
...SO THE PRINCESS RETURNED TO HER PALACE...
...AND WAS SURPRISED TO FIND THE PRINCE WAITING FOR HER AND...
ZZZzz!
AT LAST!
...AND THE PRINCE CUT OFF HER HANDS AND FEET AND MADE SOUP OUT OF THEM!

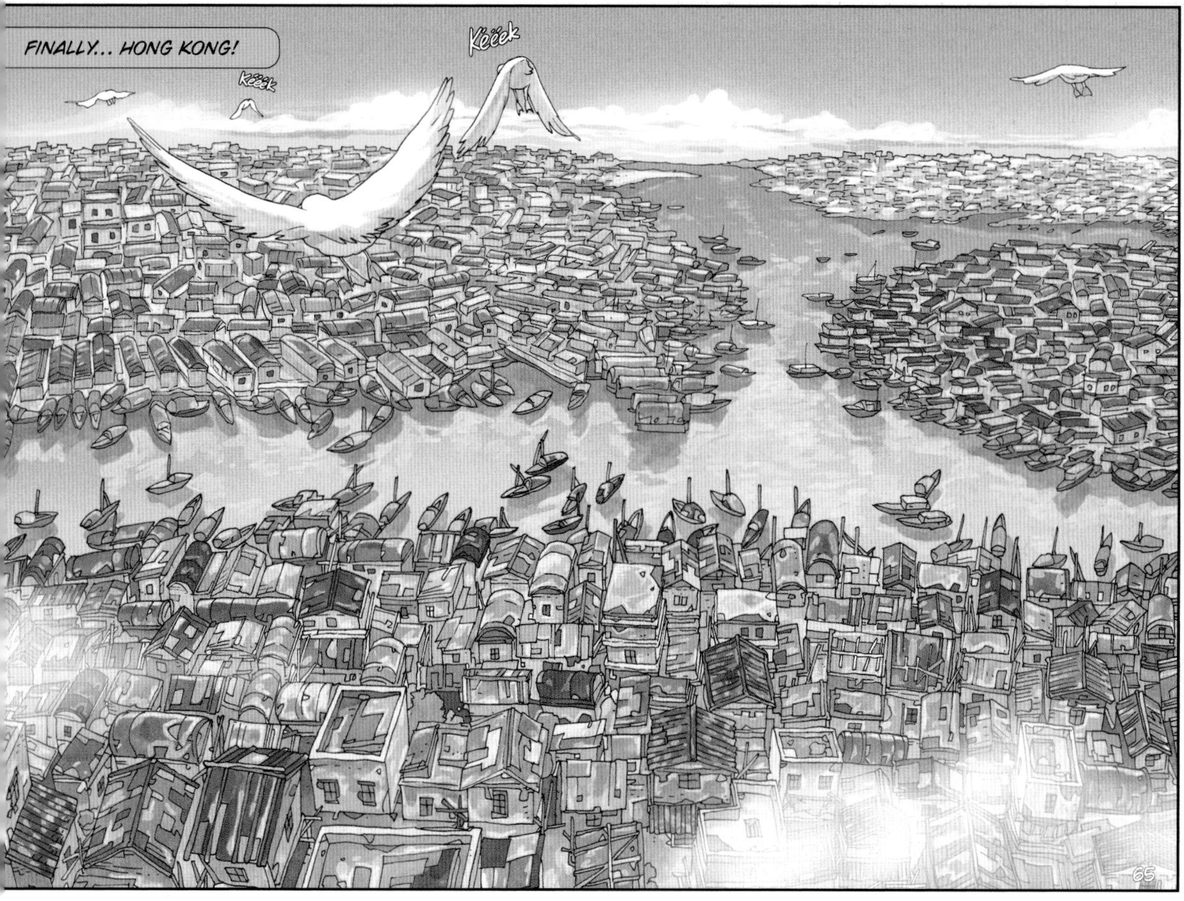
FINALLY... HONG KONG!
Kéëek
Kéëek

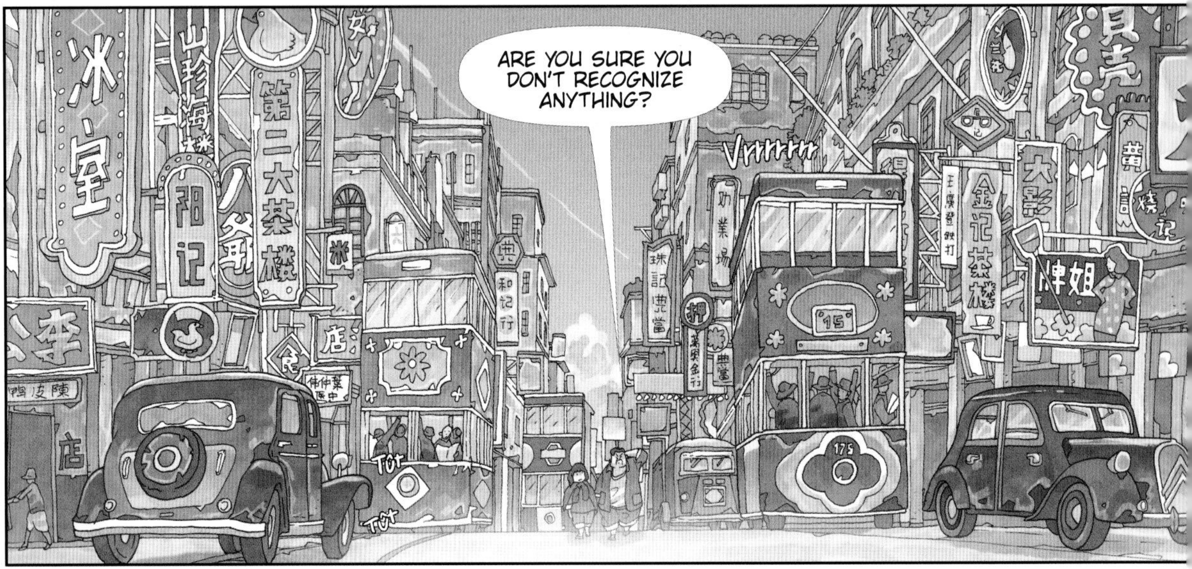
ARE YOU SURE YOU DON'T RECOGNIZE ANYTHING?

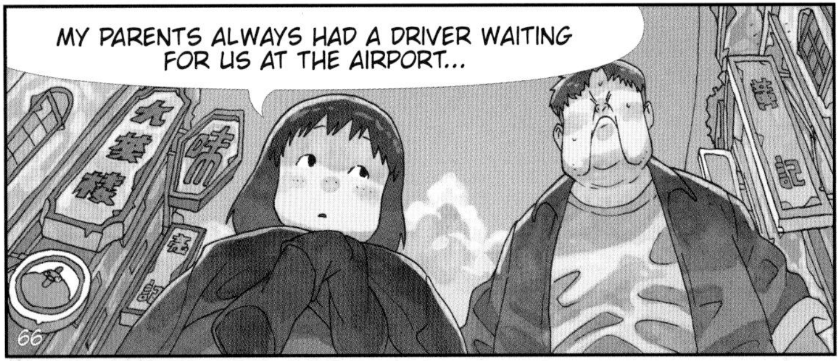
MY PARENTS ALWAYS HAD A DRIVER WAITING FOR US AT THE AIRPORT...

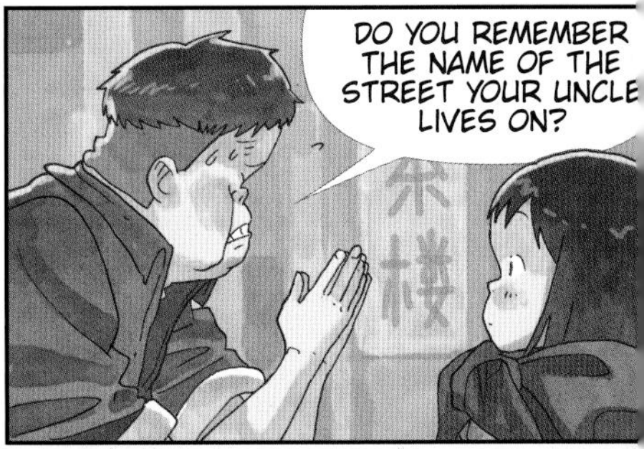
DO YOU REMEMBER THE NAME OF THE STREET YOUR UNCLE LIVES ON?

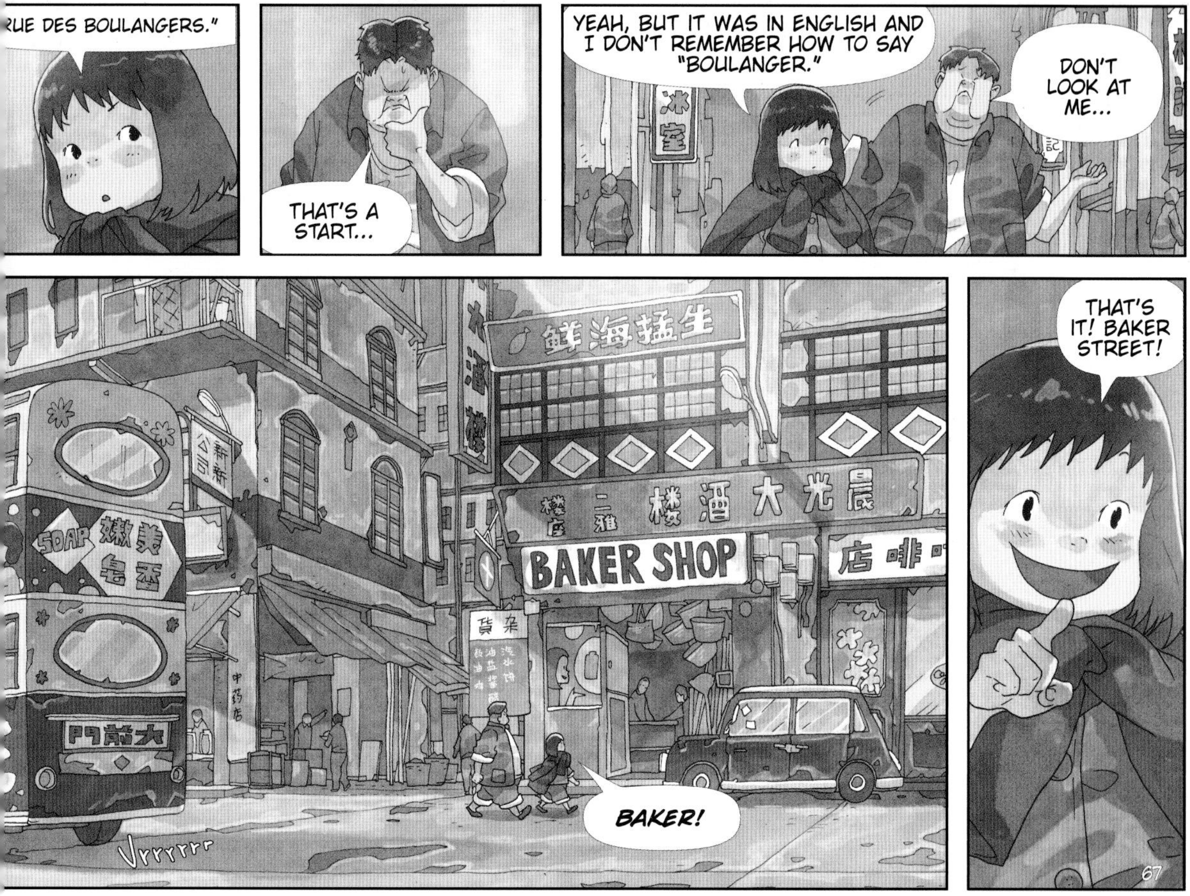
...RUE DES BOULANGERS."
THAT'S A START...
YEAH, BUT IT WAS IN ENGLISH AND I DON'T REMEMBER HOW TO SAY "BOULANGER."
DON'T LOOK AT ME...
SOAP
BAKER SHOP
BAKER!
Vrrrrrr
THAT'S IT! BAKER STREET!

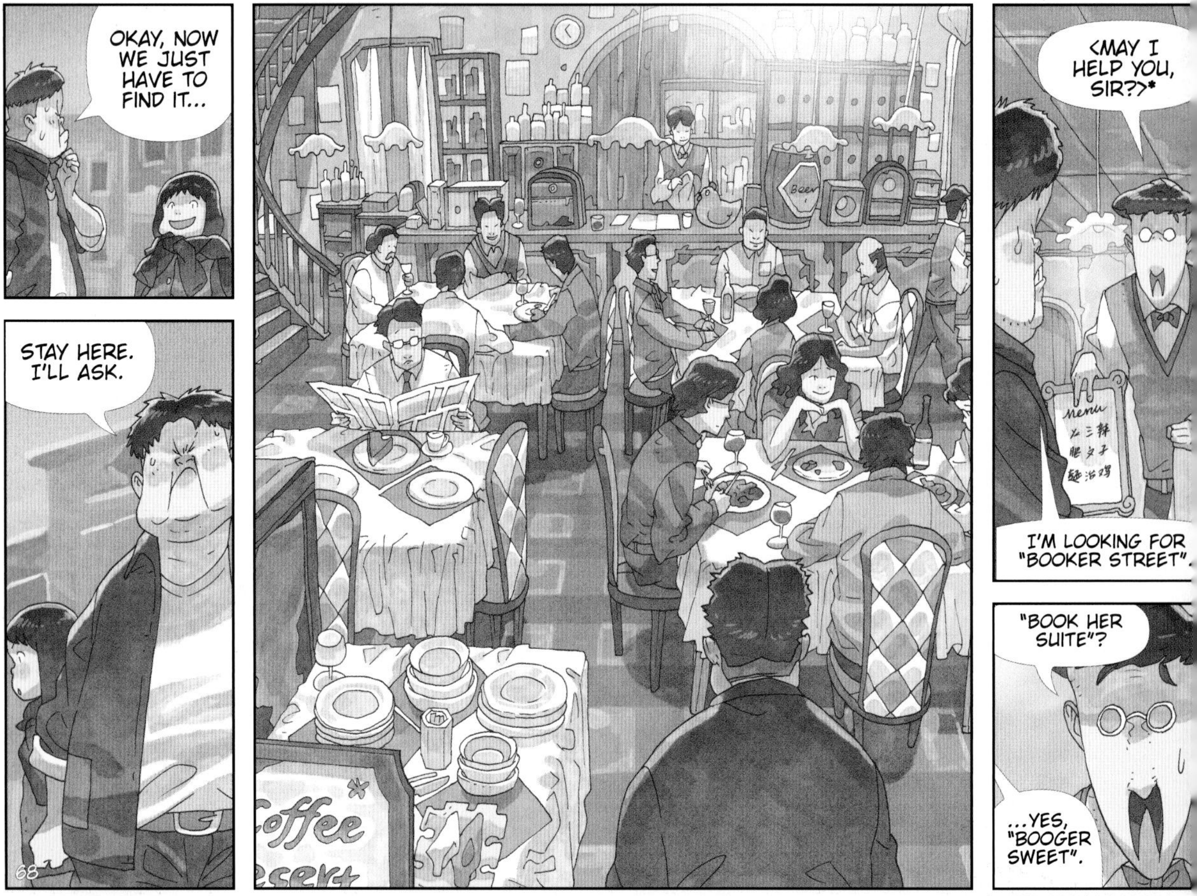
OKAY, NOW WE JUST HAVE TO FIND IT...
STAY HERE. I'LL ASK.
Beer
Coffee
<MAY I HELP YOU, SIR?>*
I'M LOOKING FOR "BOOKER STREET".
"BOOK HER SUITE"?
...YES, "BOOGER SWEET".

*<SPEAKING IN ENGLISH>

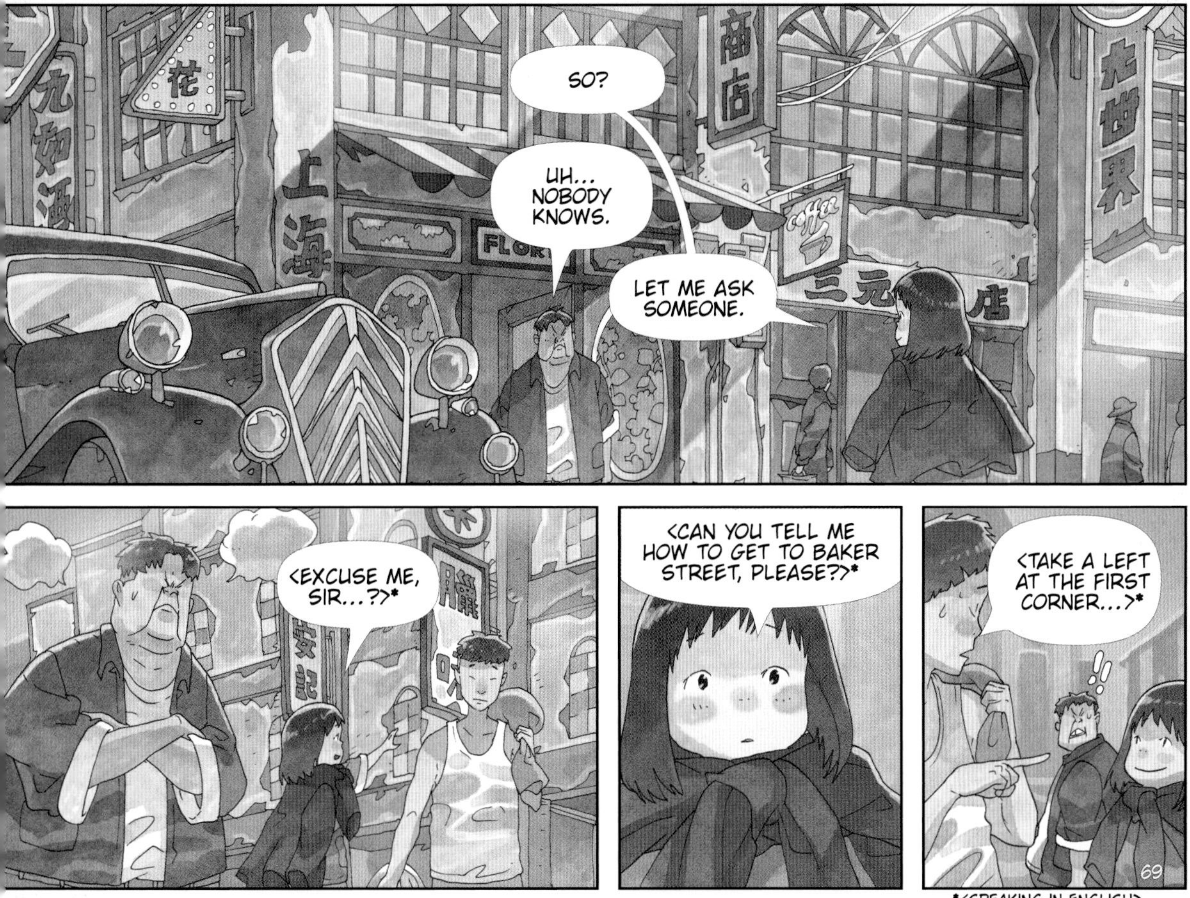
UH... NOBODY KNOWS.
SO?
LET ME ASK SOMEONE.
<EXCUSE ME, SIR...?>*
<CAN YOU TELL ME HOW TO GET TO BAKER STREET, PLEASE?>*
<TAKE A LEFT AT THE FIRST CORNER...>*
!!

*<SPEAKING IN ENGLISH>

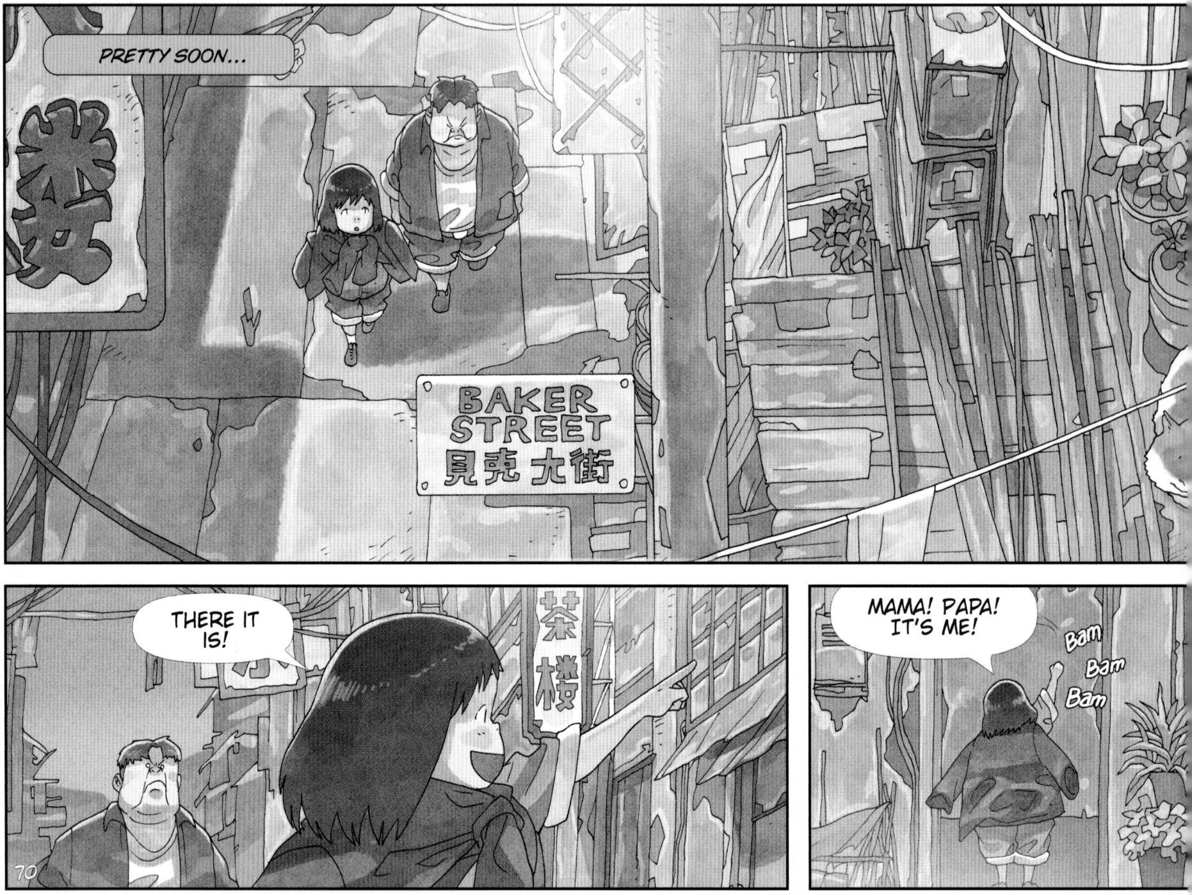
PRETTY SOON...
BAKER STREET
貝克大街
THERE IT IS!
茶樓
MAMA! PAPA! IT'S ME!
Bam
Bam
Bam

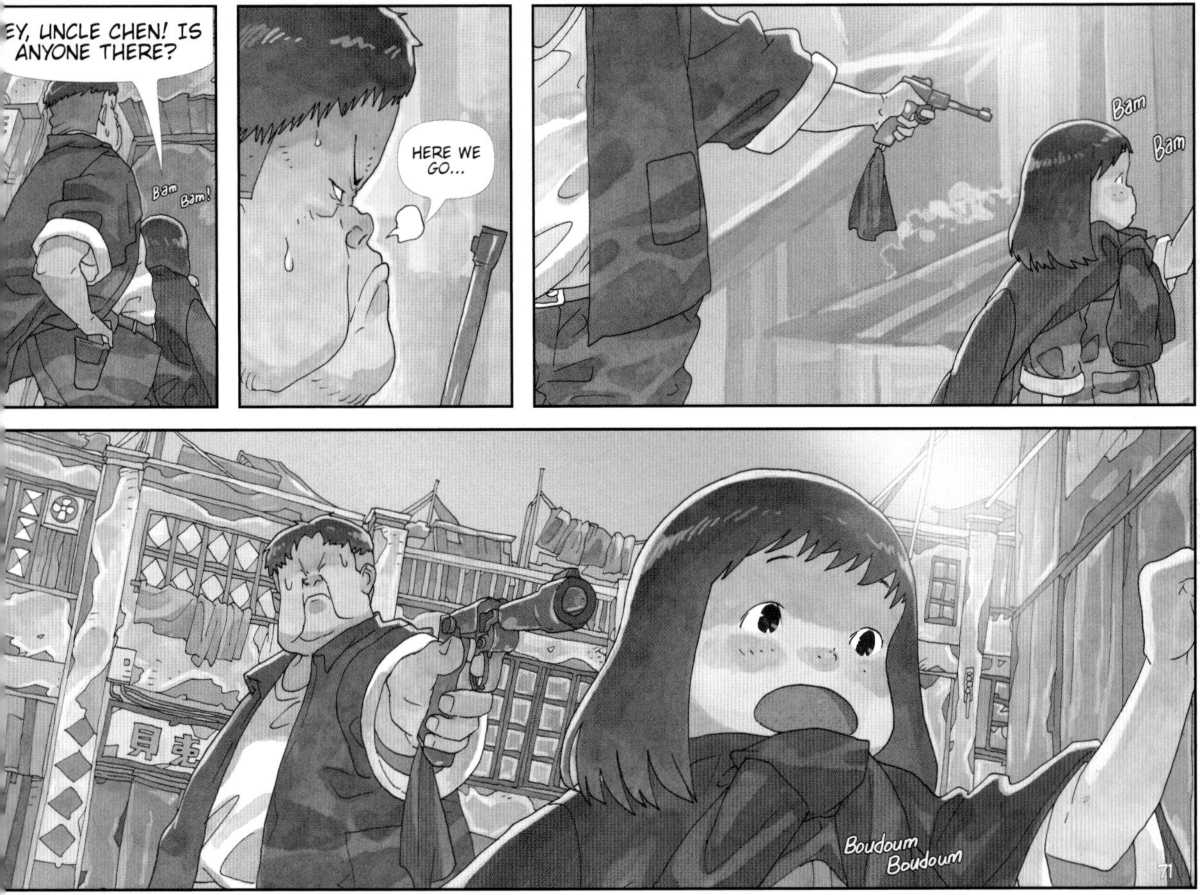

EY, UNCLE CHEN! IS ANYONE THERE?
Bam
Bam!
HERE WE GO...
Bam
Bam
Boudoum
Boudoum

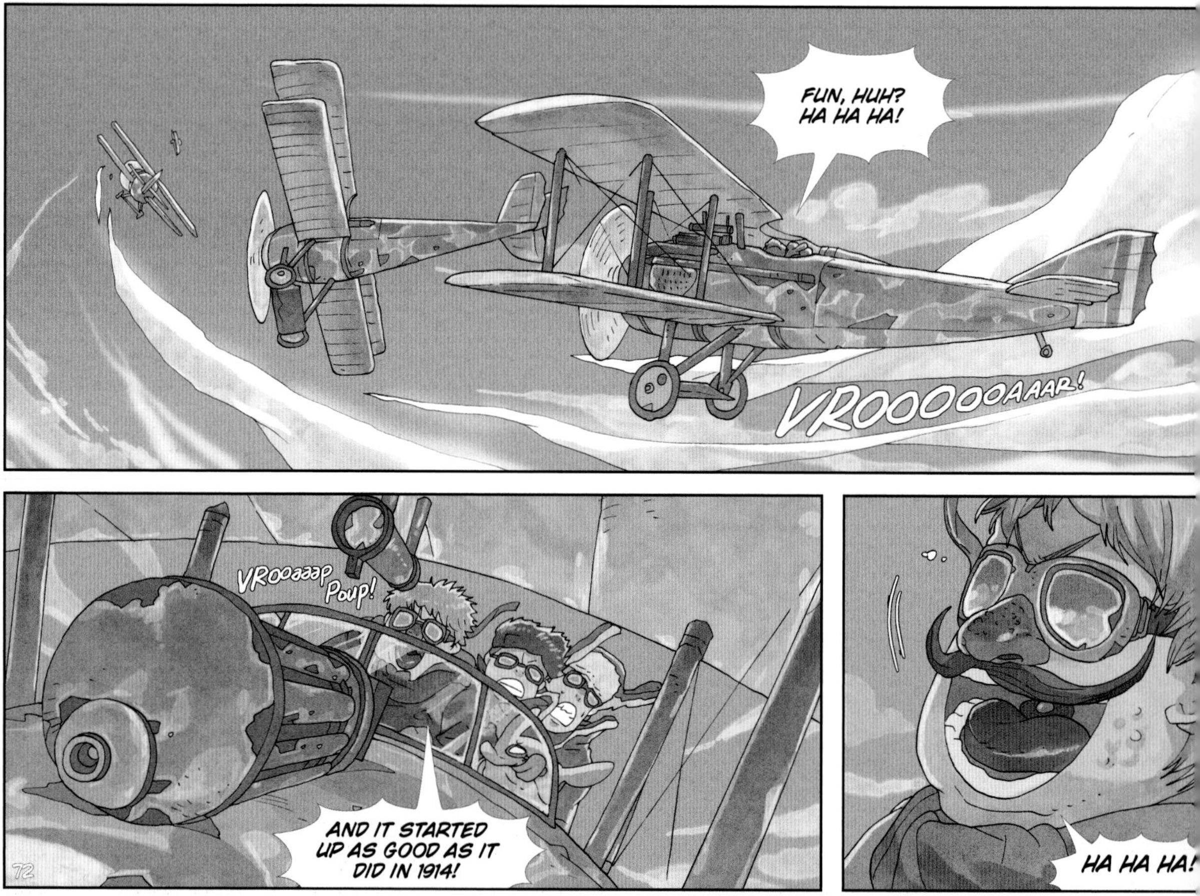
FUN, HUH? HA HA HA!
VROOOOOOAAAR!
VROoaaap Poup!
AND IT STARTED UP AS GOOD AS IT DID IN 1914!
HA HA HA!

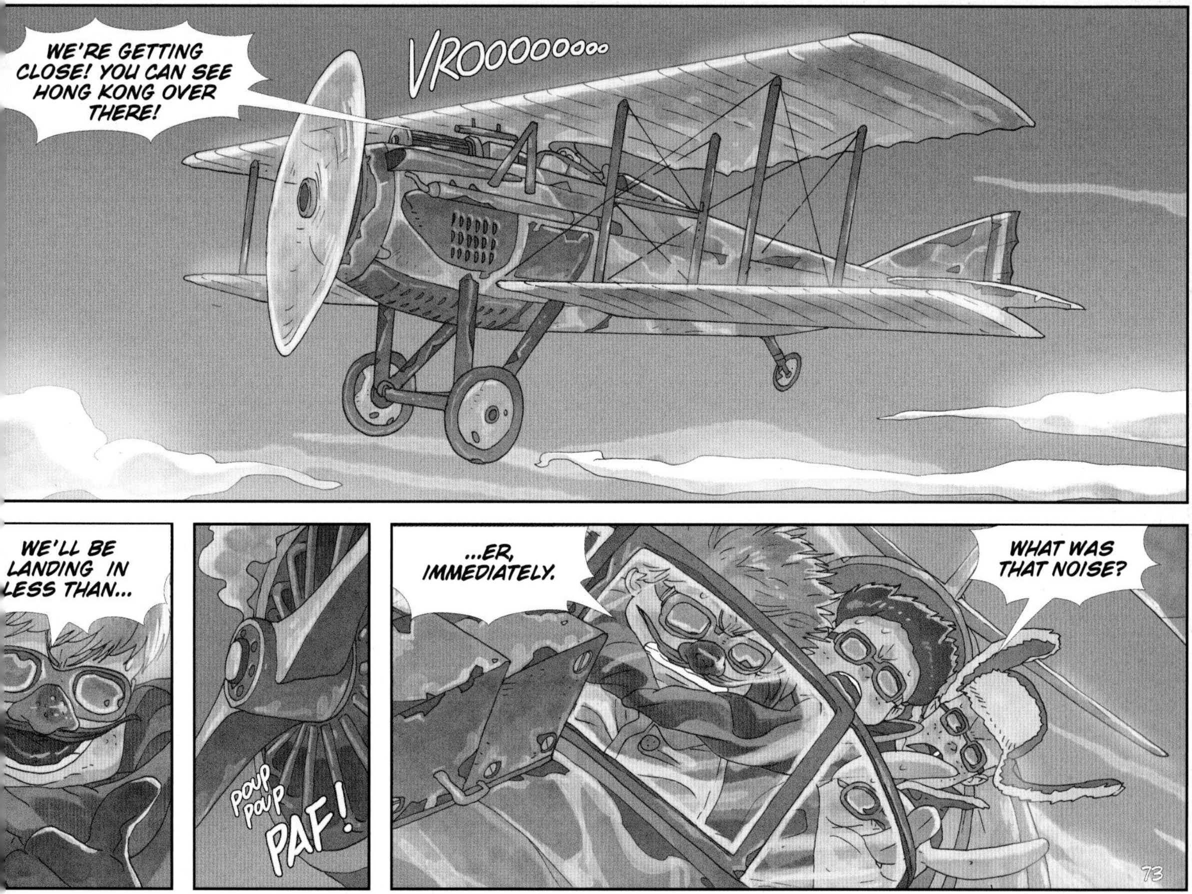
WE'RE GETTING CLOSE! YOU CAN SEE HONG KONG OVER THERE!
VROOOOOooo
WE'LL BE LANDING IN LESS THAN...
POUP POUP
PAF!
...ER, IMMEDIATELY.
WHAT WAS THAT NOISE?

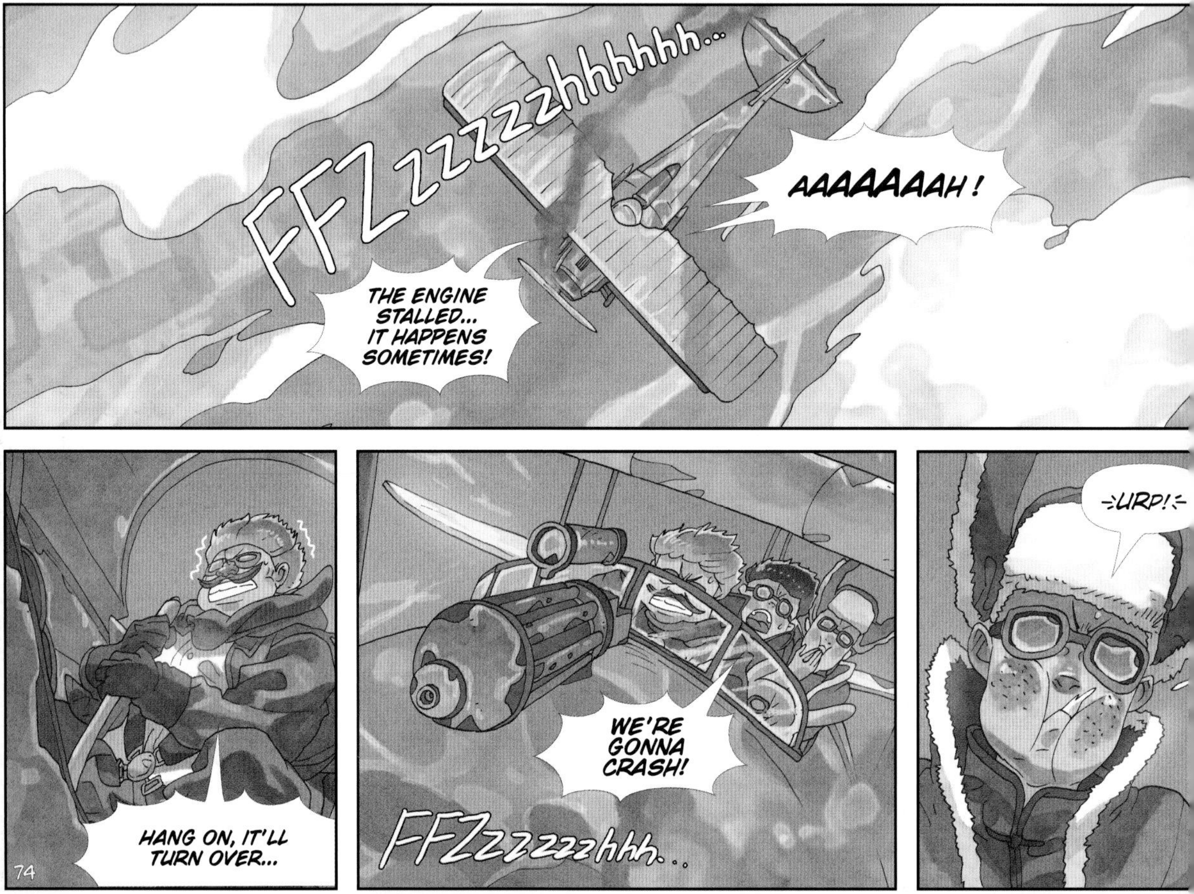
FFZzzzzzzhhhhhhh...
AAAAAAAH!
THE ENGINE STALLED... IT HAPPENS SOMETIMES!
HANG ON, IT'LL TURN OVER...
WE'RE GONNA CRASH!
FFZzzzzzhhh...
URP!

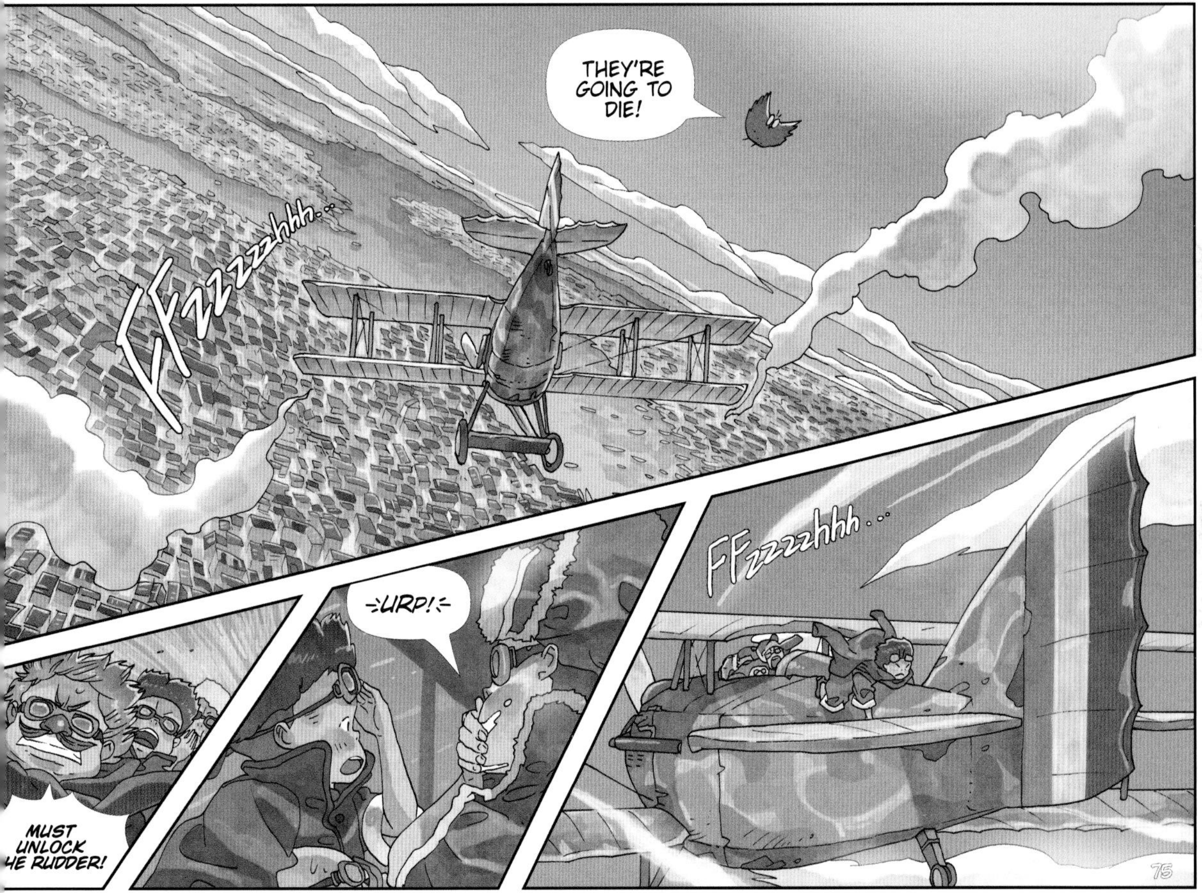
THEY'RE GOING TO DIE!
FFzzzzzhhh...
MUST UNLOCK HE RUDDER!
URP!
FFzzzzhhh...

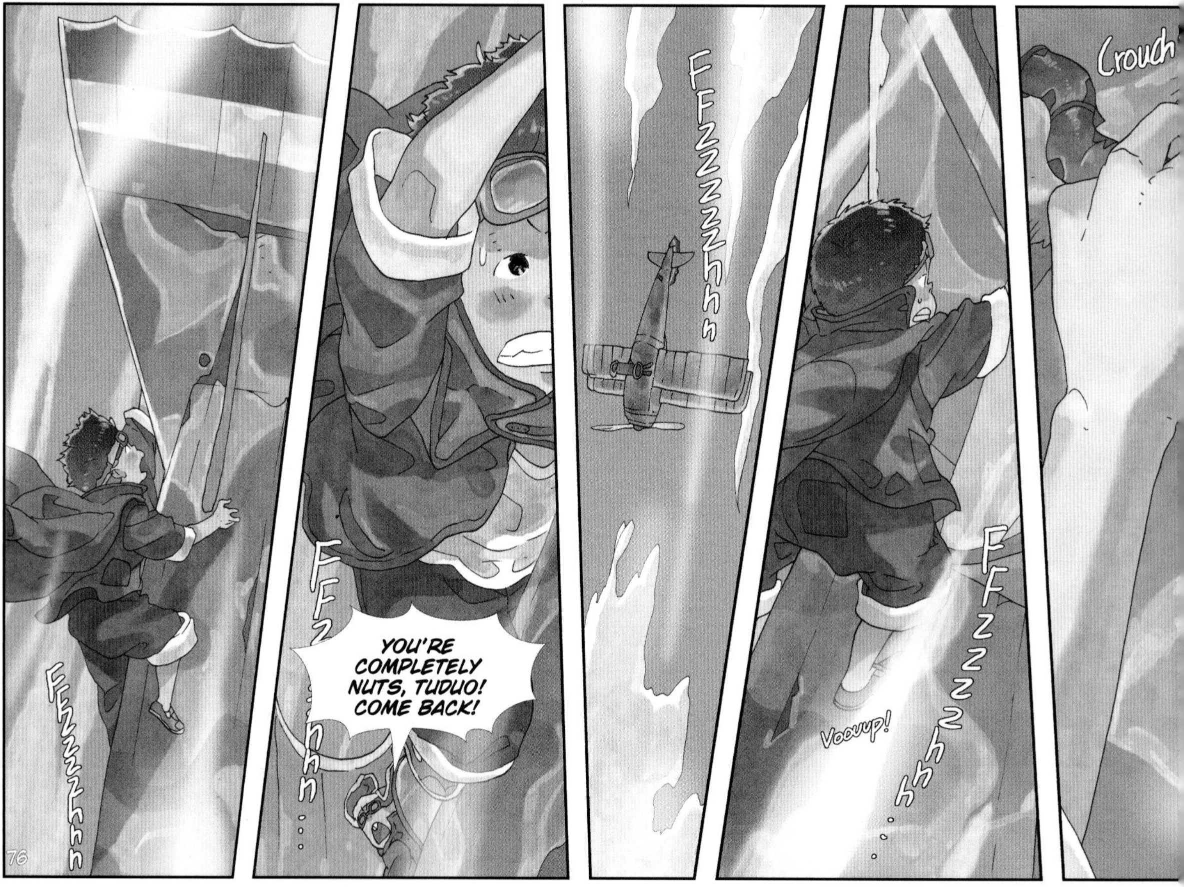
FFZZZZhhnn
FFZ
hhn...
YOU'RE COMPLETELY NUTS, TUDUO! COME BACK!
FFZZZZZhhnn
Voouup!
FFZZZZhhh...
Crouch

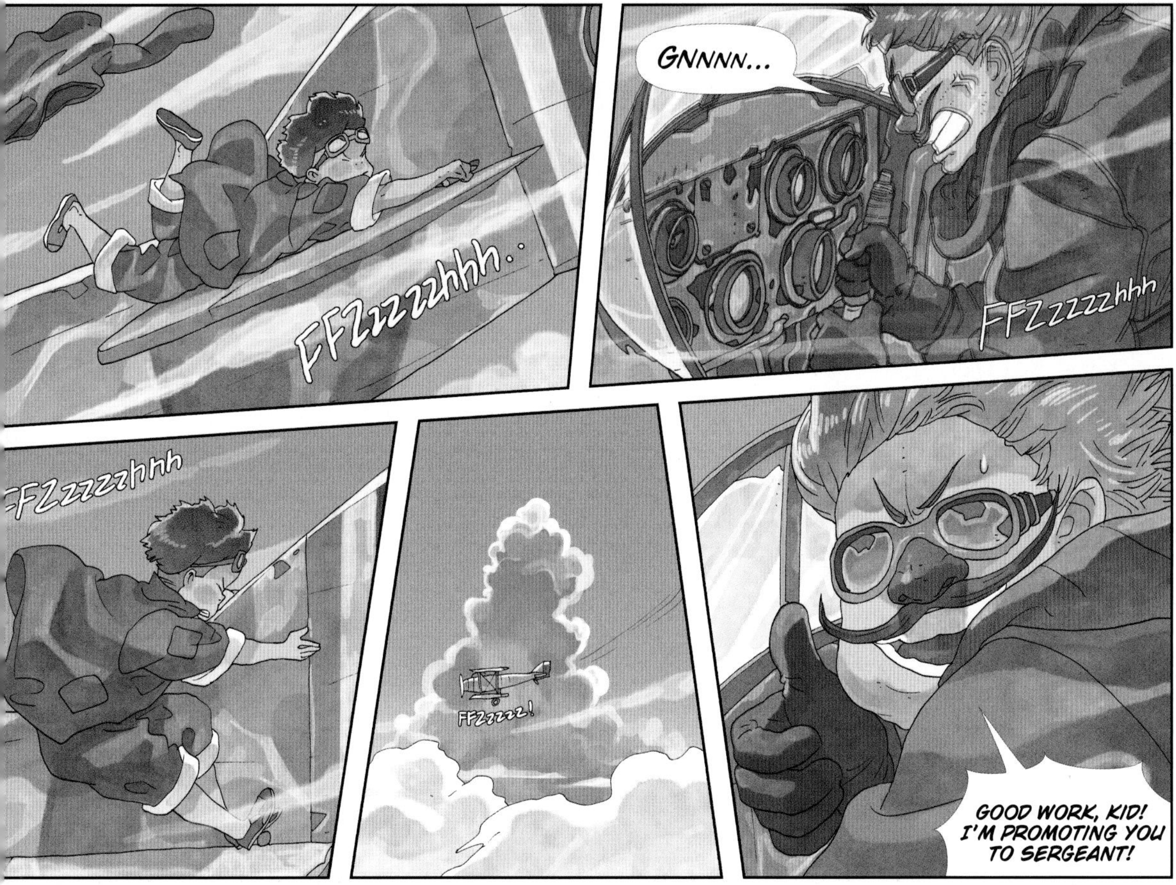
FFZzzzzhhh..
GNNNN...
FFZzzzzhhh
FFZzzzzhhh
FFZzzzz!
GOOD WORK, KID! I'M PROMOTING YOU TO SERGEANT!

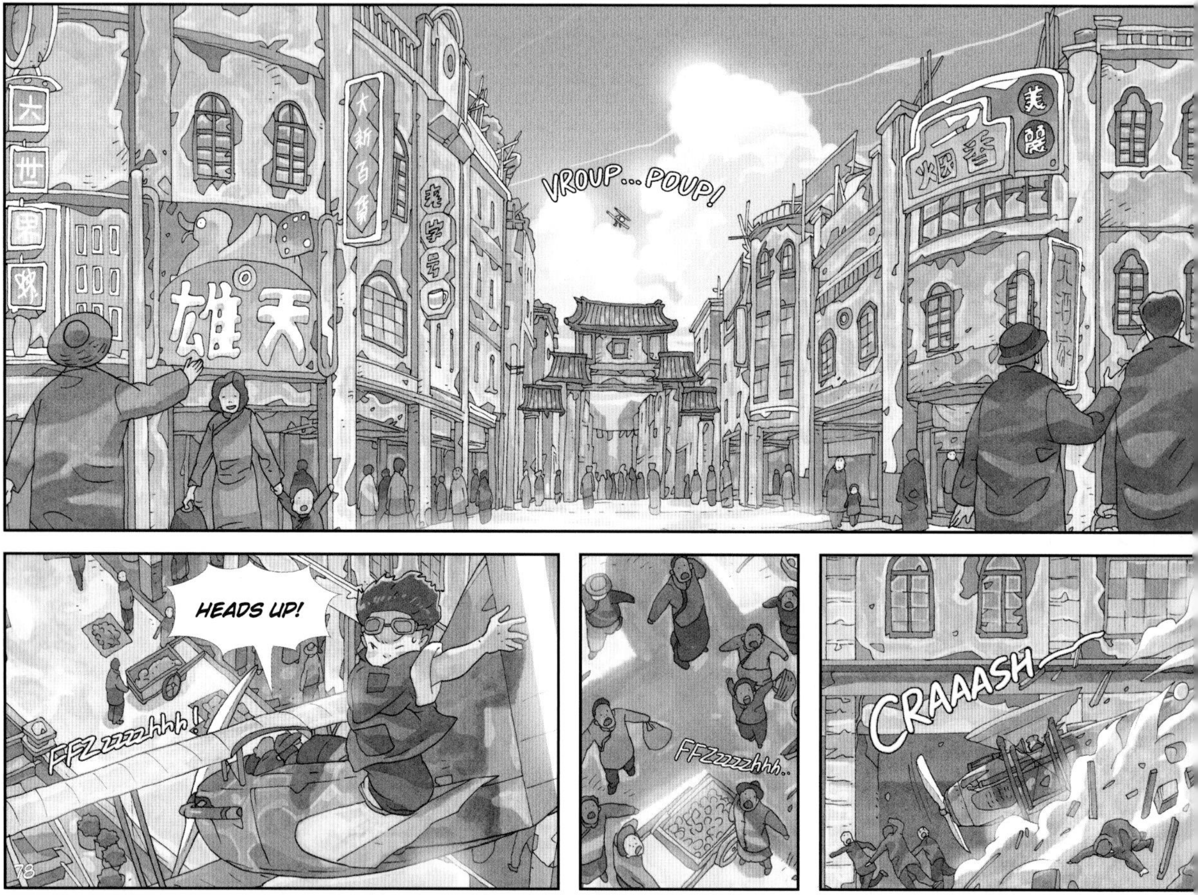
VROUP...POUP!
HEADS UP!
FFZzzzzhhh!
FFZzzzzhhh..
CRAAASH

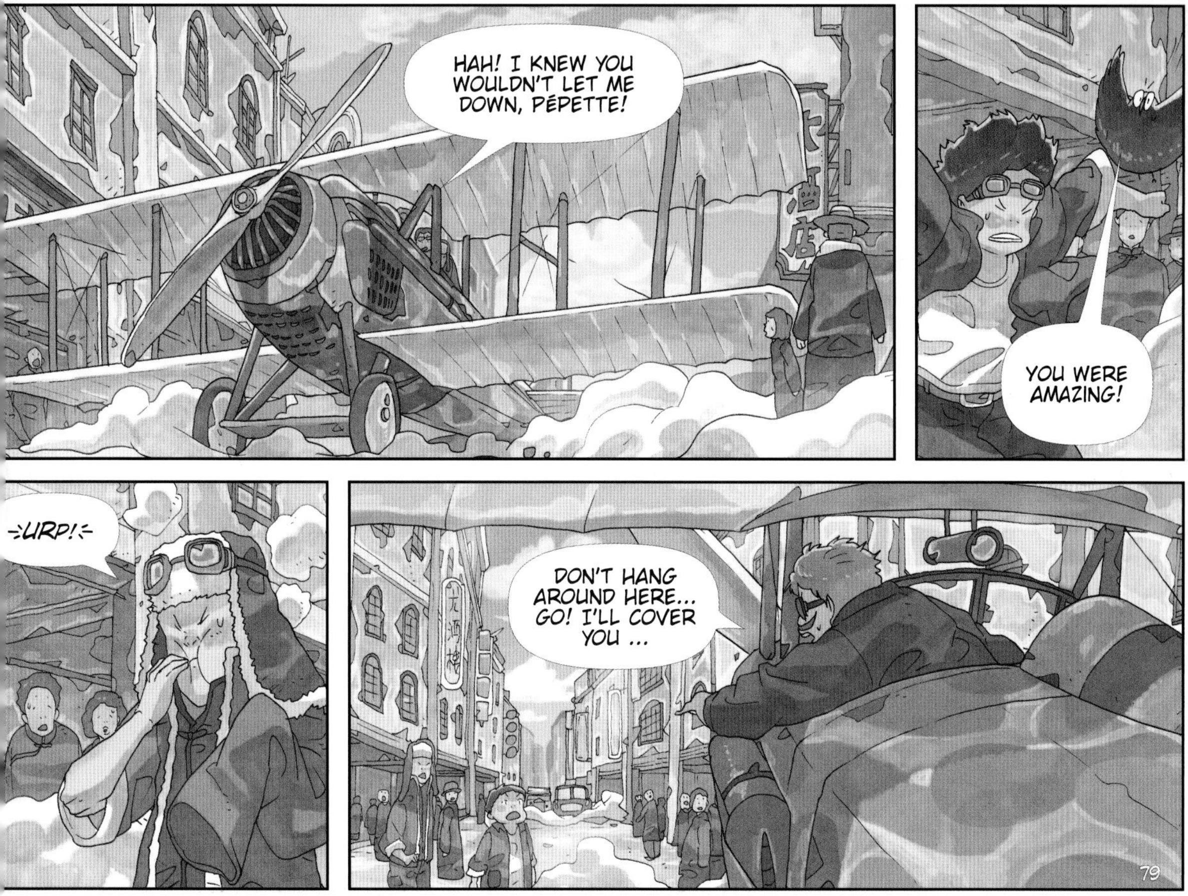
HAH! I KNEW YOU WOULDN'T LET ME DOWN, PÉPETTE!
YOU WERE AMAZING!
URP!
DON'T HANG AROUND HERE... GO! I'LL COVER YOU ...
79

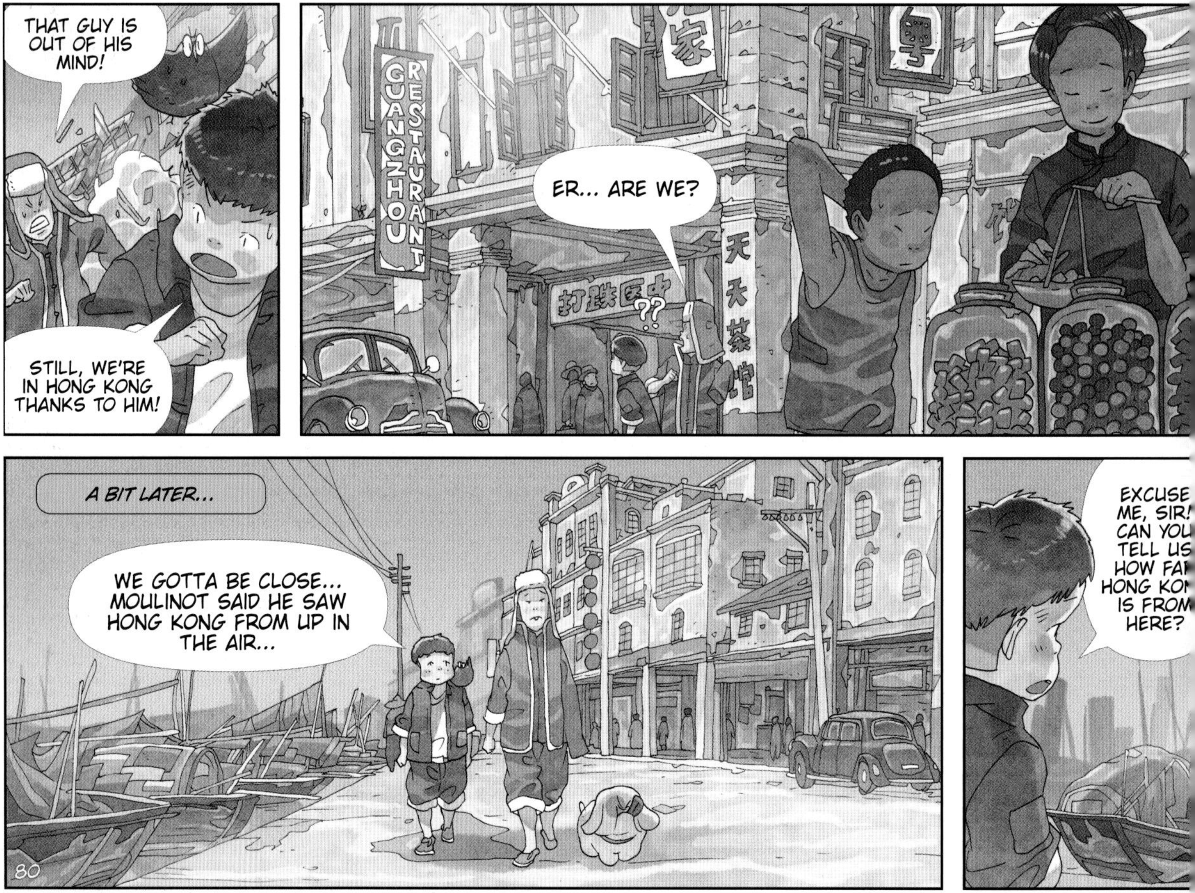
THAT GUY IS OUT OF HIS MIND!
STILL, WE'RE IN HONG KONG THANKS TO HIM!
GUANGZHOU RESTAURANT
ER... ARE WE?
??
天天茶馆
A BIT LATER...
WE GOTTA BE CLOSE... MOULINOT SAID HE SAW HONG KONG FROM UP IN THE AIR...
EXCUSE ME, SIR! CAN YO TELL US HOW FA HONG KO IS FROM HERE?

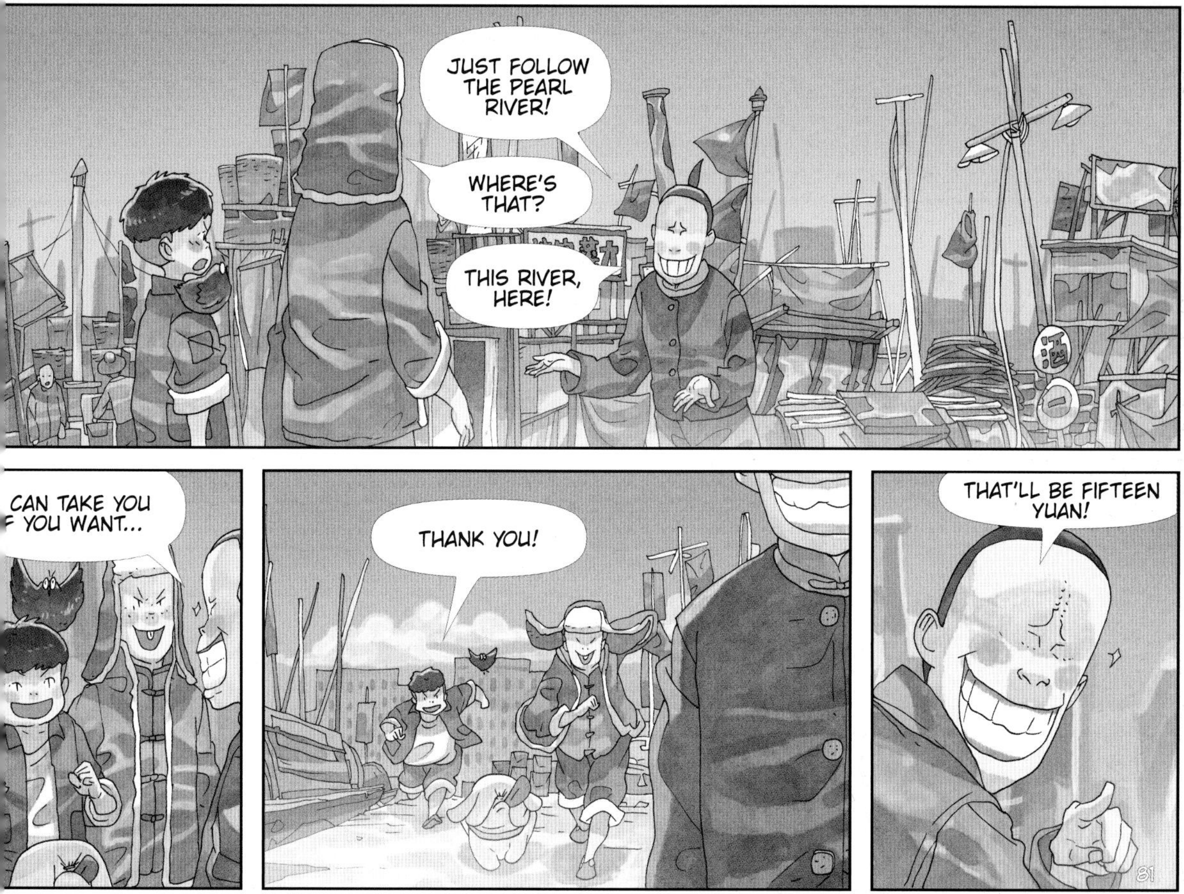
JUST FOLLOW THE PEARL RIVER!
WHERE'S THAT?
THIS RIVER, HERE!
CAN TAKE YOU F YOU WANT...
THANK YOU!
THAT'LL BE FIFTEEN YUAN!

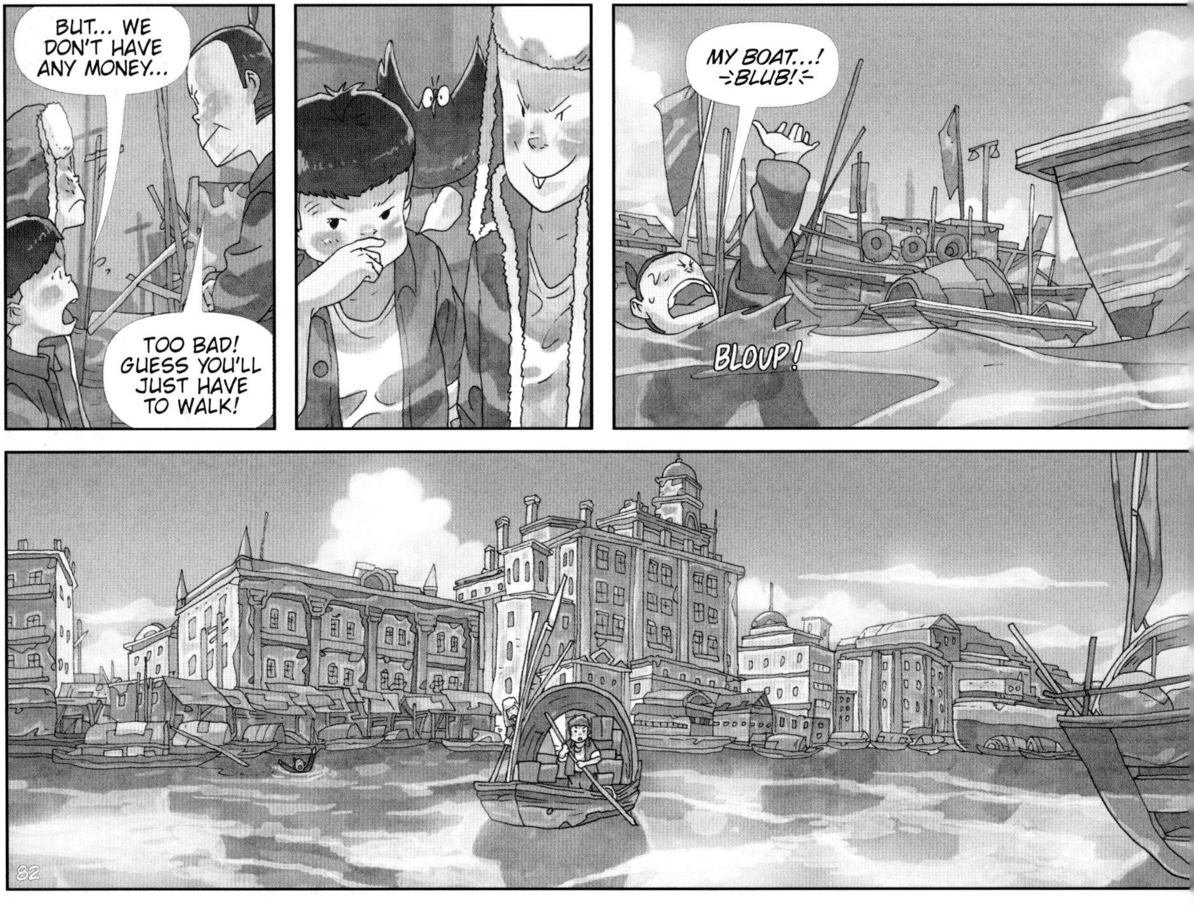
BUT... WE DON'T HAVE ANY MONEY...
TOO BAD! GUESS YOU'LL JUST HAVE TO WALK!
MY BOAT...! BLUB!
BLOUP!

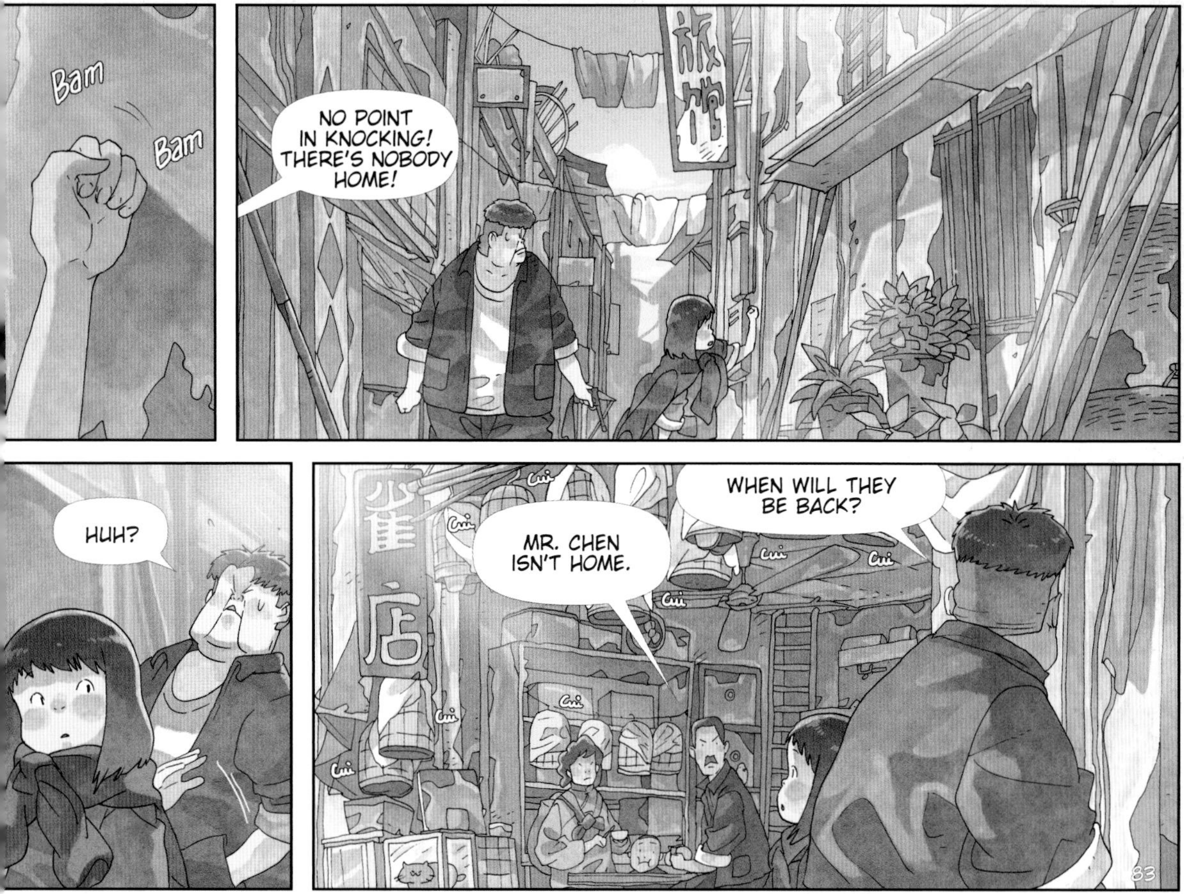

Bam
Bam
NO POINT IN KNOCKING! THERE'S NOBODY HOME!
HUH?
店
Cui
Cui
Cui
Cui
Cui
Cui
Cui
Cui
MR. CHEN ISN'T HOME.
WHEN WILL THEY BE BACK?

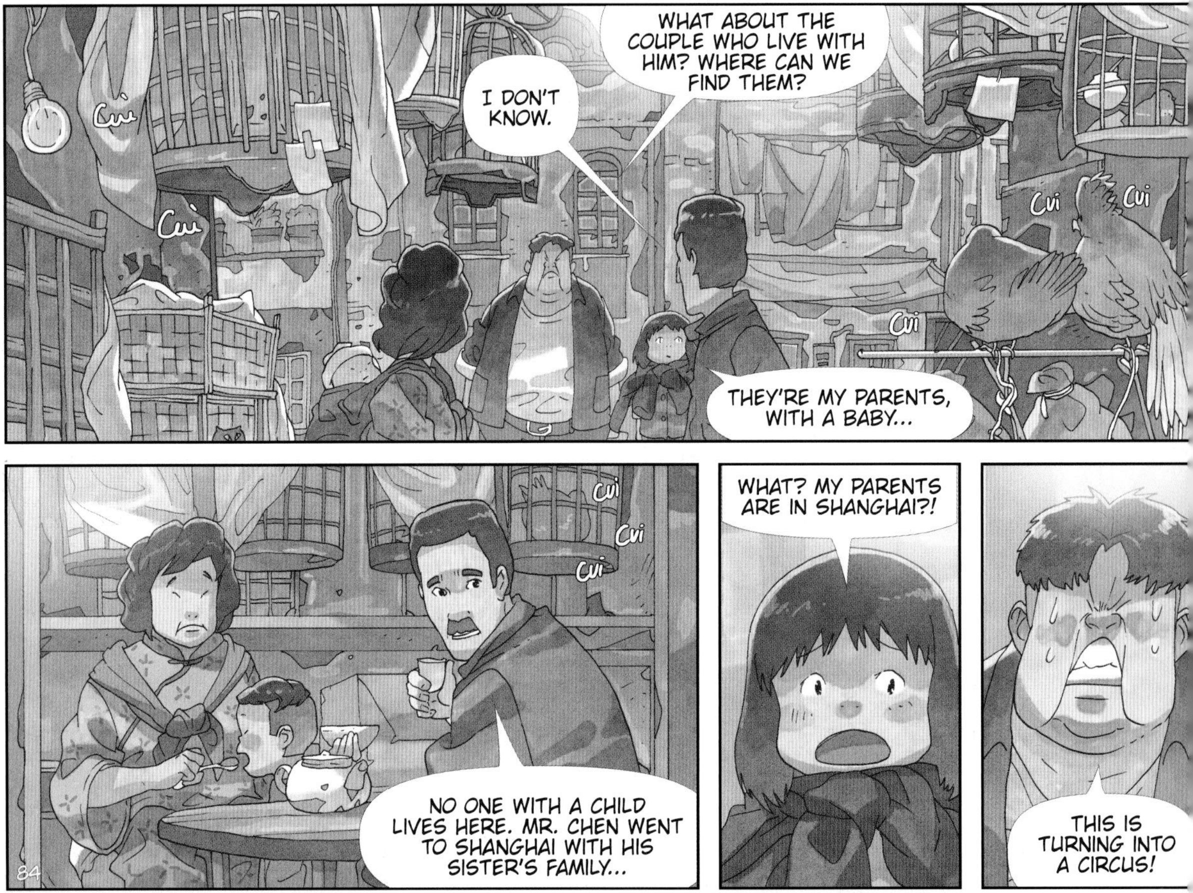
Cui
Cui
I DON'T KNOW.
WHAT ABOUT THE COUPLE WHO LIVE WITH HIM? WHERE CAN WE FIND THEM?
Cui
Cui
Cui
THEY'RE MY PARENTS, WITH A BABY...
Cui
Cui
Cui
NO ONE WITH A CHILD LIVES HERE. MR. CHEN WENT TO SHANGHAI WITH HIS SISTER'S FAMILY...
WHAT? MY PARENTS ARE IN SHANGHAI?!
THIS IS TURNING INTO A CIRCUS!

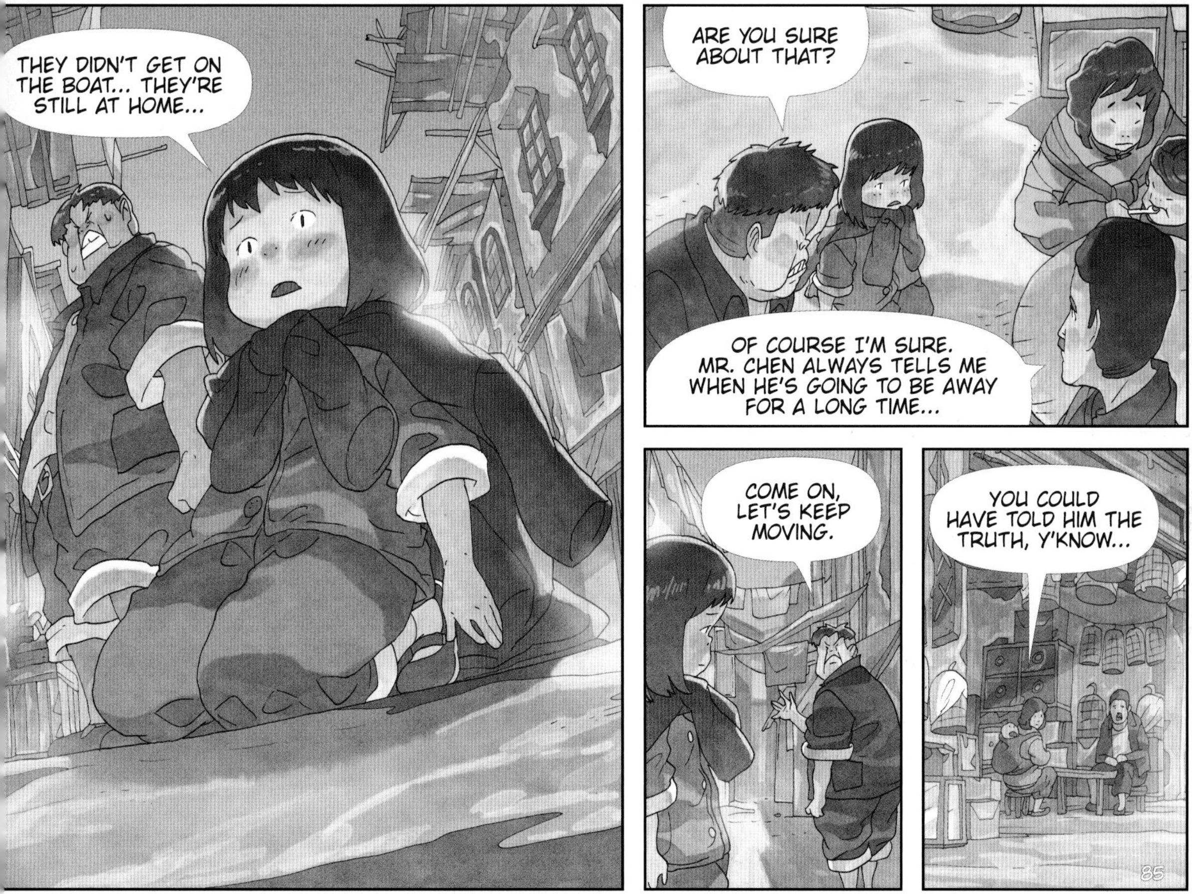
THEY DIDN'T GET ON THE BOAT... THEY'RE STILL AT HOME...
ARE YOU SURE ABOUT THAT?
OF COURSE I'M SURE. MR. CHEN ALWAYS TELLS ME WHEN HE'S GOING TO BE AWAY FOR A LONG TIME...
COME ON, LET'S KEEP MOVING.
YOU COULD HAVE TOLD HIM THE TRUTH, Y'KNOW...

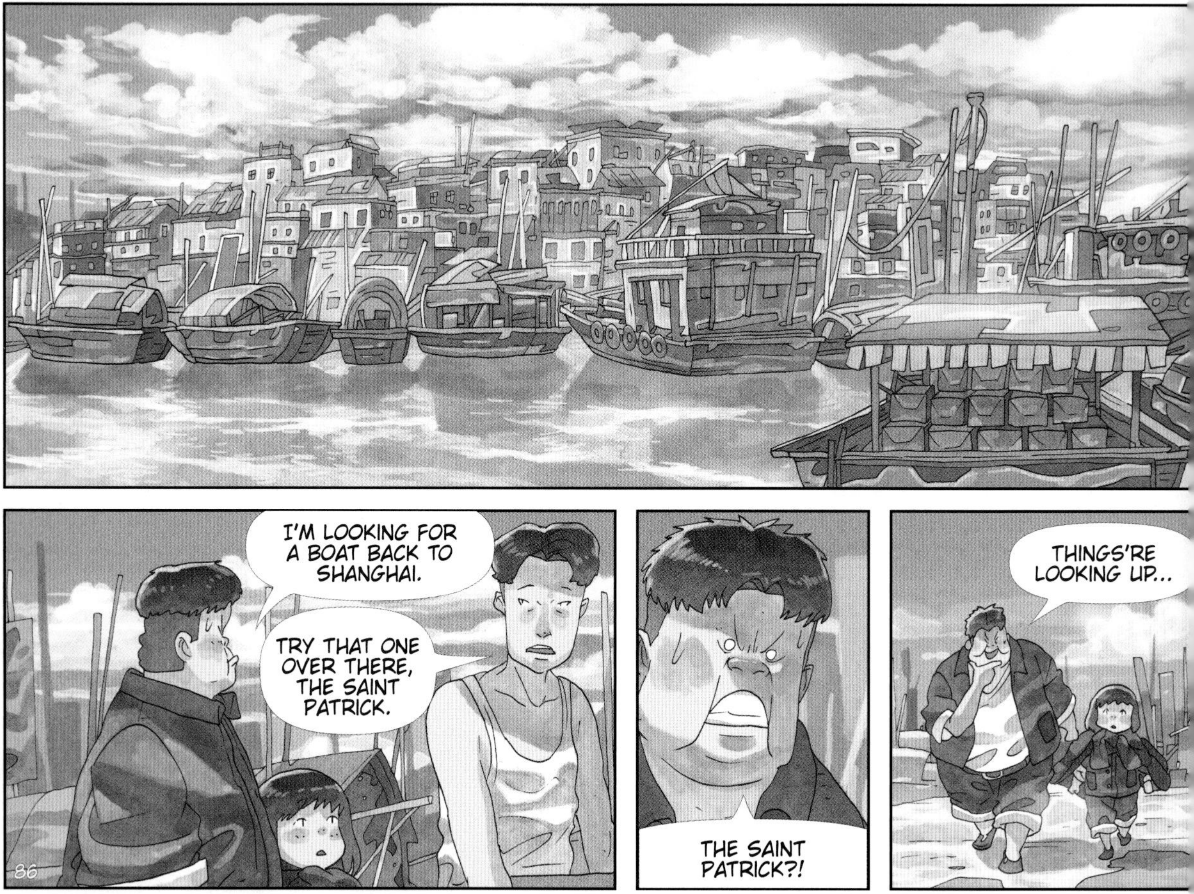
I'M LOOKING FOR A BOAT BACK TO SHANGHAI.
TRY THAT ONE OVER THERE, THE SAINT PATRICK.
THE SAINT PATRICK?!
THINGS'RE LOOKING UP...

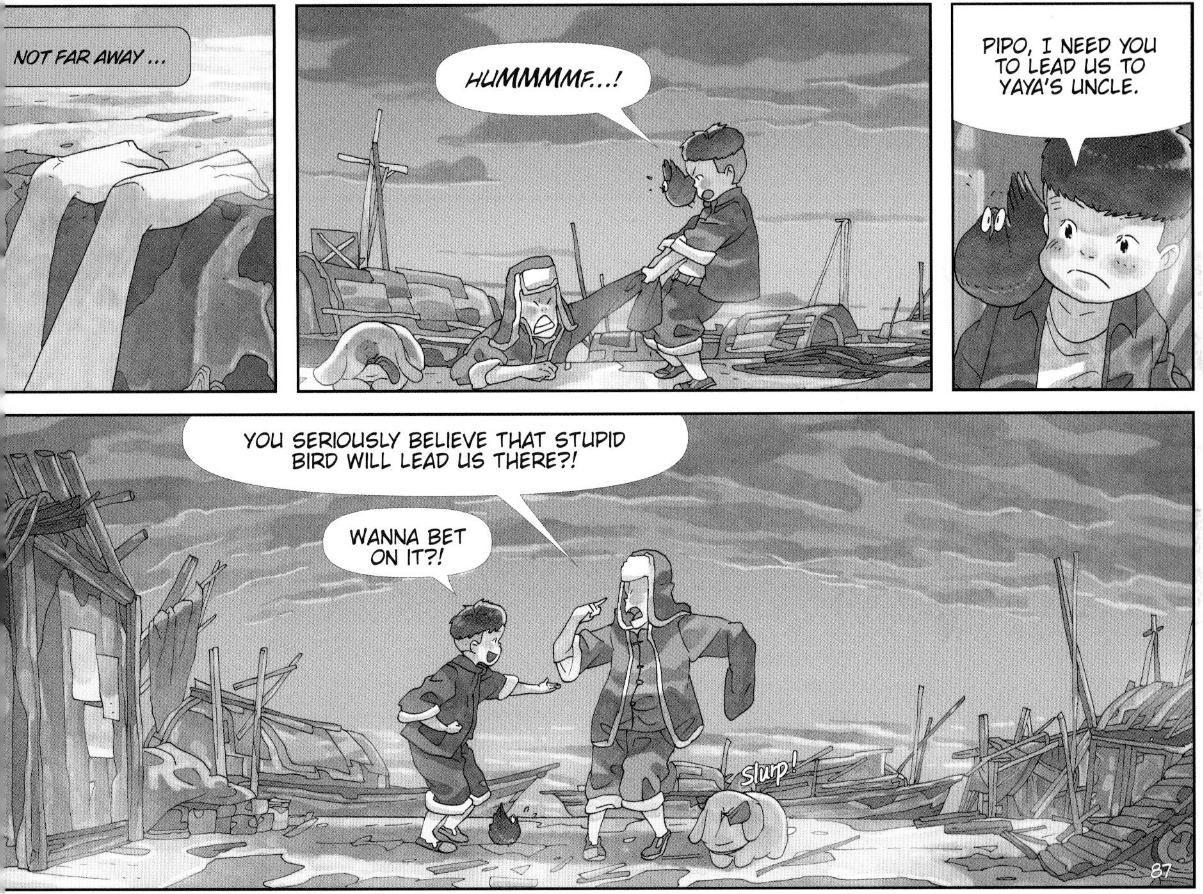
NOT FAR AWAY ...
HUMMMMF...!
PIPO, I NEED YOU TO LEAD US TO YAYA'S UNCLE.
YOU SERIOUSLY BELIEVE THAT STUPID BIRD WILL LEAD US THERE?!
WANNA BET ON IT?!
Slurp!

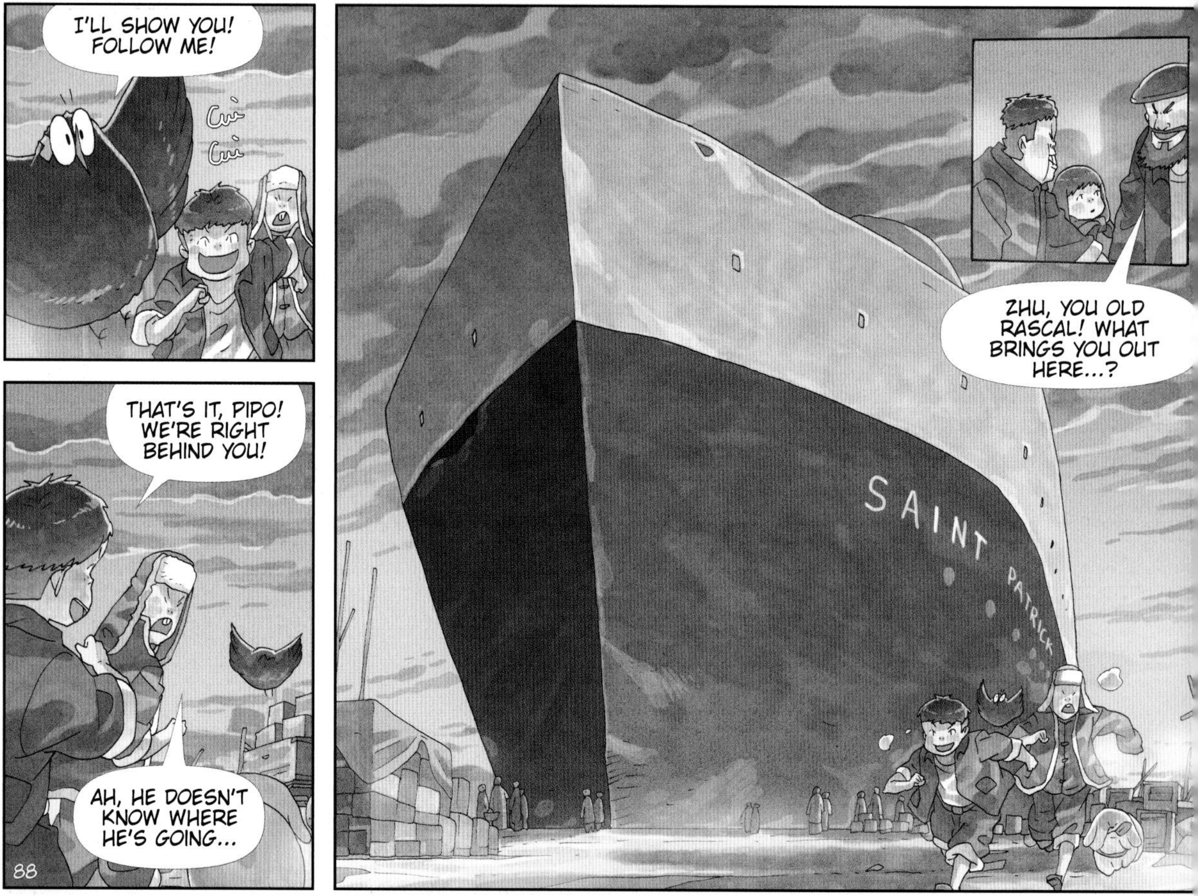
I'LL SHOW YOU! FOLLOW ME!
THAT'S IT, PIPO! WE'RE RIGHT BEHIND YOU!
AH, HE DOESN'T KNOW WHERE HE'S GOING...
SAINT PATRICK
ZHU, YOU OLD RASCAL! WHAT BRINGS YOU OUT HERE...?

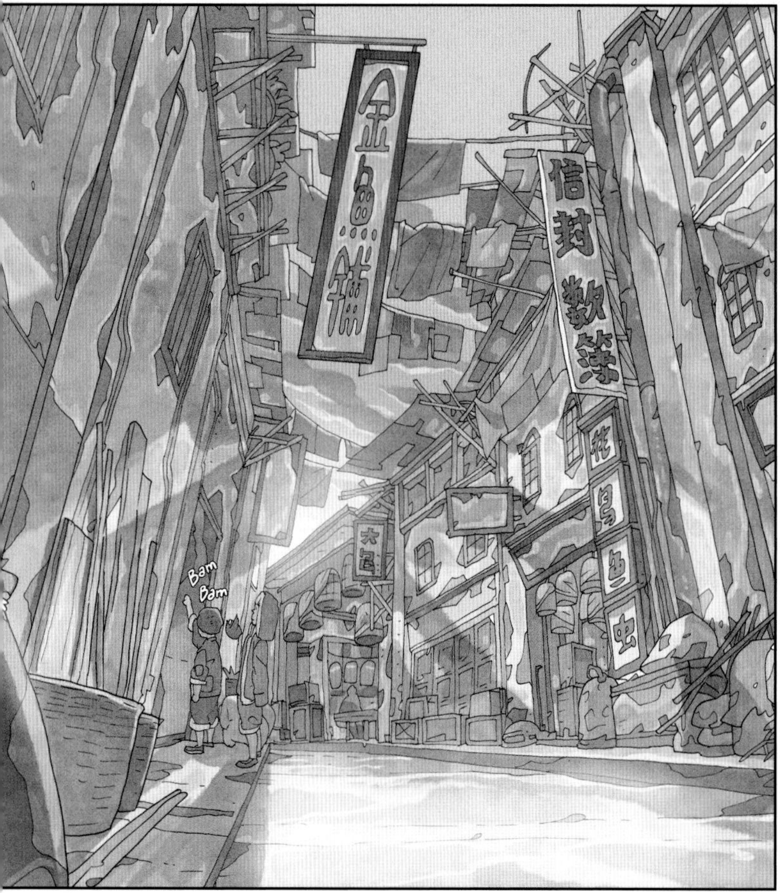
信封
Bam
Bam

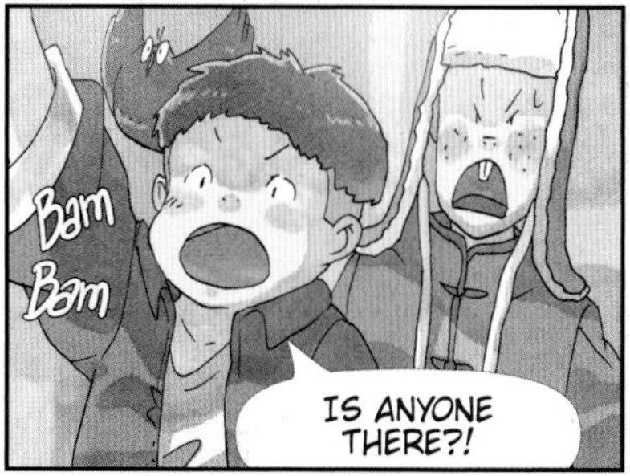
Bam
Bam
IS ANYONE THERE?!

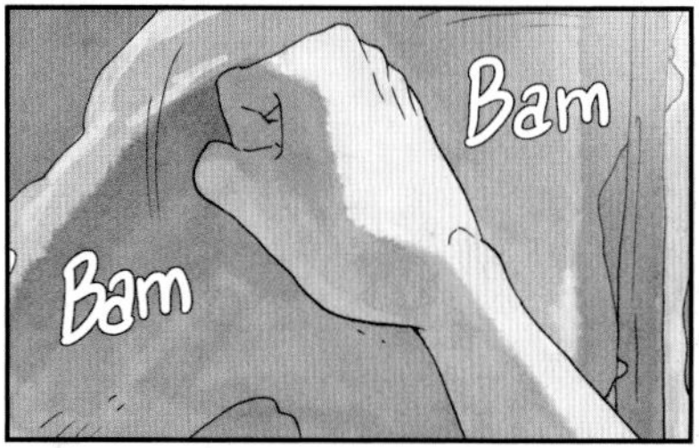
Bam
Bam

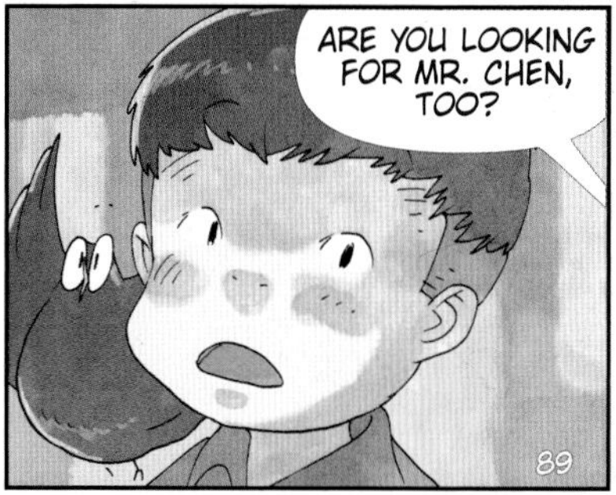
ARE YOU LOOKING FOR MR. CHEN, TOO?

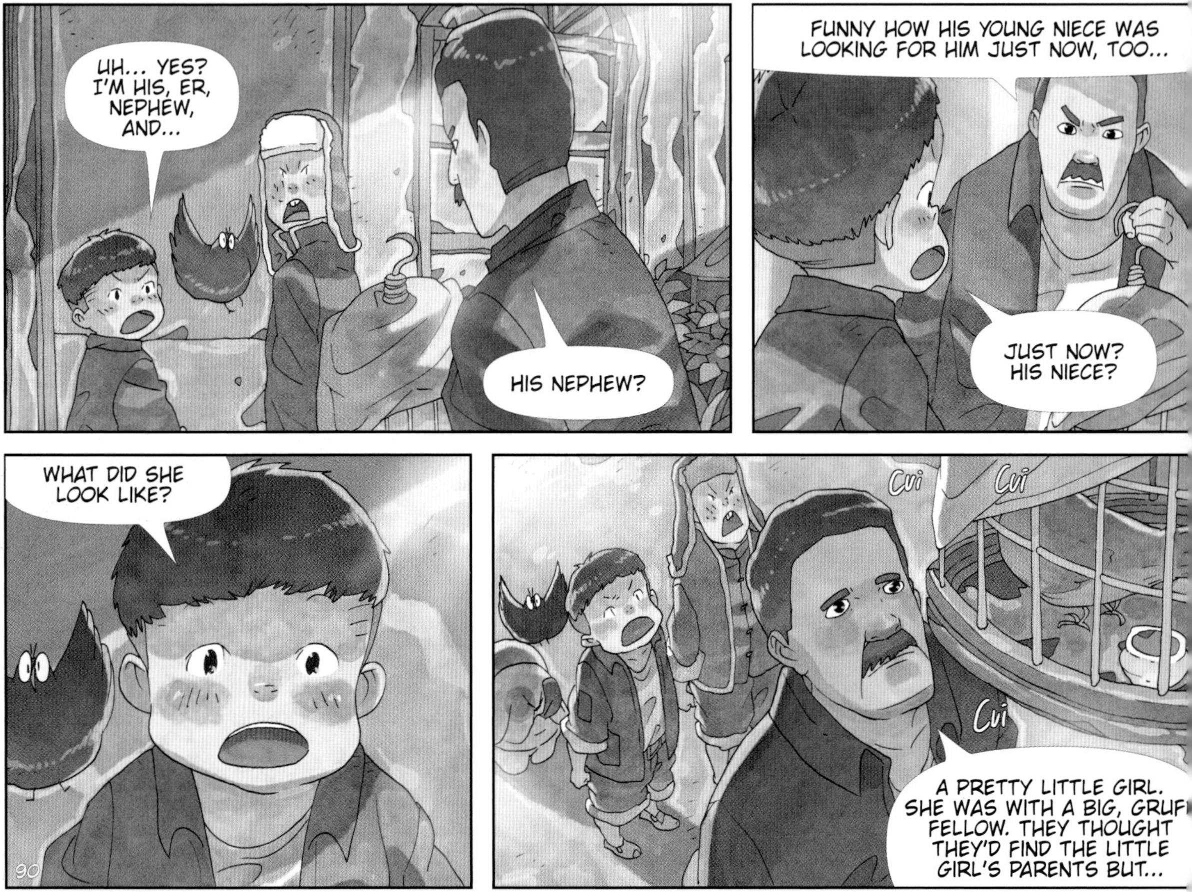
UH... YES? I'M HIS, ER, NEPHEW, AND...
HIS NEPHEW?
FUNNY HOW HIS YOUNG NIECE WAS LOOKING FOR HIM JUST NOW, TOO...
JUST NOW? HIS NIECE?
WHAT DID SHE LOOK LIKE?
Cui
Cui
Cui
A PRETTY LITTLE GIRL. SHE WAS WITH A BIG, GRUF
FELLOW. THEY THOUGHT THEY'D FIND THE LITTLE GIRL'S PARENTS BUT...

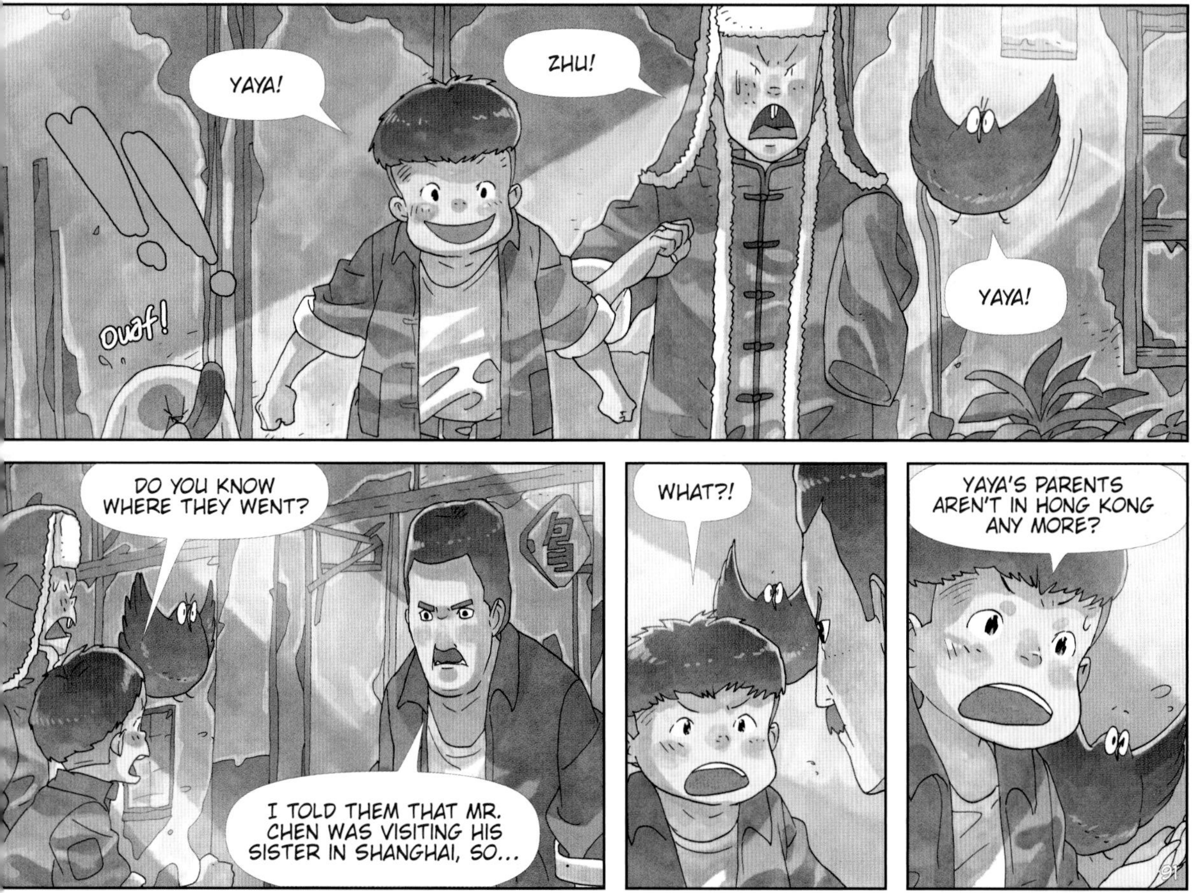
YAYA!
ZHU!
Ouaf!
YAYA!
DO YOU KNOW WHERE THEY WENT?
I TOLD THEM THAT MR. CHEN WAS VISITING HIS SISTER IN SHANGHAI, SO...
WHAT?!
YAYA'S PARENTS AREN'T IN HONG KONG ANY MORE?

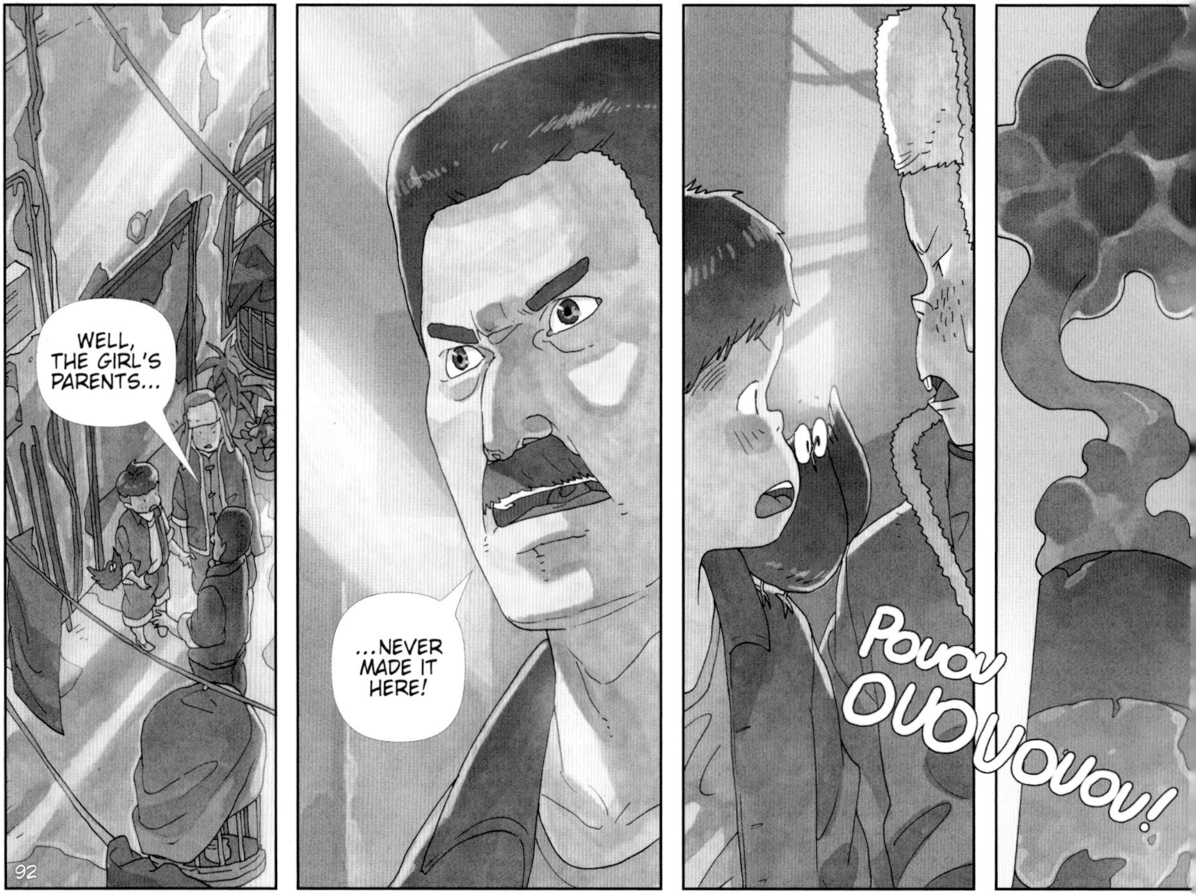
WELL, THE GIRL'S PARENTS...
...NEVER MADE IT HERE!
POUOU OUOUOUOU!

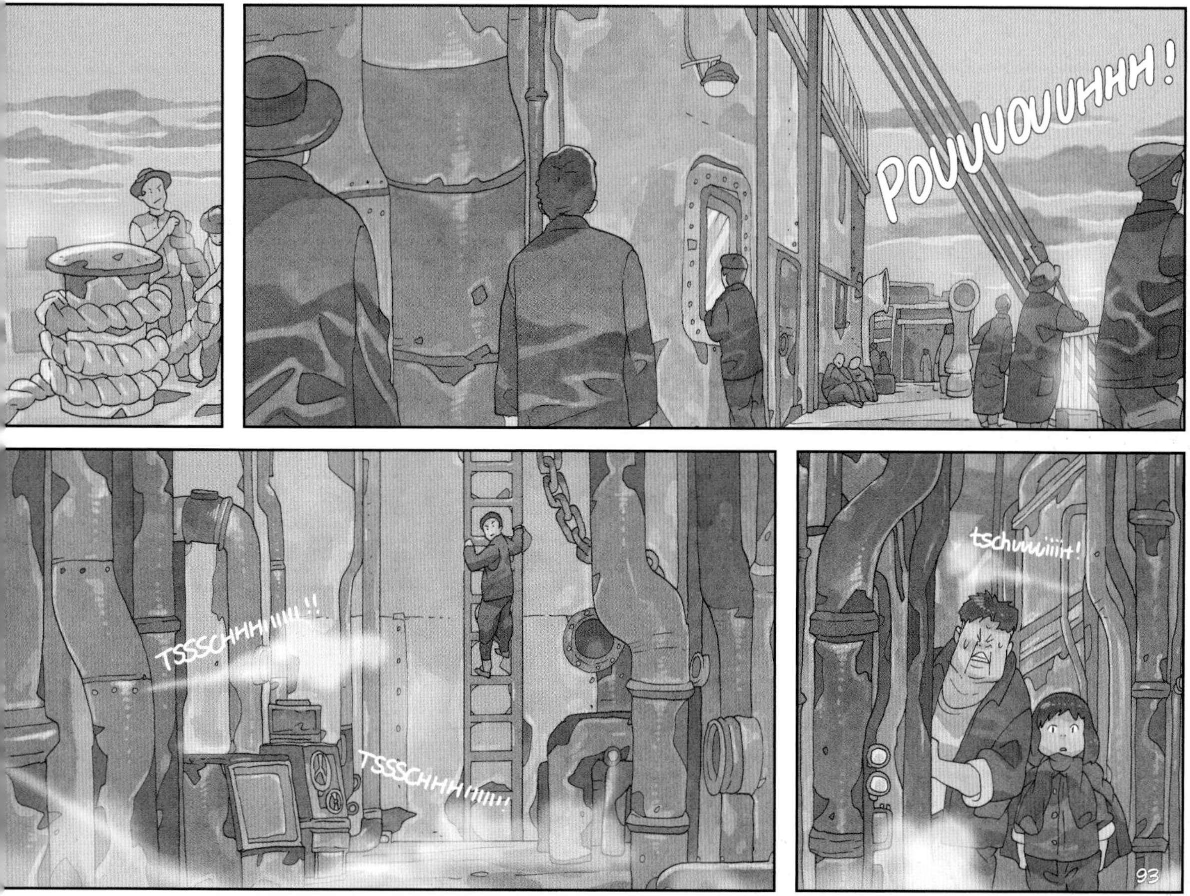
POUUUOUUHHH!
TSSSCHHHIIIIII!!
TSSSCHHHIIIIII!
tschuuwiiiit!

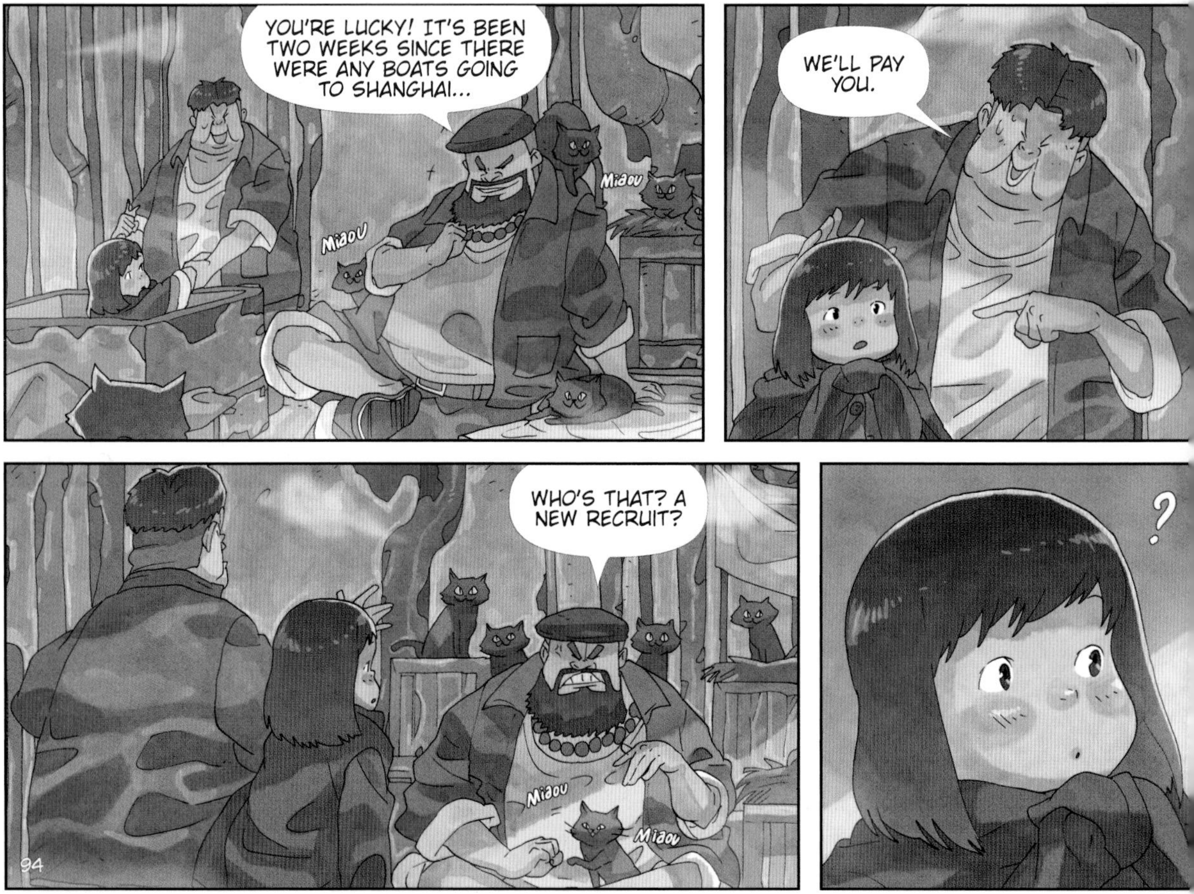
YOU'RE LUCKY! IT'S BEEN TWO WEEKS SINCE THERE WERE ANY BOATS GOING TO SHANGHAI...
MIAOU
MIAOU
WE'LL PAY YOU.
WHO'S THAT? A NEW RECRUIT?
MIAOU
MIAOU
?

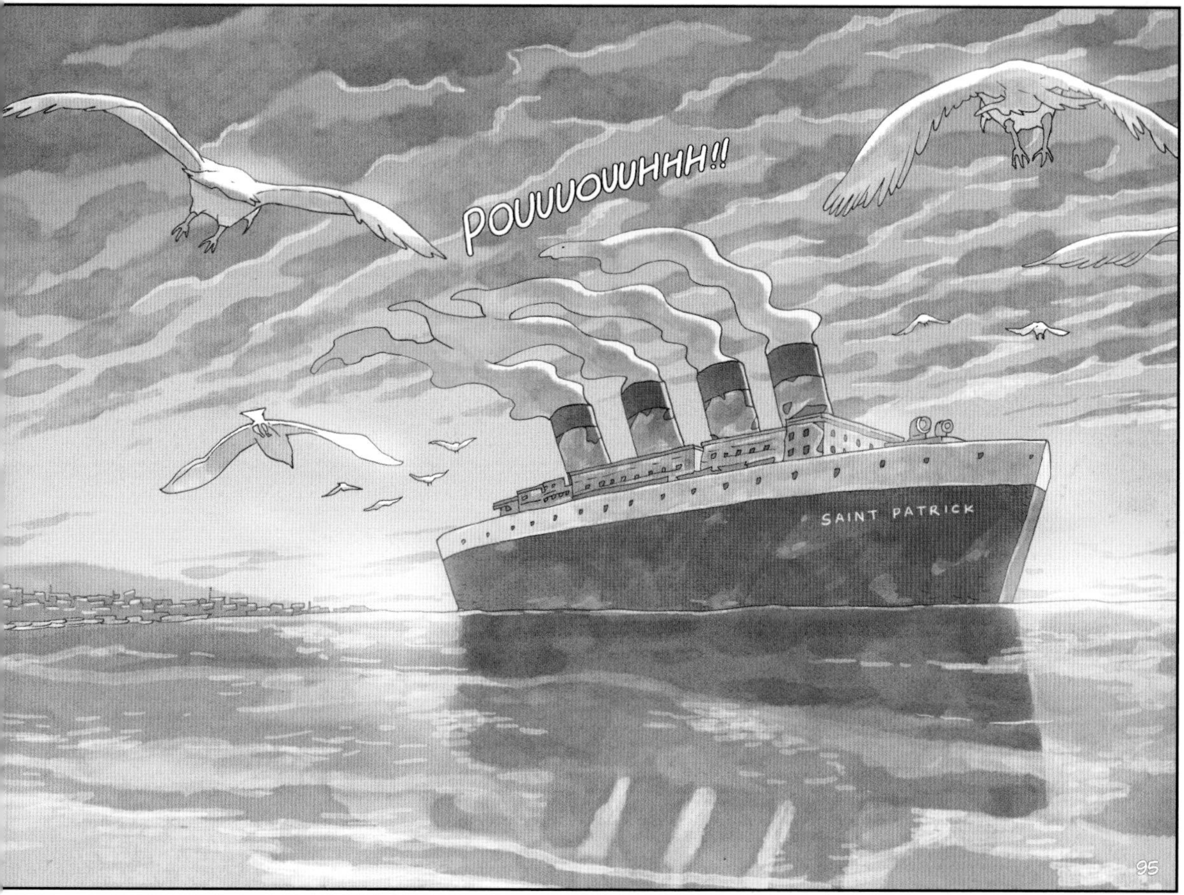
POUUUOUUHHH!!
SAINT PATRICK

YAYA IS ALIVE! BUT STILL IN THE CLUTCHES OF THAT AWFUL PILE OF TOFU, ZHU! THERE'S ONLY ONE THING LEFT TO DO: GO BACK TO SHANGHAI!

ISBN: 978-1-951719-00-5
Library of Congress Control Number: 2020915838

The Ballad of Yaya, Vol. 7: The Trap, published 2020 by Magnetic Press, LLC.
Originally published in French under the title *La Balade de Yaya 7, Le piège* © Editions Fei 2013/Golo/Omont/Marty/Girard, in partnership with Beijing Total Vision Culture Spreads Co. Ltd. All rights reserved. MAGNETIC PRESS™, and all associated distinctive designs are trademarks of Magnetic Press, LLC. No similarity between any of the names, characters, persons, or institutions in this book with those of any living or dead person or institution is intended, and any such similarity which may exist is purely coincidental.

LES ÉDITIONS FEI

Printed in China.

10 9 8 7 6 5 4 3 2 1